"Do you always go around saving dogs and kids?"

Jubal looked directly into Lisa's eyes. "Emotions get you killed." It was said in that same matter-of-fact voice, but the tightening of his jaw emphasized the words.

"Are you staying in the army?"

"Navy, Doc," he corrected, making it plain there was a huge difference. "No, I've been separated, but I don't intend to stay in a rocking chair."

The room seemed to shrink. The air between them was suddenly charged... Lisa could almost smell the ozone. Her face flamed, and heat surged through her, fueling a raw hunger.

She was only too aware he was almost naked, that his body was too near to hers, his breath too close...

Dear Reader,

It is so good to be writing you again. I appreciate each and every one of you more than I can express.

I thought this time I would say something about the writing process, or at least my writing process, because it was so important to this book.

When I start a book, I know who my two main characters are. I know everything that happened to them through childhood, adolescence and adulthood. I live in their heads.

Then I let them run free on the pages. My original premise changes. The plot changes. The end changes. Events happen that I never expected.

Never has characters' drive been as strong as in this book. I had no idea how the story would end when I started it. What possibly could satisfy an eighteen-year navy SEAL who lost his very identity after a mission gone bad and two years held as a hostage? I could only hope that Jubal would find his own way.

And then one day he was running as he did every morning, and his life—and Lisa's—changed. It surprised me as much as it did Jubal. I hope you love the iconic loner as much as I do.

And Lisa? Could she give up the goal she'd had since a child, one that had ruled her life for the past ten years? I wasn't sure myself.

I hope you love both as much as I do.

Patricia Potter

USA TODAY Bestselling Author

PATRICIA POTTER

———

The SEAL's Return

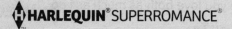
HARLEQUIN® SUPERROMANCE®

Recycling programs
for this product may
not exist in your area.

ISBN-13: 978-0-373-64013-3

The SEAL's Return

Copyright © 2017 by Patricia Potter

www.Harlequin.com

Printed in U.S.A.

USA TODAY bestselling author **Patricia Potter** has been telling stories since the second grade when she wrote a short story about wild horses, although she knew nothing at all about them. She has since received numerous writing awards, including *RT Book Reviews*' Storyteller of the Year, its Career Achievement Award for Western Historical Romance and Best Hero of the Year. She is a seven-time RITA® Award finalist for RWA and a three-time Maggie Award winner, as well as a past president of Romance Writers of America. Character motivation is what intrigues her most in creating a book, and she sits back and allows those characters to write their own stories.

Books by Patricia Potter

HARLEQUIN SUPERROMANCE

Home to Covenant Falls

The Soldier's Promise
Tempted by the Soldier
A Soldier's Journey

HARLEQUIN BLAZE

The Lawman

HARLEQUIN HISTORICAL

Swampfire
Between the Thunder
Samara
Seize the Fire
Chase the Thunder
Dragonfire
The Silver Link
The Abduction

Other titles by this author available in ebook format.

Dedicated to all the nonprofit organizations—large and small—that help veterans heal through interaction with dogs, horses and other animals.

PROLOGUE

Nigeria

JUBAL PIERCE KNEW he probably wouldn't live to see the next dawn. It wasn't that he had seen many dawns in…what was it? One year, two years? Maybe longer since he'd been taken prisoner by a band of terrorist rebels?

He knew his time was limited because his most frequent guard had brought him something more than a small dish of insect-filled rice.

"Gift," the tall, thin figure said in the limited English he'd picked up while guarding Jubal.

Jubal grabbed the bowl with his chained hands. The usual rice, but this time there was also some kind of meat. There was no spoon. He was expected to eat with his fingers. He was allowed nothing that could be turned into a weapon. His sole possessions were the filthy pants and remnants of a shirt he was captured in.

"Why a gift?" he asked, using his hands to help the guard understand.

The man simply shrugged.

Jubal bowed his head in thanks. The guard

left, closing the door to the tiny windowless hut that was home. There were enough cracks that he could hear activity outside. Excited chatter. A lot of movement.

Jubal ate the food, licked the sides of the tin bowl, then struggled to get to his feet and walked the length of the chain attached to the wall. He was so damn weak from lack of food. He figured he had lost nearly half of his two hundred and thirty pounds. With pure strength of will, he finally stood and peered through a crack.

His eyes slowly adjusted to daylight. Most of the fifty-some members of this particular group were scurrying around like ants. Tents were being loaded in an ancient truck. Three men, including his keeper, gestured wildly.

They were leaving. Something had happened and it didn't bode well for him. The terrorists didn't know who he was. If they did, Jubal knew he would be dead. All they knew—or thought they knew—was that he was a doctor.

His SEAL team had been sent to rescue a medical unit caught between warring tribes in Nigeria. They were too late. The medical civilians and their patients had been killed, and enemy soldiers were waiting for them.

His fellow team members had been killed as well, and Jubal was badly wounded. But so was one of the rebel leaders. When Jubal claimed to be a doctor instead of a soldier, he was tasked with saving the life of the wounded leader. He had enough medic training to stop the bleeding and was taken along to care for the leader.

When the man recovered, Jubal was kept prisoner to provide care for others in the tribe. After several escape attempts, he was kept chained.

Jubal was quite sure that he, like his teammates, was believed dead. There had undoubtedly been a search, but the clinic had been burned with the bodies of his team and medical unit members inside. All identifying objects had been stolen as souvenirs.

He knew that he could die any day, especially after the supplies they had taken from the clinic ran out and his patients started dying. He heard the loud debate outside his hut after one fatality. But the head man, whose life he had saved, prevailed. Jubal knew, though, that time was running out...

Now something—or someone—had alarmed his captors. A rival tribe? A government raid? The question was whether they were taking him with them or planning to kill him. He suspected the latter. He was in no shape to move. That meant they would either kill him directly or leave him locked in the hut to starve to death.

His guard stepped inside, threw him a chunk of bread, then left without a word. Another "gift."

He heard the truck take off, then the three jeeps

followed with armed men hanging onto the sides. No one looked back at the hut…

To them, he was already a dead man.

CHAPTER ONE

Chicago

DR. LISA REDDING woke instantly at the loud ring of the telephone. She glanced at the clock. Three a.m.

Her heart skipped a beat. It couldn't be the hospital unless there had been a horrible accident. She'd just come off her twenty-four-hour stint as a resident three hours earlier.

"Dr. Redding?" the voice on the other end of the phone said.

"This is Dr. Redding," she replied.

"I'm Officer Kent Edwards, Chicago Police. I understand you're the guardian of Gordon Redding."

"Yes. What happened?" She tried to keep her voice calm as her heart started to race. She had arrived home after midnight and hadn't bothered to check on her brother and sister. Her aunt, who looked after them, was probably still asleep downstairs.

"He's been arrested. He's down at our station."

Lisa's heart slowed. Not dead, then. That was

her first thought after seeing so many maimed juveniles in the hospital. Then it sped up again. Gordon? Arrested? "What are the charges?" she asked with an audible tremor in her voice.

"Car theft and possession of drugs," the officer said.

She took a deep breath. She knew Gordon was having a tough time, but this? "Where is he?" she asked in a voice she'd trained to be professional in the worst of situations.

The officer gave the name and location of the precinct, and she was relieved it was one just three miles away. She knew it, in fact. She even knew some of the officers since they often visited the hospital to talk to both victims and offenders. "I'll be there in twenty minutes," she said.

She hurriedly dressed, went downstairs to wake her aunt, who'd been staying with them since Lisa's mother had died nine months earlier.

Lisa knocked at Aunt Kay's door and when her half-awake aunt opened it, she explained what had happened. "I'm going down to the precinct now, but I didn't want you to wake up and find two of us missing."

"I stayed up until he went to bed at ten," Aunt Kay said. "He must have left after I fell asleep." She shook her head. "I just don't know what happened to that boy," she said. "But I don't think I can handle him."

Lisa's heart dropped. She was home enough

to know how difficult Gordon had become. She had hoped he would snap out of it. But the death of their mother had sent him on a downward spiral. He had become rude and dismissive of both her and Aunt Kay, who'd moved into the Redding home to take care of her youngest niece and nephew while Lisa finished her residency.

Lisa gave her a quick hug. "I understand," she said. "I don't know when I'll be back but we'll talk then. Try to keep everything normal for Kerry." Lisa grabbed her purse and car keys and drove toward the precinct. The late summer air was still hot, the sky dark with clouds. She concentrated on the empty road ahead and tried not to think what this would mean for Gordon, or Kerry, or her career.

She reached the precinct and identified herself, and almost instantly a young man in uniform hurried over to her. "Dr. Redding? I'm Kent Edwards. I understand you're Gordon Redding's sister."

Lisa simply nodded.

"I've seen you at the hospital," the officer said. "I'm sorry this happened, but your brother isn't helping himself."

"What happened?"

"At two-thirty this morning, my partner and I stopped a car that was reported stolen. Your brother was a passenger. The driver is also a teenager but is known to us. Drugs were in the car. Prescription pills. Weed."

"What kind of pills?" Lisa asked sharply.

"A hallucinogen known as Adam on the street."

She was familiar with it. It was also one of the date-rape pills. "Were they on him?"

"Not on his person but they were in the car under the seat. Your brother won't say where they got them."

"So he's an accomplice who might, or might not, have known there were drugs."

"It would help if he would talk to us. He's not saying anything. Look, he's a first-time offender. If he would tell us who supplied the drugs, we could probably get him probation."

"I can tell you now he won't tell you anything. If nothing else he's loyal to a fault." She hesitated, then added, "Our father died eight years ago in a plane crash. Our mother died nine months ago of cancer. As a resident at the hospital, I'm gone more than I'm at home. He's angry and rebellious, but until this year he's always been a good kid."

The officer nodded. "You can see him in the interview room. Talk to him."

"What about the boy with him?"

"He's eighteen with a previous record. Mostly small-time stuff. Fights. Vandalism. Now he's graduated to a felony."

"Can Gordon go home?"

"The sarge wants to hold him for twenty-four

hours. He thinks it might do some good if he gets a glimpse of what the future might hold if he doesn't help himself now. You should probably call a lawyer."

Her heart sank. The thought of Gordon in jail was like a jagged knife in her heart. She had failed their mother. Failed Gordon by not being there for him. For not understanding how bad things really were. "Will he be in jail?"

"Juvenile detention."

"Can I see him?" Lisa asked.

He escorted her to a room. Gordon sat in a chair at a table, his wrists in handcuffs.

He looked up at her. His longish blond hair was mussed and his green eyes were red. He visibly swallowed as she entered the room, then his mouth tightened. Gordon was a good-looking boy, tall and lean. He had been on the soccer team until their mother died and he missed too many practices.

"We going home now?" he said while avoiding her gaze.

"I don't think so. I've been advised to get a lawyer we can't afford."

For the first time, fear crept into his eyes but his voice was defiant. "That's horseshit. I didn't do nothin'. I was just riding…"

"In a stolen car?"

"I didn't know that. This guy just called and

asked me to go to a party. He picked me up. I didn't know the car was stolen."

"And you didn't know about the drugs?"

His gaze wouldn't meet hers.

"Do you know how much trouble you're in?" she asked. "That was a date-rape drug in the car."

"I said I didn't do anything."

She just stared at him. "You were just in the wrong place at the wrong time, right?"

He nodded.

"Unfortunately, the police do not buy that. It's not like school," she added. "I can't talk you out of this…situation. They're going to keep you here for twenty-four hours. I'll get you a lawyer, but you have to understand that being in a stolen car with drugs means more than a a slap on the wrist. A criminal record can destroy your chances for college, for a career."

"Whatever," he said, but she saw a growing awareness behind the word she'd heard too often this year.

She stood. "Think about cooperating with the police. You don't owe that…guy anything."

The fragile mask came off his face. Gordon blinked then, and she thought she saw tears gathering in his eyes. Her heart started to melt. He was just a kid who lost his father and then watched his mom die. She softened her voice. "I'll do everything I can to help you," she said. "I love you. Aunt Kay loves you. And Kerry…she would be devastated if anything happened to you. I know it's been a hell of a year but Kerry and I need you. We can't lose someone else."

She left then, before she started crying. Once outside the room, she leaned against the wall and let the tears flow.

THREE DAYS LATER, Lisa reluctantly approached the office of the director of Medical Education at the hospital where she was finishing her third year as a resident. She paused, stiffened her shoulders and knocked.

"Dr. Redding," Dr. Rainey said as he opened the door. "You wanted to see me?"

The words stuck in her throat. She had to force them out and keep the tears in place behind her eyes. "I have to turn down the pediatric surgical fellowship," she said. "I hope it's not too late to find a replacement."

"May I ask why?" Dr. Rainey asked with a raised eyebrow.

She hesitated. She knew there were a hundred applicants or more for each fellowship at the hospital. It had been an honor to receive it, and now...

He waited for her answer.

She started haltingly. She told him about Gordon and her family situation. "The good news is the other boy admitted he bought the drugs on his own, that Gordon had nothing to do with it. He claimed, though, that Gordon knew the car was stolen. Gordon said he didn't, but he must have had his suspicions."

After she finished, she couldn't speak for a moment. She'd fought hard to get this residency and then to be selected for the coveted fellowship. It was her long-held dream, but she couldn't sacrifice what was left of her family for it.

"My sister and brother need more than I can give them now," she finally said. "My brother... I'm afraid Gordon is headed for disaster. He's just so...angry. My sister is still grieving, and her grades are diving. My aunt has been staying with us and doing her best, but she has to leave. I...just can't be away all the hours required for the fellowship. I can't give you or my siblings my best with..." Her voice trailed off. Every word had pain dripping from it.

"They've lost two parents," Dr. Rainey said. "That's a lot to handle."

"My brother was...very close to Mom, considered himself the man of the house, and then he had to watch her die. He's angry at the doctors who couldn't save her, and I'm one of them. He feels I deserted him, as well." She hesitated, then said the words she had practiced. "I promised Mom I would take care of Gordon and my sister, and I haven't been able to do that."

Dr. Rainey leaned forward. He seemed to hesitate, then said, "I don't want to lose you. You're one of the best residents we have and I think you would make a fine pediatric surgeon. I'm told by the attendings and nursing staff that your instincts are excellent."

It was a rare compliment from Dr. Rainey and made what she had to do even harder.

Gordon's arrest, though, made a change in lifestyle imperative. Gordon had been released with a number of conditions, including a curfew. His hearing would be in three weeks, and the attorney she'd hired had talked to Gordon's caseworker. It was possible that he would be given a year's probation and then his record could be cleared... expunged...if he stayed out of trouble.

She knew he wouldn't. She'd caught him sneaking out after curfew last night. She knew as sure as the sun rose in the morning that he'd try again.

"What are you proposing to do?" Dr. Rainey asked after a few seconds.

"A position with stable day hours," she said. "Maybe a clinic. Maybe after Gordon finishes high school, I can..." Her voice drifted off.

Dr. Rainey sat back in his chair and tapped a pen on his desk.

"I have a friend," he said, "a general practitioner in a small town in Colorado. He's had heart surgery. It leaves the town without a doctor within a hundred miles. He hopes to find someone to replace him while he recuperates.

Lisa was stunned. She hadn't known what to expect but it certainly wasn't what she realized what was coming.

"I've been to the town," Dr. Rainey continued. "It's small and friendly. You can step into a fully equipped practice. It would be good experience for you and a great environment for kids. There's a lake, mountains, skiing. The school draws from the surrounding ranches and is said to be quite good."

He paused. "The town will provide a house within walking distance of the office. If, at the end of a year, you're still interested in the fellowship, I'll try to bring you back."

IT SEEMED TO be an answer to a prayer. She was exhausted from the hours at the hospital together with the ongoing drama at home. Still, she hesitated. "Our house…"

"If I remember correctly, you live near the hospital. I'm sure a resident or incoming staff member will be more than happy to rent it for a year." He wrote down a number. "If you're interested, call Eve Manning in Covenant Falls. She's the mayor and can give you more details." He looked up at her from his desk. If you're interested, I'll need to let my friend know ASAP."

"Thank you," she said, surprised at his understanding, even more so by the proposal. She had never lived anywhere other than a large city but right now a slower pace seemed inviting.

She thanked him and said she would certainly consider it. The more she thought about it during the day, the more feasible the idea seemed.

During a break, she looked up Covenant Falls on the web. The site featured a photo of a sunrise spreading gold across a pure blue lake with white-tipped mountains behind it. There were insets, including photos of a football field, a community center, an attractive main street and two teenagers riding horses.

From that moment, everything happened swiftly. She called the mayor, liked her instantly on the phone. She found herself relaying all her concerns, especially regarding the two rebellious teenagers, and by the end of the conversation was convinced Covenant Falls might be an answer.

She tried not to think of the fellowship. This was something she owed her parents, a debt she couldn't ignore.

Two days later, Lisa used her day off to fly to Denver, full of apprehension, for a one-day visit to Covenant Falls.

She was picked up by Eve Manning and driven to Pueblo to meet with Dr. Bradley at the hospital there. He was hooked up to a monitor and his color was poor, but his eyes were challenging as they met hers.

"Dr. Rainey said you're a good diagnostician,"

he said. "But it takes more than that to be a small-town doctor. You need an instinct about people. You have to really care about them. They know if you do. And if you don't. It's not like a hospital where you see them once or twice before sending them to someone else."

"I realize that," she said, "and it appeals to me. It's frustrating to treat a patient and never know what happens later. I intended to go into a private practice after completing my fellowship."

"Cliff Rainey said you're experiencing family problems?"

"Siblings. Teenagers," she said frankly, and gave him a brief summary of what had happened. "What makes it hard is I've been absent when they needed me most. I thought my aunt could fill in, but it isn't the same. I didn't realize that until my brother, Gordon, was arrested."

He nodded. "Sometimes we doctors are so busy taking care of our patients, we don't have time to take care of our own families. I'm guilty, as well."

He then asked medical questions, queried about diseases, treatments and protocols. "We have an older population with the ailments that come with it, but we also have our share of pregnancies, broken bones, flu and rattlesnake bites. We usually have a couple of those each year. We keep anti-venom in the office but then the patient has to be transported to a major hospital that maintains a larger stock."

"As to staff," he said, "I have a very competent nurse, but she isn't qualified to write prescriptions. There's also a part-time bookkeeper who works out of her own house. She can take care of most of the paperwork for Medicare and insurance companies." He studied her for a moment. "I can't pay you much, but the town is providing a home, and the experience will be useful."

She nodded.

"Let me know what you decide after you visit Covenant Falls and see the clinic. The position is yours if you want it. If Cliff Rainey recommends you, that's good enough for me."

She breathed easier as she left. She glanced at her watch. It was one-thirty in the afternoon. She had left Chicago on an early flight that morning, but then there was the long drive from Denver. She understood it would be another hour and a half drive to Covenant Falls, then the drive back to Denver for another early-bird flight to Chicago.

Her aunt was staying with Kerry and Gordon. She hadn't told them about the possibility of moving. She didn't want to say anything until she felt reasonably confident the position was a real possibility.

"What do you think?" Eve asked when Lisa joined her in the hospital reception area.

"He said the job is mine if I want it," she said.

"So now it's my job to convince you to want it," Eve said. She explained that the town was cradled on one side by mountains and the other by the plains. "There's approximately three thousand people in the area, including ranches that aren't in the city limits but contract for city services."

"I'm going to be taking my sister and brother out of the schools and activities they know," Lisa said. "What is there for them here?"

"The school is highly rated and will open in four weeks. We have football, baseball, basketball and track along with a terrific music and drama department. Then there's skiing clubs, Boy Scouts and Explorer Scouts, community baseball and football. There's also a lot of special-interest groups—music, mechanics, computers, a horseback riding club."

"It sounds great. To me. I'm not sure it will to them. They love the city."

"Maybe because they've never experienced anything else," Eve said.

Lisa was silent the rest of the drive into town. Rolling plains reached toward the mountains. The two-lane road was bordered by fences with occasional breaks leading to houses and barns. As they entered the town of Covenant Falls, it looked even smaller than she'd imagined. She counted all of three stop signs. Eve parked in front of an attractive building she identified as city hall, and they walked across the road to the Covenant Falls Medical Clinic.

She met the nurse, Janie Blalock, who didn't look much younger than Dr. Bradley. The nurse was friendly and showed her around the office, including a small X-ray room. It was, Lisa thought, probably well equipped for a small-town doctor but she would miss all the state of the art diagnostic technology available in Chicago.

"Time for lunch," Eve announced when Lisa finished the tour.

Lisa thanked Janie, then she and Eve walked half a block to a glass-fronted building with a big sign proclaiming it to be Maude's. The diner was nearly empty, and they took a seat next to the window. A large motherly looking woman immediately came over.

"This is Maude," Eve said. "She owns this place and it has great food."

"This the new doctor?" Maude asked.

Lisa looked helplessly at Eve.

"She's looking us over," Eve said lightly.

"You're a sight prettier than Doc Bradley," Maude said. "Your meal is on the house," she added. She studied Lisa solemnly. "Seems to me you need a bit of meat on you. How about a steak?"

"They're good here," Eve said. "My husband swears by them."

Lisa wasn't sure. The last few days of uncertainty and worry had her stomach in turmoil. But she also had to eat and she still had a long day ahead. She nodded. "A steak and salad with dressing on the side, please. And an iced tea."

"I'll take the same," Eve said.

When Maude left, Eve turned to her. "What do you think?"

"I like Dr. Bradley. I like the clinic. I like the mountains. But I'm not sure Kerry and Gordon will feel the same."

"My son lost his father when he was four," Eve said. "I know how difficult it is for a child to lose a parent. And you and your siblings have lost both. But this town supports its own, and that would include you. We'll do our best to keep your family safe and happy."

They couldn't do any worse. Their Chicago neighborhood that had once been a safe place to live now bred gangs. It wasn't home sweet home anymore. She just wasn't sure Gordon saw it that way.

"I'll show you the house after lunch," Eve said. "The owner passed away and the heir agreed to let us use it and much of the furniture for a year if we did the repairs and voided the overdue taxes. It's a good deal for us both. My husband and his group of vets painted the house and fixed everything that needed fixing."

"Group of vets?"

"We have a lot of veterans here," Eve explained.

"In fact, a military nurse recently moved here. She was wounded in Afghanistan and wasn't ready to go back to nursing, but she's available in an emergency."

Lisa absorbed that. Since their mother died, Gordon had threatened to go into the military when he was old enough, and she had done her best to dissuade him from that path. Would a town full of vets sharpen his interest? One count against coming here.

The food came then, Lisa's stomach's turmoil ending at the smell of the steak. Once bite proved Eve's recommendation. It was excellent and the salad good. The prices were amazingly low, even if the meal hadn't been free. One count for moving here.

Eve continued to plug the town as they ate, then drove her around for a tour. They drove by a wooded park with a gazebo in front of a sprawling building. "That's our community center and library," Eve said. "And there's a small museum and a beach, as well."

"Where do the kids usually gather?"

"School. Maude's. The falls. The community center or sports field. Or they go horseback riding as incentives. Nearly every kid in town can ride. I have two horses that your brother and sister can ride."

A plus for Kerry, the animal lover. Lisa wasn't

so sure about Gordon. His sport of choice was soccer and he'd quit playing in the spring.

Eve took a corner just three blocks from the clinic and stopped in front of a white house. It was a two-story with a connected garage. A white picket fence stretched around the property.

She and Eve walked onto the small porch. Eve unlocked the door and they went inside. The house was not unlike her parents' house in Chicago: a large living room with a fireplace, a kitchen with plenty of cabinets and a small dining room. There was a master bedroom and bath downstairs and two nice-size bedrooms and a bathroom upstairs. It looked newly painted and the furniture, though a little more formal than she liked, looked comfortable.

She looked out the kitchen window and saw a large fenced area. "Pets are welcome, too," Eve said.

Lisa hadn't thought of that. Kerry had always wanted a dog, but it never happened for one reason or another. Maybe…

She realized she was making a life-changing decision for all of them. A huge decision. Kerry may be happy with it, especially with a dog and horseback riding. Gordon, the other hand, would hate it. She would be taking him away from his so-called friends and all he knew.

She thought of the argument they had when

she caught him trying to sneak out of the house after his release from jail.

"You can't tell me what to do," he'd said, his face red with anger. "You're not my mother. You're not even my real sister."

It was a barb that hurt more than she let him know. She had been adopted when her mother failed to conceive after years of trying. Eleven years later, her mother delivered Gordon, and Kerry arrived four years after that.

Lisa had mothered them, especially after their father was killed, and her mother went to work in a real estate firm. She loved her siblings with her whole heart.

And now…she would be turning their lives upside down. Again. She hadn't told them she was flying to Colorado. They would just assume she was at the hospital. "What do you think?" Eve said, breaking into her train of thought.

Lisa hesitated. "It's very nice."

"I sense a reservation," Eve said.

"I think you should know why I'm considering this," Lisa said slowly. "You might change your mind about wanting us." She'd told Eve on the telephone there were problems, just not how severe they were.

Eve didn't say anything, just waited.

Lisa spelled out the story, from her mother's death to Gordon sneaking out after his arrest. "I hoped the arrest would scare him, but it didn't."

She hadn't meant to say that. It was another failure on her part and she wasn't used to failing. She should've noticed Gordon's problems, just as she should've caught her mother's illness before it was too late.

"Losing two parents is a lot for a kid to handle," Eve said slowly. "I can't imagine my son dealing with losing me after already losing his father."

"I should have been there for him," Lisa said. "I have to do it now and hope it's not too late." She paused, then added, "I talked to the caseworker handling his case. She said she would ask for probation and suggested it might be possible to transfer supervision here. Can you do that?"

"We can. We have a new police chief who's great with kids."

"It's okay, then?"

"I'm sure it will be," Eve replied. "Sometimes magic happens in Covenant Falls."

"It would have to be pretty major magic."

"That happens, too. Someday I'll have to tell you how I met my husband." Eve paused then asked, "So what do you say? Does the house and clinic work for you?"

Decision time. "Yes," Lisa said, her stomach tightening. She was gambling and she didn't like to gamble. She didn't see any other choice. "I'm happy to accept the offer."

CHAPTER TWO

JUBAL PIERCE PLUCKED the letter he'd received yesterday from the trash can. He'd read it then and discarded it. This time he reread it slowly and considered the proposal.

His first inclination had been *Hell, no.*

That was his answer to almost everything these days.

He took a swallow of Jameson Irish whiskey as he glanced around the San Diego apartment he shared with two other SEALs. He was the only one in residence now. The others were on missions. He usually saved the Jameson for the end of successful missions. Now it signaled the end, period.

He couldn't stay here now. His career as a navy SEAL was over. He knew it. His superiors knew it. His body had been too damaged by two years of near-starvation and captivity—not to mention what it had done to his mental health.

He'd been a SEAL half his life. It had been his entire identity until that rescue mission had gone to hell, and he was taken.

He'd crawled out of a jungle with the last of his strength. After his captors abandoned him, he'd found a key to the chain around his wrists in the bread that his guard had thrown at him. One act of mercy, maybe because he'd saved the man's life a year earlier. The tribesman probably didn't think he would make it through the jungle alive. He barely did. He didn't want to think of those days spent crawling through the jungle more dead than alive.

He'd been offered a slot as a SEAL instructor but turned it down. Too many memories. Too many friends dead. Too many sleepless nights because of nightmares. He looked at those young, fatigued warriors who were trying to survive the almost unsurvivable SEAL training and he saw the faces of his dead teammates. He didn't have the heart to drive the candidates to be what you had to be to win the coveted trident, the SEAL symbol.

Problem was he didn't have the heart for anything. He looked down at the glass of whiskey. The Jameson was a reminder of other days when he and his team members had splurged after a successful mission. A last salute to a life he was leaving. If there had been ice, it would have made a merry noise from the shaking of his hand.

He looked back at the letter from Clint Morgan, a helicopter pilot who had once rescued his team from one hell of a bad situation. They had gotten very drunk together that night with Jameson, and although they rarely saw each other after that, they'd stayed in touch. When they did manage to meet, it was usually a boisterous celebration with a lot of drinking. Their last meeting was three months before his last mission…

He picked up Clint's letter again.

Hey, cannot tell you how happy I am to hear you're still among the living. I'd heard you were missing, presumed dead, then a few weeks ago heard you'd turned up. I toasted you in absentia with our favorite whiskey. I should have known no mere terrorist could keep you down. David Turner told me you were leaving the navy but he wasn't sure what you planned to do.

Don't know if you heard, probably not, but I left the army because of a head injury. I was in limbo until I ended up in a small Colorado town called Covenant Falls, and believe it or not, I'm now its police chief. I'm also a married man as of a month ago. I can hear you laughing now.

In case you're at loose ends as I was, there's a cabin available here that is handed down from vet to vet who's leaving the service and trying to figure out what's next. It's on a lake and backs up to the mountains. Fishing and hiking are great. The town is full of veterans and there's a weekly poker game along with a fine watering hole that caters to us. What more could you want? The cabin, by the way, would be all yours. I lived there for several months and can vouch for its comfort.

The town itself is small, rather quirky, but it has good people. The last three vets who used the cabin decided to stay here, including the former Ranger I mentioned, a battlefield military nurse and yours truly. Anyway, come for a few days at least so we can tell lies, toast friends and drink a bottle of Jameson.

Jubal put the letter down. He'd changed a lot since the last time he'd seen Clint. He hadn't gained back all his weight and he often woke in a cold sweat. After all the isolation, he was uncomfortable in crowds and had difficulty carrying a conversation. He was mentally adrift.

And then there were the nightmares. He relived the ambush over and over again. He wondered why he lived and those who'd been with him didn't. One of the things he needed to do was visit the families of his teammates who'd died in Nigeria. He hadn't been mentally able to do that yet. Maybe visiting Clint could be the beginning of that journey.

No one had loved flying more than Clint, and

he'd planned, like Jubal, to be a lifer in the service. If he could make a successful transition, maybe Jubal could, as well. He heard Clint's humor in his letter. There would be no pity. No sympathy. No expectations. No questions.

No reliving hell.

He picked up his cell and punched in the number Clint had provided…

EIGHTEEN DAYS LATER, Jubal stuffed some clothes in his duffel along with several books. He drove straight through from San Diego to Covenant Falls, Colorado, stopping only long enough for coffee, hamburgers and gas. He had no trouble staying awake. Sleep never came without nightmares, so he tended to avoid it, anyway.

A little more than a thousand miles and twenty hours later, he reached his destination midmorning.

He followed Clint's instructions through a small town to a road that ran beside a lake. Clint hadn't been kidding when he said the town was small. He couldn't imagine Clint, who was always the life of the party, being happy here. Even less could he imagine his friend as its police chief. That must have been one of Clint's jokes. He'd been a full-blown hell-raiser back in the day, made even Jubal look like a saint.

It was just after ten in the morning when he found the place, the last one on Lake Road. He drove down a gravel lane to a cedar-sided cabin with a large screen porch stretching across the entire front of the structure. He stepped out of his car, a dark blue Mazda, and took a deep breath. The air was scented by the giant pines that surrounded the cabin. The clear blue lake was visible through the trees.

Clint had told him the cabin would be unlocked, the keys inside on the kitchen counter. Jubal grabbed his duffel from the backseat of the car and took the three steps up to the porch. He opened the screen door, then the door to the interior of the cabin, and looked inside.

As Clint promised, it was cozy. A stone fireplace filled one side of the main room and a wall of windows another. He looked outside. There was a rock grill surrounded by several comfortable-looking lounge chairs. Then the yard ended in what appeared to be forest stretching upward.

He checked out each room, then retreated to the kitchen where there was a thermos of coffee and a plate of cinnamon rolls waiting for him, along with a note.

Tradition dictates the cabin comes with fridge full of food. I added some beer and, knowing you, some damn good whiskey. Help yourself. Call me when you're settled.

Jubal didn't call. Instead, he took the thermos

of coffee and rolls and headed toward the front porch. He sipped the coffee, which was still hot, and ate two rolls, then decided to explore further. He walked out to the road, glanced at a dock, which looked new. To his right, he noticed a path winding up a mountain. He took the path and climbed up to a spot where he had a good visual of the land around him.

Habits die hard. It was still part of him, this reconnaissance of his immediate environment, a suspicion of strangers, a springboard reaction to the slightest noise.

He was tired. It had been an exhausting drive from San Diego, and he hadn't slept in more than forty-eight hours. There had been a time when he would still be going strong, but he hadn't regained the stamina he once had. It had been one reason he'd rejected the job of trainer. He couldn't imagine driving candidates to do something he could no longer do himself.

He was working on that stamina. His weight had gone from two hundred and ten pounds on a six-foot-three frame to little more than half that during his long months of captivity. It was up to a hundred and seventy-five now, all of it hard muscle after a strict exercise regime, but there had been enough permanent nerve and joint damage to end his career as an operating SEAL.

After returning to the cabin, he relaxed in one of the lounge chairs outside and watched as the sun reached its zenith and started back down again. He appreciated the fact trees shielded the cabin from the dwelling next to his. He was used to isolation.

At least this isolation was of his choosing.

His mind flipped back to Africa as it did too often. He'd been left alone for long periods of time, unless one of his guards came into whatever cave or hut they kept him in. And then it was only to beat, taunt, threaten or sometimes do all three. A gun was held against his head or a knife across his throat. He had scars all over his body from repeated torture.

The only thing that kept his captors from killing him was their belief he was a doctor and could be of use to them. He advised them on what medical supplies to take from the clinic before they burned it, to reinforce his lie.

Jubal took a deep breath. He was in the States again, the master of his own fate once more. Problem was, he had no idea what he wanted that fate to be. That was a first for him and he didn't like it.

He knew he should call Clint, but he kept putting it off. He didn't want to answer questions. He didn't want to deal with small talk. He certainly didn't want to talk about the last two years.

As a SEAL, he never thought about the next week or the next month, just the next mission. It was better that way. Think about the future and you start making mistakes.

Now he had to consider it.

He heard a car pull into the drive. He looked at his watch. It was nearly six. Clint, most likely. He'd probably been waiting all day for his call.

Still, he didn't move as Clint appeared from around the cabin. A scarred pit bull was at his heels.

"Hey, Reb." Clint used the nickname Jubal's fellow SEALs had given him when he joined his first team. His grin was wide as ever.

Jubal looked at him. Clint wore a tan uniform and carried a sidearm, but he looked relaxed. The exhausted lines Jubal remembered around his eyes were gone. He turned his gaze to Clint's scarred companion.

"Who's your friend?" Jubal asked without moving.

"Bart. He rides along with me." Clint leaned down and whispered something into the dog's ear. The dog came over to Jubal and looked at him solemnly with deep brown eyes.

"I told him you're a friend. He's saying hello."

The dog was among the ugliest Jubal had seen. Like himself, the dog had scars all over his body, but the animal waited patiently for a response.

Jubal immediately felt a kinship with the dog's obvious brutal past. He leaned over and rubbed behind his ears. "Hello, Bart."

"He adopted me last year," Clint explained. "I had no choice in the matter, but I thought he would be a good icebreaker today," Clint said. "I wasn't sure I'd be welcome since you didn't call."

Jubal relaxed slightly. He sounded like the old Clint. "I just needed a few hours' rest. I drove all night," Jubal said without elaborating. Then he looked Clint up and down. "You weren't kidding about being a cop?"

"Nope. Some of those MPs we encountered would have strokes if they knew. Okay if I get a beer?"

Jubal didn't bother to get up. "Since you supplied them, I'd be a real jerk to say no."

"Now that's the wholehearted 'Hello, great to see you' that I expected," Clint groused good-naturedly. "But I accept the invitation." He headed for the cabin, disappeared inside and reappeared with a beer. He slouched down in the lounge chair next to Jubal. "Like that scruff on your face," he said. "It's a hell of a lot more civilized than the last time I saw you in Afghanistan."

"I didn't want to scare the natives," Jubal replied.

"I don't remember you being that sensitive."

"It's only on your account," Jubal said. "I'm your guest. I wasn't sure you weren't kidding when you said you were police chief. Didn't think it would look so hot if I turned up looking like a biker."

Clint shrugged. "They're kind of used to us now. Nothing bothers them much."

"Us?"

"Vets occupying the cabin. We've kinda been adopted by the town folks."

"What if you don't want to be adopted?"

"That's okay with them, too. The people in town don't ask questions or impose, except maybe to quietly drop off a pan of brownies or cinnamon rolls. That's rule number one in town."

"Dropping off brownies or not asking questions?"

"Okay, rule one *and* two," Clint corrected himself.

Jubal looked at him curiously. "How did you come here? Doesn't look like your kind of place. Seem to remember you liked big cities with lots of bars."

"The shrink at the military hospital where I was treated recommended it," Clint said. "Dr. Payne. He was Josh Manning's doctor at Fort Hood, and they became friends."

Clint hesitated before continuing. "This is Josh's cabin. He inherited it—along with a traumatized military dog—from his best buddy who died saving his life. He admits to being in pretty bad shape when he arrived with a lot of survivor's guilt and a bad case of PTSD. All he wanted was to be left alone and wallow in grief and guilt."

Jubal understood that. He waited for the rest of the story.

"The town mayor somehow lured him out of hermitsville. A very pretty mayor, too. Single mom to a young son. She's a force of nature in a soft, unassuming way," Clint said. "Sounds contradictory, but there it is. I'm sure you'll meet them at some point.

"To make a long story short," Clint continued, "Josh and Eve married and he moved into her ranch house. He asked Dr. Payne if he knew a vet who needed a temporary place to stay. That was me. Then Andy came through before moving in with her fiancé. She'd been a surgical nurse in a forward base. The cabin was sitting here vacant when I heard you were leaving the navy…"

"I'm not staying," Jubal broke in. "I thought to be here just long enough for a bit of hell-raising, but I guess that's out of the question seeing you're the law these days."

"The two things are not mutually exclusive," Clint retorted. "What are your future plans?"

Jubal shrugged. "Haven't thought much about it."

"Haven't wanted to, you mean," Clint corrected. "Been there, done that."

Jubal wanted to change the subject away from himself. "You said in the letter you had a head injury. A chopper crash?" The question was out before he could withdraw it. He usually didn't ask personal questions because he didn't like them directed at him. He wouldn't have with anyone other than Clint, but since the day Clint rescued his team, they'd been like brothers.

"I did something stupid," Clint said. "I was at Fort Hood between deployments. I'd practically rebuilt an old Corvette and wanted to try it out on a road a friend said no one used. I was going pretty fast when an old truck pulled onto the road and I had to turn suddenly to miss it. The car went into a ditch and my head hit the side of the interior. I suffered a concussion with brain trauma. I had continuing blackouts and headaches. For a while I couldn't even drive, much less keep a pilot's license."

Clint said, "I haven't had a blackout in a month and I'm hoping to get a clean bill of health from the doctor to fly again, but this time I'll be fighting fires. We had a bad one a few months ago. Good news is I *can* drive. If I do feel a blackout coming on, I can turn off the highway and call a deputy. Can't do that in the sky."

Jubal heard the pain in his voice. It hadn't been as easy as he tried to make it sound.

"I'll be honest," Clint said. "It was rough in the beginning. I wasn't very happy about coming here until I ran into a redheaded veterinarian who almost killed me the day we met, and a mayor that duped me into teaching computers to senior citizens."

Jubal raised one eyebrow. His mind couldn't comprehend it. The image of daredevil pilot and woman-magnet Clint teaching elderly women the basics of computers was just too…crazy. Maybe even more crazy than being police chief.

"Don't you miss—"

"Hell, yes. There's still those times I hunger for a throttle in my hand, the lift of a chopper. Bringing guys back." He paused, shrugged. "But I love my fire-breathing wife, and I like this town. We have a lot of veterans here and we help each other."

"You're planning to stay here, then?" Jubal asked.

Clint nodded. "Stephanie loves it here, and I have good friends, including Josh and a number of other vets. And dammit, I like my job."

"What does a cop even do here?" Jubal asked curiously.

"We've been having some old-fashioned cattle and horse rustling. That's keeping me busy now."

"Rustling? You're kidding."

"Nope, but now it's done by trucks rather than horses. There are petty robberies, too, bar fights, domestic disputes, accidents. We also assist county and state agencies if needed," he explained. "It's a small department of ten. Three dispatchers and seven officers, including me. Mostly, though, it's being diplomatic."

"And you don't get bored?"

"I might if it weren't for Stephanie. You don't get bored with Stephanie. I'm working with her now to become qualified in canine search and rescue." He seemed to notice Jubal's dubious expression as he glanced down at Bart.

"Not with Bart," he explained. "He doesn't qualify. He's too timid, although he's getting better. Stephanie has two trained golden retrievers. I'm the one that needs qualifying, not the dogs. It's embarrassing." He paused, put his hand down on Bart's head. "But Bart's helped me a lot. More than I have him." He paused, then added, "I know a great dog if—"

"No," Jubal said. "I've been avoiding attachments all my adult life. They don't go with what we do."

The answer was automatic. One he'd given many times to avoid any lasting relationships, especially with women. SEALs worked in small teams and often disappeared with an hour's notice, leaving whoever loved them not knowing where they were going, or when they might be back—if they came back at all. It was hell on marriages.

He was grateful Clint didn't remind him he wasn't a SEAL anymore. Jubal still thought like one. Hell, he'd been one for twenty years. He'd learned to close the door on his emotions.

He just didn't know how to open it again. Wasn't sure he wanted to. He took another sip of beer only to find it nearly gone. He unwound his body from the chair. "I'm getting another beer. You want one?"

"Sure. I'm off duty."

Jubal snorted loud enough for Clint to hear. He went inside, pulled two beers from the fridge, opened them and returned to the lounge chair after handing one to Clint. The setting sun was streaming layers of gold and crimson flames across the sky.

Clint was silent, apparently satisfied that Jubal seemed to appreciate the sunset at least.

"What else is there in Covenant Falls?" Jubal asked after several swallows of beer.

"We have a couple of great bars, including one that's veteran-owned. We all get discounts and never get kicked out for being rowdy. There's Monday night poker games. Horseback riding." He glanced at Jubal. "You ride, don't you? Didn't you tell me you did some riding in Afghanistan?"

"Yeah, but it wasn't exactly pleasure riding. Those horses were ornery as hell." He didn't want to explain more, though the memory wasn't all bad. Those horses had been ornery, all right, but he'd relished the challenge of riding over narrow mountain paths in the dark with some of the most ferocious warriors in the Middle East.

Clint stood. "I'll go and let you get some rest. How about we hit that bar tomorrow night?"

He nodded. "I'll probably head out the next day."

Clint looked disappointed but nodded. "In the meantime, the fridge is loaded with food and beer. Help yourself. If you need anything, there's a general store, grocery store and pharmacy in town. My phone numbers are next to the phone. The middle room is kind of a library. Feel free to take or add any books. Lastly, we do have internet. It's slow but it usually works."

Jubal stood, as well. He'd been damned unappreciative. He thrust his hand out and Clint took it in a tight grip. "Good to see you."

"Likewise. I'd better warn you," Clint said. "Neighbors might leave tins of cinnamon rolls or brownies on your doorstep."

"And I have to be polite?"

Clint shrugged. "I was. Josh wasn't. He scared the hell out of the first person who tried."

"I think I would like Josh."

"I know you would," Clint said. "Get some rest, buddy. Call me if you need anything."

Jubal watched Clint walk toward the side of the cabin before turning around the corner. He had changed. Become civilized.

Still, he was glad he came. He had done more talking this afternoon than he had since his return. But Clint was an old friend, a warrior, and the fact that he, too, was separated from the service he loved made talking easier. He was one of the few people who understood having a foundation ripped away.

He sank back down in the chair and mulled over the conversation. Three vets had occupied this cabin. All three were married or engaged or close to it. Covenant Falls was beginning to sound like a Venus fly trap. If that was what the town did to a warrior like Clint, then he—Jubal Pierce—didn't belong there.

CHAPTER THREE

LISA REDDING WAS thinking along the same lines as she listened to Gordon and Kerry complain on the drive through Covenant Falls to their new home.

It had been a whirlwind four weeks. First came the professional problems. She couldn't practice in Colorado or write prescriptions on her own without a Colorado medical license. She *did* qualify—she'd passed a nationally recognized exam, had thirty-six months of postgraduate training and numerous reference letters—but it would take the medical board sixty days or more to verify the information and check for malpractice problems.

She'd started the process immediately after returning to Chicago, and Dr. Bradley had assured her he had friends on the board and would do what he could to expedite the licensure. But there would be at least a month when he would have to be available to "supervise" and write prescriptions.

He assured her he could do that from his home, which was close to the clinic.

After that problem was managed, she told Kerry and Gordon they were moving.

"I'm not going," Gordon announced. "I'll bunk with someone here."

"Think again," she said. "In the first place, we're moving to keep you out of juvenile detention. If you don't go, you'll violate your probation and go back to detention." It had taken several weeks of heavy-duty bargaining with the juvenile court judge, caseworker and probation officer in cooperation with the Covenant Falls Police Department before Lisa received permission to take Gordon to Colorado.

Still, he would have to adhere to certain restrictions, including a curfew, no alcohol or drugs and regular school attendance. She had the impression that Chicago—and Illinois—was only too happy to shove a problem kid to another state.

"I don't have to do what you say," he retorted. "You aren't even my real sister." It was the same old comeback he always used.

"Regardless, I *am* your guardian and we *are* going," she said, shutting him down while trying to hide the hurt she felt.

Kerry wasn't any better. Upon hearing the news, she wailed, "You're ruining my life. What about *my* friends? Just because Gordon did something dumb, I'm being punished."

Kerry's complaints grew even louder after she checked out Covenant Falls's website. "It doesn't even have a movie theater," she whined, then went in her room and slammed the door. *Woe of all woes.*

Aunt Kay, though, was relieved. She'd been hoping to move in with her sister, who recently lost her husband. Now that Lisa would have the time to take care of her siblings, she could do so.

With Dr. Rainey's help, Lisa leased the family home to the doctor who was replacing her at the hospital. He had a wife who also worked at the hospital. It was a mutually beneficial arrangement. She would have someone responsible taking care of the house, and the couple had a partially furnished home near the hospital.

The drive to Covenant Falls had been a nightmare. She'd rented a U-Haul trailer for what little furniture they were taking. Several of her friends helped load it while Gordon stood by, glaring.

She'd hoped that on the long drive to Covenant Falls, Kerry and Gordon might become interested in the scenery and local history. They weren't. They ignored her every effort to point out interesting landmarks. Both her siblings were stone-faced in the backseat. Gordon played with his phone, and Kerry's nose was stuck in a book even though it made her carsick.

At least it was an improvement over Gordon's bitter threats to run away and stay in Chicago. Only the knowledge that he might be sent to juvenile detention had kept him with her. But his resentment was like a poisonous haze in the car.

They reached Covenant Falls at noon on the second day, after an uncomfortable night at what she considered a "Bates" motel. Lisa drove directly to their house, parking in the driveway. She stepped out of the car and onto the porch. The key was under a flowerpot as promised.

Kerry left the car and joined her, looking around with a curiosity she obviously tried to downplay.

"We have a fenced yard," Lisa said. "Maybe we can get that dog you've been wanting."

Kerry's face lit up. "Really?"

Lisa had planned to wait until they were settled to make the peace offering, but Kerry was too far under her brother's angry influence. "I already asked if it would be okay. I think you're old enough now to take care of one."

A smile touched her sister's blue eyes. "When?"

"In the next few days. I understand there's a dog rescue group here, and they have adoptable pets."

"Traitor." Gordon had left the car and approached from behind. "Bought off by a dumb dog," he said derisively to his sister.

Lisa spun around. "I've had enough, Gordon. We're here because of you. You either shape up and stop making our lives miserable, or go back to jail in Chicago. Your choice!"

He looked startled, and Kerry looked scared. Lisa immediately regretted the words. She loved Kerry. Loved both of them. They were good kids, but they'd had one blow after another with the death of their parents.

"Come inside," she told Gordon in a softer tone. "I'm not your enemy. I know I haven't been around much, but I'm here now and I'm going to do everything I can to help you."

It was a plea that didn't change Gordon's face. He shrugged. "As if I have a choice."

"After getting your things put away inside, why don't you take your bike and look around?" she suggested. "There's a lakeside park, community center and ball fields less than a mile away. There's also a drive-in in the same area."

"I don't have any money," he complained.

She gave him ten dollars when he finished bringing in his stuff. "Be back at five p.m. for dinner, okay?"

He grunted something that she took as agreement.

It was better than nothing.

She only hoped it was a start. A new beginning in a house where memories and grief weren't in every corner.

JUBAL JERKED AWAKE a little after midnight. Plagued by smothering nightmares, he preferred sleeping outside in the comfortable lounge chair to being confined by four walls.

He was stiff, but walked down to the lake. Moonlight painted the surface silver. The water was probably ice cold, but he doubted it was any colder than the frigid Pacific where he had done his SEAL training and where he had continued to swim whenever he returned to base.

He went back to the cabin and changed into his swimming trunks. He grabbed a towel and jogged out to the lake. There was no sign of life anywhere around him, and the lake water was clear and still.

He judged the water to be five feet deep at the end of the dock. He made a shallow dive and started swimming.

The contact was like an electric shock to his body that woke all his senses. His strokes grew stronger, and the chill subsided. He swam to the other side of the lake, relishing every stroke as he skimmed through the water. The exercise stimulated him and chased the ghosts from his head as he concentrated on each stroke.

When he returned to the dock, he easily lifted himself onto the planks. He shivered now he was out of the water, and jogged back to the cabin. After a hot shower, he still felt energized from the swim.

It was time to explore his new location. He planned to stay two or three days at the most, but exploring a new territory was second nature to him. He slipped on running shorts and a T-shirt.

Jubal stepped outside and started running. His vision was not as good as it once was, but there was enough moonlight that he could see as well as most civilians could during daylight.

He ignored the pain that persisted in his joints from months of beatings and near-starvation. He tried not to think about that time. It already haunted his dreams; he wouldn't allow it to haunt his waking hours.

He started at a slow pace, then increased his speed. He'd studied the town from the mountain and memorized the street patterns. He intended to start making an outside circle of the town, then ever smaller circles until he ended up at the park.

There were several streetlights in that area. He noticed an obvious memorial but decided to check it out later. He ran north of Main Street, past what appeared to be the prestigious area of town. Most of the homes were brick two-story structures with either wraparound or broad front porches.

Then he turned east, ran through another residential neighborhood. Smaller homes, smaller lots, but all neat and well maintained. He continued eastward past larger lots and ranch houses, most with small stables or barns. He remembered Clint telling him the mayor owned horses.

He turned back toward the south. Then saw a police car following him. He stopped. Waited.

A man running in the wee hours of the morning would, most likely, raise suspicions.

The car slowed. A young man poked his head out. "Mr. Pierce?"

Jubal nodded.

"Thought so. Just wanted to say welcome. I'm Cody Terrell if you need anything. Have a good run." Then he sped ahead.

No questions about running half-naked in the middle of the night. News did get around fast. Of course, Clint was chief and probably spread the word. Jubal didn't know whether he should be irritated or amused. He continued to run and hit the business district—if it could be called that.

He noted the doctor's and veterinarian's offices. There was a light on the second floor of the vet's office. He passed a grocery and hardware store, then headed back toward the cabin. When he was four houses away, he noted movement on his dock. Not *his* dock, but the dock where he was currently staying. He glanced around. No parked cars. No lights in any of the nearby dwellings.

His training and instinct kept Jubal close to the trees as he approached the dock. He saw a flicker of light. A match. The figure was kneeling, and now he saw whoever it was kneeling over a pile of what looked like broken branches. The intruder was so involved in what he was doing he obviously didn't see Jubal.

Jubal looked around. He sensed more than saw

the slightest movement among the trees behind him. It was a skill that had saved his life more than once. He turned and spotted a second figure who wouldn't make first grade in surveillance school.

Jubal heard a warning whistle from the lookout behind him before the figure took off down Lake Road.

Jubal didn't wait any longer. The wood on the dock was dry. And as long as he was staying here, he was responsible. He ran toward the dock as the figure stood up. Tall. Slender. Young.

The figure on the dock was silhouetted against the lake like a deer in headlights. There was no place for him to go except the water, and Jubal knew how cold it was.

"Don't even think about jumping in," he shouted as he started down the dock. "I can swim better than you. And put out that damn fire. Kick the wood in the water."

The boy—Jubal was sure he was a boy now—froze.

Jubal moved down the dock until he faced the culprit. "Do it," he said.

"Do it yourself," the boy replied heatedly. "No one lives here. None of your damn business."

"*I* live here," Jubal corrected him. "Now put out the fire."

Defiance and bravado oozed from the boy as he stood his ground. "You gonna make me?"

Jubal noted the boy was probably sixteen or seventeen. And he was really pissing Jubal off now. He knew he probably didn't look that threatening. He hadn't regained the weight he once carried.

"You need to cool off, kid." He flipped him into the water, then kicked the kindling off the other side of the dock, stomping out the few remaining sparks. The flames had never really caught. The kid knew nothing about starting fires. Nor, obviously, when to take a threat seriously.

The water came up to the kid's nose even as his feet found the bottom. He struggled to breathe, lost his footing and went under. Jubal jumped in, lifted the kid onto his shoulders and carried him out of the water. The kid was shivering when he regained his footing.

"What's your name?" Jubal demanded.

The kid hesitated and Jubal gave him a look that usually silenced arguments.

"Gordon," the boy finally said.

"Well, Gordon, we are going to have a little discussion, unless you want me to call the cops right now."

"No...no."

Jubal marched the boy to the cabin and forced him inside. Both of them were dripping.

"Let go of me," Gordon demanded.

"Will you run?"

There was no answer.

"At least you don't lie," Jubal said. He steered the kid into the bathroom. "There's towels in the cabinet. Take a hot shower."

"Then what?" Gordon asked.

"I'm not sure yet. Depends on whether you do as I tell you."

"Who the hell are you, anyway? They said nobody lived here."

"So that makes it okay to burn someone's property?"

"It's only a stupid dock."

"Which cost money to build and maintain. What right do you have to destroy it?"

The kid looked down at the floor. "Whatever," he mumbled.

"Take a hot shower," Jubal said.

"You some kind of pervert?"

Jubal gave him a look that had cowed a hell of a lot meaner adversaries. "I'll lend you some dry clothes. I'll expect them back. Clean."

"You aren't going to call the cops?"

"Did I say I wasn't?" Jubal closed the door and went to hunt for something the boy could wear. He finally picked a pair of sweatpants with a stretch waist and an old T-shirt. The kid would probably drown in them, but there wasn't any help for that. Jubal changed into a pair of jeans and a sleeveless sweatshirt.

He would sit the kid down and read him the

riot act. Scare the hell out of him. Like someone had scared the hell out of him years ago.

Why would he start a fire on a dock? What in the hell did the dock ever do to him? It might be interesting to find out. Then he would take the kid to his parents.

He planted himself outside the bathroom. He wasn't going to give the kid a chance to escape. There were consequences to actions.

The sound of running water stopped.

Jubal opened the door and threw in the clothes. "Dress and then we'll have a little chat about arson."

He closed the door and took up his post. The door didn't open. He would give the kid five minutes. No longer.

The door opened after four and a half minutes. Gordon was indeed swallowed in Jubal's clothes. He was maybe five foot nine to Jubal's six-three. He was lean, had an athlete's supple frame but not the muscles. He was holding his wet clothes at arm's length.

"Into the living room," Jubal said.

"Why?" Gordon said with attitude. The shower apparently gave him courage.

"Okay," Jubal said. "If you're going to play it that way, I'll call the cops now. Let them sort things out. Your parents know you're out this late?"

"I don't have any parents," Gordon said defiantly.

"You just dropped from above?" Jubal asked.

"They died."

"Then who looks after you? Or who is supposed to?"

"I'm seventeen. I don't need anyone to look after me."

"After seeing you tonight, I'd disagree," Jubal said calmly. "Where do you live?"

"Where do you think?"

"I'm not fencing with you." Jubal's voice hardened. "It's three in the morning, and you've disrupted my peace and tranquility. I didn't plan on confronting a juvenile punk and taking another swim."

"I was doing okay. You didn't have to come in the water."

"That so?" Jubal said with a raised eyebrow. "In any event, you think I was just going to let you stroll away?"

"Why not? It was just a small fire. No harm done."

"Only because you obviously don't know how to build one. I take it you're not a Boy Scout?"

"That's for losers."

"Losers who clearly have more sense in one finger than you have in your entire body."

Gordon stared at him. Jubal noticed the boy's

gaze seemed more careful now, hesitating when he saw the tattoo on his arm. "What's that?"

"I thought you were smarter than anyone else," he said. "You tell me."

"Military?"

"Yeah."

"My sister thinks they're all fascists."

"So your sister is the source of all your information? You live with her, then?"

"Yeah."

"Tell me where you live, or I'll call the police. Maybe those fascists can straighten you out."

The boy's face paled. "We just wanted to see if it would burn," he said. "He said no one lived here."

Jubal raised an eyebrow. "Who told you that? Your chickenshit buddy who ran out on you? I saw him run."

Gordon didn't say anything.

"Okay, have it your way." Jubal took his cell out of his pocket. "The police chief is a friend of mine and I have his number. I didn't know I'd need it so soon."

"Don't!" Gordon said, adding a belated, "Please."

"You don't want him to know a juvenile pyromaniac is running around the community?"

"I'm not… I mean, you can't call the police."

"Why not?"

"I'm…" Gordon's voice trailed off.

"Yes?" Jubal said, and raised his eyebrow.

"I'm…on probation," Gordon admitted with obvious reluctance.

"Burn someone else's house down?"

"No!"

"Anyone missing you right now?"

"No."

"Why don't I believe that?" Jubal said.

"My sister doesn't give a shit what I do. She's too busy…"

"Too busy doing what?"

The boy's lips closed.

"You're not getting out of here until you tell me where you live."

The defiance in Gordon's eyes faded away. "She's the new doctor."

Jubal studied him for a moment. "I'll make a deal with you."

"What?" Gordon said cautiously.

"Give me her address. I'll drive you there, watch you go inside whichever way you got out. In return, you'll give me ten hours of work. Productive work, and I decide what counts as productive."

The kid looked disbelieving. "Ten hours?"

"You think it should be longer? Maybe you're right."

The kid looked trapped.

"You *have* a choice," Jubal said. "I can call the police chief. I imagine you'll be charged with arson. That won't be the least of your problems if, as you say, you're on probation."

The last remnant of defiance drained from the kid's face. "What'd you want me to do?"

"I'll think of something. Yard work. Painting the dock. You start tomorrow. Be here at two p.m."

Jubal watched the calculating look on the boy's face. Despite his abject firebug skills, the kid wasn't dumb. All he had to do was point out a house, then make a dash for an alley and disappear.

"I'm a hell of a lot faster than you," Jubal said, checkmating that particular scheme. He kinda liked the kid. He didn't give up. And he wasn't afraid of former SEAL Jubal Pierce. Damn, had he changed that much?

"Who are *you*?" the kid asked.

"Name's Jubal. Jubal Pierce."

"That's a dumb name."

Jubal shrugged. "My dad was a rodeo rider. Jubal wasn't all that unusual among that set." He had no idea why he explained that, except maybe it would make an impact on a kid.

Gordon's face showed more interest. "*You* ever ride in a rodeo?"

"Nope. And no more diversions. Deal or no deal?"

The kid nodded sullenly.

"A deal's a deal," Jubal said. "You break it, there will be consequences."

"Why do you give a shit about a tiny fire?" The kid tried one last tact.

"Because I live here, and while I live here, I respect the property and the man who loaned it to me. It's a matter of, shall we say, honor."

"You come from the dark ages, man," Gordon retorted.

Jubal shrugged. "Come on, let's go. And take your wet clothes with you."

The kid almost tripped over the dragging legs of Jubal's sweatpants, but he followed Jubal to his Mazda. At least he couldn't run, not without tripping.

He asked the kid for directions and retraced one of the routes he ran earlier. Gordon slouched in the corner of the car, his sullen voice barely audible.

"That's it," the kid said, pointing at a neat two story house. When Jubal stopped, Gordon opened the door.

"I want my clothes back," Jubal warned. "Washed."

"Whatever," the kid said.

"Don't use that word with me again," Jubal warned. "It's offensive and stupid."

The kid's lips clamped shut, then, carrying his wet clothes, he walked to the side of the house and disappeared in the back.

Jubal waited several minutes, saw a light go on upstairs, then decided the kid really did live there. He said his sister was the doctor, and he believed that. It would be too easy for him to check it out, and Covenant Falls was not big enough to hide in. He did wonder, though, if the kid would show up tomorrow, or was it today now?

Jubal also wondered what in the hell he was doing. He'd planned to leave in the next day or two. He was starting something he couldn't finish unless he hung around longer than he intended.

He always finished what he started if humanly possible. It was in his DNA.

So why had he started something that might keep him here longer than planned?

The answer came too quickly.

He recognized that kid. It was him twenty years ago.

CHAPTER FOUR

LISA WOKE TO SILENCE. No sound of heavy trucks passing or the blaring of a horn. It took her a moment to realize where she was.

The flower print on the wallpaper was not the comforting light blue of her former bedroom. New house. New town. New job. She should be excited. She wasn't. She was too worried about Gordon.

She looked at the clock. A little after seven a.m. That was late for her. She thought about the day ahead, mostly about Gordon.

Gordon *had* appeared at dinner yesterday and shoveled down his share of a casserole Lisa had found in the fridge along with eggs, milk, cheese, bacon and other basic items.

Although he ate well, he did it with a scowl and grunts when she'd asked him whether he'd met anyone his age yesterday afternoon. Then, completely ignoring both his sisters, he disappeared into the bedroom with his phone and tablet.

She'd checked on him at ten before she went to her own bedroom. His light was off.

She'd gone to sleep then. She was exhausted from the long drive yesterday, then unpacking most of what they'd brought with them. Some items still remained in the trailer.

So much to do today. First on the schedule was a meeting with Dr. Bradley, who was back home in Covenant Falls. Then she intended to drop by the clinic to look over scheduled appointments for the next several days and familiarize herself with the office.

Also on the "to do" list was a visit to the veterinarian's office to look at adoptable dogs. Kerry, along with Gordon, had gone through two terrible years. They both deserved more than she'd given them. She was intent on remedying that.

Kerry, she knew, would be easier than Gordon. Her sister loved animals and reading. She was a good student, though her grades had also fallen in the past year.

Gordon was more difficult. He had been a strong student until their mother became so ill. He was good with his hands and had built a fort in their backyard when he was twelve. It was still sound. He could also look at any puzzle and solve it in half the time it took someone else. But since their mother died, everything had been different.

Lisa rose, put a robe over her nightshirt and headed toward the kitchen. To her amazement, she smelled the aroma of coffee and was even more surprised to see Kerry at the kitchen table eating a bowl of cereal.

Kerry turned around, sensing her presence. "I made coffee," Kerry said.

"I smelled it. Thank you." Lisa made a beeline for the pot on the counter. Coffee was her lifeblood.

"Can we go over to the veterinarian clinic and see if they have dogs for adoption?" Kerry asked after Lisa dropped two slices of bread in the toaster.

"Maybe this afternoon if she's there. I have to meet with Dr. Bradley this morning and go over records."

"What will I do this morning?" Her voice was plaintive.

"What about going to the library? You can ride your bike. Maybe you'll meet some kids there."

Kerry shrugged. "Gordon says they're all weirdos."

"And what, pray tell, qualifies someone as a weirdo?"

Kerry nibbled on her cereal and shrugged, ignoring a question she probably couldn't answer. "Will you call the vet this morning and see if we can come this afternoon?" she persisted.

The eagerness in Kerry's face warmed Lisa. She hadn't seen it in far too long. She located the list of phone numbers Eve provided and found Dr. Stephanie Morgan's number.

Lisa looked at her watch. It was eight a.m. "She might be in now. Maybe Gordon will come with us and help pick one out."

"He probably won't even be around," Kerry said dismissively. "And it'll be my dog, anyway. Will you call now, Lisa?" she begged.

To Lisa's surprise, Stephanie answered on the second ring and must have recognized her name on phone ID. "Hi," she said. "Dr. Redding? Eve said you might call. What can I do for you?"

"Eve said you might have some dogs available for adoption."

"Music to my ears," Stephanie said. "I have a couple of really good rescues. Would you like to come over today?"

"That would be great. My sister's very excited."

"What about noon?" Stephanie said. "I have a break between appointments then."

"I'm meeting with Dr. Bradley at nine but lunchtime should be fine."

"I'm really glad Doc found someone to fill in for him. His doctors told him he shouldn't be working at all, but he's insisted on seeing patients since there's been no one else."

"I'll try to make sure he doesn't need to see them now," Lisa said.

"Good. I'll expect you and your sister at noon." The phone clicked off.

Lisa looked at her watch. Nearly eight. She

needed to take a shower and dress. She had no idea what to wear in town. Black pants and a short-sleeved fitted blouse would probably do. She would take one of her white coats and drop it off at the clinic.

She went upstairs and knocked on Gordon's door. He'd been far too quiet since he went to his room last night. He had a backlog of movies on his tablet along with games but...

No sound inside.

She opened the door. He was still sleeping. She looked around. To her surprise there were no clothes on the floor. She closed the door, then knocked. Hard.

Mumbling came from inside. "Just a minute." Finally, Gordon appeared. His long hair was a mess. He was blurry-eyed as if he hadn't had any sleep. "Wh-what do you want?" he asked rudely.

"I have to leave to meet with Dr. Bradley," she said. "I may not be back until noon, and then I'm taking Kerry to look at some dogs. Want to go with us? Maybe help Kerry pick one?"

"You gotta be kidding. We'd never agree. She'll want some little prissy thing. Besides, I have things to do. Going on a hike with a kid I met."

"Where to?"

He shrugged his shoulders. "I don't know. I don't live here. Just going to show me around."

Lisa swallowed hard. Nothing had changed.

"You're supposed to check in with the police department."

"Tomorrow," he said.

"I'll make an appointment for you."

"Whatever," he said, and closed the door.

She wondered if he'd ever forgive her for bringing him here. It didn't matter that she was trying to help him—help both of them. She'd hated to take them from the house they'd lived in all their lives, but it had become a house of ghosts.

She went back downstairs and took a hot shower, trying to erase all the doubts she had, the failure she felt. She washed and dried her hair and pulled it back, fastening it with a clasp. Not very fashionable or stylish but fast and practical.

She checked her watch again. Seven minutes until nine. The doctor's office was just six blocks away but she was running late. She grabbed her white coat, the car keys, her laptop and stopped by the living room where Kerry was watching a talk show. "I'm not sure when I'll be back but I promise it will be before noon. Try the library or maybe just explore this morning, okay?"

She gave Kerry her allowance in case she wanted to go into town. She knew from her own teenage years how important it was to have at least a few dollars for a soft drink or emergencies. She hoped Gordon would find a part-time job as she had as a teenager.

JUBAL TRIED SLEEPING inside the cabin but woke up drenched in sweat. He'd been in the hut again. No light. No air. Only half a cup of filthy water to drink. His wrists were bound with rusty chain that tore into the skin, and he bled from several gashes inflicted by one of his captors.

Forcing the images from his head, he glanced at the clock. A little after four a.m. He knew he wouldn't go back to sleep. He stood and walked to the bathroom, turning on the light. He looked at himself in the mirror with disgust. Why in the hell had he bargained with that kid last night? Maybe he wouldn't show up.

Or, Jubal thought, he could forget about it and leave now. He hadn't promised Clint anything but a quick visit, and he certainly didn't owe the juvenile delinquent anything.

He swore as he took a shower, washing away the sweat. He couldn't take enough showers these days after two years without. When he'd reached civilization six months ago, he had a beard half-way to his chest and layers of dirt.

Jubal was too awake now to try to sleep. He always thought better when running or swimming, and the shock of cold water should clear his mind. He considered skinny-dipping since he doubted anyone was awake. But then Clint was his host; it probably wouldn't help his job as police chief if his guest was reported for indecent exposure.

He resisted the urge and pulled on his swimming trunks before jogging out to the dock. He plunged into the cold water and his thoughts strayed back to the kid. Even if he did show up, what would he find for him to do?

Hell, he kept questioning himself. Why did he let himself get involved? The kid had a nice house from the look of it. Yet Jubal couldn't escape seeing himself years ago. He'd lived in a nice house, too, but he'd been filled with resentment and bitterness. His mother had taken him away from the father he adored, the father who died a year later with no one to mourn him but a son who lived two thousand miles away.

Maybe that was why he inserted himself in someone else's life, something he'd never done before. He remembered his own pain when his father died, the rebellion he felt against his mother whom he'd blamed for his father's death. Wouldn't have happened if he had been there, if his father knew he was looking on. This kid had not only lost a father but a mother as well. He didn't know the whys or hows, but he recognized the hurt and loss inside and the urge to strike out.

It was obvious the boy was headed for trouble.

After returning to the cabin, he did his usual quota of push-ups, showered again, and at eight decided the hour reasonable enough to call Clint.

"Hey," he said. "I'd like to meet the owner of the cabin."

"Josh? Sure. He'd like that, too."

"Can we make it just him and me?" Jubal asked.

"Sure. Either Josh or I will call you back."

That was one of the reasons Jubal had always liked Clint. No questions. No explanations needed.

The phone rang within minutes. "Jubal? Josh Manning here."

Short. Jubal liked that. "Thanks for the use of the cabin."

"Happy to have you there. Clint suggested it was time to meet. How about lunch?"

"I don't want to interrupt anything."

"You won't," Josh said. "Eleven okay? I'd like you to see the town's main attraction, then we'll go to Maude's. Great diner."

Jubal had planned to stay around the cabin to see whether the kid turned up early, but hell, it was the kid he wanted to discuss with Josh. "Sure."

"Good. I'll pick you up."

"Thanks," Jubal said.

Jubal made coffee and toasted several pieces of bread from the full larder. He had more than a few thanks to give Josh Manning in addition to his questions.

With another three hours to kill, he checked his laptop for recent news, particularly about the Middle East. Friends were there. He wished

he were there, as well. He felt like a fish flop-
ping on land in this peaceful town in the middle
of nowhere.

One website led to another until he heard an
approaching vehicle. He closed the laptop and
went to meet his temporary host.

The top was down on a Jeep and his visitor
was accompanied by a Belgian Malinois. Jubal
recognized the breed from his SEAL days. It was
the service's dog of choice because of intelligence
and size.

Even if he hadn't known Josh Manning had
been a soldier, he would have instantly recognized him as one. Although there was a slight
limp, Manning walked with an assurance that
came with being a career warrior.

They shook hands, each sizing up the other.

"This is Amos," Josh said. "He's also a veteran."

The dog lifted his paw politely and Jubal
leaned over and shook it. Jubal knew instantly
he was going to like both his host and the dog.
"Thanks again for the use of the cabin," he said.

"Glad to have someone here to take care of it."

"That's what I wanted to talk to you about,"
Jubal replied.

Josh raised an eyebrow. "Okay. Let's talk while
I show you around. Maude's a great diner but it's
not a good place for private conversation. News
and rumors travel with the speed of light."

"I discovered that when one of your officers stopped while I was running and knew me by name."

"Drove me crazy when I first came here," Josh said. "Now I just accept it. People here are interested in what's happening in their universe, and Covenant Falls *is* their universe. But there's no malice about it." He paused, then asked, "You walk up the mountain yet?"

"Yeah. Right after I arrived."

"Me, too." He turned a corner. "I thought I would show you the falls. It's our main attraction. It'll take a little more than an hour going and coming. We can talk, then stop at Maude's for lunch. I'll never hear the end of it if I don't take you there."

Jubal mostly listened as Josh drove through town. They passed what looked like an old, rustic saloon with a dozen cars in the parking lot. "That's the Rusty Nail," Josh said. "It's our watering hole. The owner is a vet and makes sure we feel welcome. He's also a member of our Monday night vet poker game."

They passed an inn with a sign portraying a whimsical camel that looked toward the mountains. "The Camel Trail Inn?" Jubal asked.

"My pride and joy," Josh said. "My partner—another vet—and I finished rehabbing the inn two months ago. We're getting tourists, but unfortunately we don't have enough activities to keep them here more than a day or two. We want to start a wilderness adventure business but we have to have the right person." He glanced at Jubal. "Would you be interested?"

"Thanks, but I don't plan to stay more than a few days."

"Heard and understood," Josh said. "I'll say no more."

After a few more miles, Josh saw a large sign: The Falls of Covenant Falls. Josh turned left and followed a winding road through a virgin forest. Then he stopped in a parking area. "The falls are just beyond the bend."

Jubal heard the roar ahead and walked with Josh around the corner to a picnic area. It was empty. The falls were grander than Jubal had imagined. Torrents of white frothy water cascaded over rocky outcrops into a gorge below. Water vapor hung in the air forming a rainbow.

"Impressive," he said. He'd seen a lot of waterfalls, but there was a pristine beauty about this one that touched something inside him. He understood now why Josh wanted him to see it. "I would think there would be more visitors."

"The locals come here on the weekend and special events," Josh said, "but we're trying to attract more out-of-town visitors and new residents. For a long time the majority of the town leaders didn't want change or growth, but that policy resulted in a town that was dying off. My wife and others are trying to reverse that."

"A new mission for you?" Jubal heard the longing in his own voice.

"Something like that. I didn't know how much I needed one until I came here. But that's not why you wanted to see me. I gathered from Clint that you have something on your mind."

In the short time they'd been together, Jubal sensed he could trust Josh's discretion. He told him about the kid.

Josh listened without commenting until Jubal finished. "He's probably the brother of Lisa Redding, the new doctor in town," Josh said. "I understand he got into some trouble back in Chicago."

"It's your property," Jubal said. "I thought you should know."

"And you want my input?"

"It's your town. Your cabin. Your dock. I don't want to do anything that would put you in a bad spot."

"Can't see how unless you intend bodily harm."

"Other than throwing him into the lake?"

Josh chuckled. "Haven't heard anything about it this morning so I think your kid is keeping silent."

"He's not 'my' kid."

Josh met his gaze. "I would have done the same

thing—except maybe throwing him in the lake. I don't like cold water."

"Yeah, but he's the brother of your new doctor, who, I'd imagine, is important to the town."

"She is. We've been looking for a doctor for months and Dr. Redding is said to be a very good one."

"And," Jubal continued, "according to the kid, she considers the military 'fascists.'" He paused. "I wouldn't want to be responsible for her leaving because of this."

"Well, I get the impression she's made of stronger stuff than to turn and run. She also has a contract. As for the 'fascist' comment, I met her several weeks ago and she seemed perfectly fine with me, and I'm pretty sure she knows I'm ex-military. Eve did say Lisa was concerned about Gordon and it was the main reason she moved here.

"As for the kid himself," Josh said, "he may not show up. If he doesn't, I would forget about it. You probably scared the hell out of him. And if you didn't, the lake probably did."

"And if he does?"

"It would be a step in the right direction."

"What could he do around the cabin?"

"Maybe build a bench on the deck?" Josh suggested. "I've always kinda wanted one."

"And say nothing to the sister?"

"We probably should," Josh said with a wry

smile. "But then he might get defensive and act out more."

"I know," Jubal said. "Been there. Done that."

Josh chuckled. "Me, too."

"What will your wife think about this? I hear she's the mayor."

"Truth be told, I'm not sure. She keeps surprising me. She has a devious soul underneath an innocent facade. She can be more concerned about the end rather than the means. I think she would approve, unless we lose the doctor. Then there will be hell to pay."

Jubal didn't answer. He felt trapped in a spiderweb but then he was the one who decided to reform the kid on his own. He just damn well couldn't figure out why he cared as much as he did.

Josh looked at him sympathetically. "Just don't become a cause with my wife. You'll never know what hit you. When I came here, I was a confirmed loner, mad at the world. Now I have a ranch, a wife, a son, five dogs, two horses and a crazy cat. And, God help me, I'm a businessman with a huge bank loan."

Jubal had no idea what Josh had been like before, but now his eyes were alive with humor and, obviously, love. For the slightest sliver of time, he felt envy.

Josh interrupted the thought. "Now it's time to introduce you to Maude's steaks."

LISA KNOCKED ON Dr. Bradley's door. A kind-looking woman who appeared to be in her seventies opened the door.

"You must be Dr. Redding," the woman said. "I'm Gloria Bradley and I'm so pleased you're here. A physician who has been filling in for him had to leave three weeks ago. Janie can handle a lot of the problems, but my husband took several calls. It worried me to death."

She led the way into a comfortable-looking living room. Dr. Bradley sat in a wheelchair next to a table piled high with folders.

"'Bout time," Dr. Bradley groused as she was shown a chair next to him. "Thought you were going to be here three days ago."

She would have been had there not been complications in Gordon's court case. There was no qualified probation officer in Covenant Falls. An arrangement was worked out with the office in Pueblo whereby the local police in Covenant Falls would keep in contact with Gordon and report any probation violations. But she didn't want to go into all that with Dr. Bradley. "I'm sorry," she said. "We had last-minute complications."

He turned then to the stack of folders on the table. "These are the records of our chronically ill patients. Heart disease, diabetes, cancer." He discussed each case, often adding a wry comment about personal quirks of the patient.

She took notes on everything and silently

vowed to do more research on ailments specific
to the community. "I was thinking about holding
an open house," she ventured.

He raised a bushy white eyebrow. "Don't know
if that would be a good idea," he warned. "The
entire town would come to meet the new doctor.
And if you had a series of them, you would have
to figure out a way to string out the invitations
as to not offend anyone. And they would expect
to be fed."

"Maybe not such a good idea?" Lisa winced.

"Don't think so. If you want to get to know
people, go to the churches. You'll meet a lot of
our patients there. You'll be invited to a lot of
homes, but again, people will be unhappy if you
go to Mrs. Smith's house and not theirs."

She was getting a headache. This country
doctor thing was more complicated than she'd
thought.

"One more thing," he said. "A lot of people
here don't have much money, but they have a lot
of pride, so my billing system might seem a bit
peculiar to someone who hasn't been in private
practice. Janie can fill you in on that."

She nodded. They had already worked out the
terms. She was to receive a salary, not rely on
income. The salary wasn't high but it was better
than a resident's salary and even the fellowship's.
And she had free rent and what looked like a very
low cost of living compared to Chicago.

Dr. Bradley looked tired, too tired.

"I'd better go," she said. "I promised my sister a dog today."

"Great idea," Dr. Bradley said. "It's amazing what they can do in reducing stress."

Maybe she needed two—or more—dogs. She nodded, even as she wondered whether he meant more than the words indicated. "Thank you for giving me this chance. I'll keep in close touch."

"Good. Don't hesitate to call me if you have a question."

But she *would* hesitate. He didn't look well at all. He skin looked pasty and pale, and his breathing was labored. She'd already stayed too long.

She said goodbye and left.

Kerry was waiting for her when she arrived back at the house.

"Where's your brother?" Lisa asked.

"He didn't say."

Lisa didn't press her. She didn't want them tattling on each other. That, she knew, was no way to build trust, which was already sorely lacking.

"Did he eat anything?"

"Some toast, then took off."

Lisa closed her eyes. Secrecy had become a way of life with him.

At least he couldn't get in trouble in a town this small. She suspected she would hear about it instantly. She comforted herself with the thought that he was exploring the town, not huddled in his bedroom with his cell phone.

Still, she called him. To her surprise, he answered almost immediately.

"Where are you?" she asked.

"Just hanging around."

"Meet some kids?"

Silence.

"When will you be back?" she tried again.

"Don't know exactly."

"What about lunch?"

"I'm not hungry."

"You're always hungry."

"Not since you made me leave Chicago." Bitterness was thick in his voice.

She ignored the dig. "I'll be at the clinic this afternoon," she said. "And home by five. I want you there for dinner."

"All right. Gotta go." He hung up.

He gave up too easily. It worried her.

Lisa looked at her watch, noted the time. She ran a brush through her hair and added a touch of lipstick. Then she went into the kitchen. "Let's go see about that dog, kiddo," she said.

The delighted look on her sister's face lightened her heart. She hoped they could find a suitable dog. At least her sister would have some happiness and maybe her brother would, as well.

CHAPTER FIVE

IT WAS TWELVE on the dot when Lisa and Kerry arrived at the veterinarian's office. Punctuality had been drilled into Lisa's head as a child and fortified by college, medical school and residency.

They were greeted by a young woman behind a counter. "Hi," she said. "You must be the new doctor. Stephanie's expecting you. I'm Beth Malloy, her vet tech. I'll tell her you're here."

"Thank you," Lisa said, and looked around the office. It was a pleasant setting with comfortable chairs and light blue walls. She looked at a large bulletin board. There were "lost and found" flyers on dogs and cats and "for sale" flyers for horses. Toward the bottom were photos of dogs with For Adoption headings.

"Hi," came a voice from behind her. She turned around and saw a tall, lithe redhead.

"I'm Stephanie," she said. "Welcome to Covenant Falls, Dr. Redding." Without waiting for an answer, the veterinarian turned to Kerry. "And you must be Kerry. I'm sorry I missed you yesterday. I hear you like animals and might be interested in one of my rescues."

"Yes…ma'am." It was obvious, at least to Lisa, that Kerry was nervous.

"Have you had a dog before?" Stephanie asked.

"No."

"But you know an animal is a lot of responsibility?" Stephanie studied Kerry's face.

Kerry nodded.

"I have several dogs here in need of a family," Stephanie said. "Two are puppies, but that takes even more care and time." She looked at Lisa for guidance.

"Oh, can we have a puppy?" Kerry said just as Lisa was about to announce her preference for an older, well-trained addition to her family.

"Let's take a look at them," Stephanie said. She opened the door between the waiting and office areas and led the way to the back. She opened another door and they walked into a large room. Two golden retrievers stood and frantically wagged their tails. "These two are mine," Stephanie said. "Sherry and Stryker. They're search and rescue dogs."

"Can I pet them?" Kerry asked.

"They would be offended if you didn't," Stephanie replied with an infectious grin. "Sherry is the one on the right."

Lisa noticed that Stephanie watched carefully

as Kerry knelt and rubbed her hands through the thick fur of each dog. They responded with thumping tails and happy wriggles.

Stephanie nodded with approval. "They're good judges," she said. She went over to one of the kennels and opened it. "Now this little girl," Stephanie said as she brought out a blond bundle of fur, "was found in a hoarding situation where there wasn't enough care. She's about six months old. She's very sweet and smart, but she's been neglected and needs a lot of attention. I've been looking for just the right person to take care of her," Stephanie said.

"I can do that," Kerry said as she took the small dog in her arms. The dog promptly licked her face.

Lisa-the-doctor inwardly flinched, but Lisa-the-sister didn't have the heart to say no. Kerry hadn't looked so happy since months before their mother died.

Stephanie looked at Lisa with a question in her eyes.

Lisa hesitated, then nodded.

"What's her name?" Kerry asked.

"I've been calling her Susie, but if you take her, you can rename her," Stephanie said.

"I like the name," Kerry said. She looked at Lisa, her heart bursting with affection. "Can I have her, Lisa?"

"You'll have to feed her, keep her dishes clean and walk her often," Lisa said. "She'll be your responsibility."

"I've started her house training," Stephanie said, "and she's doing very well, but you have to take her out often and clean up if she makes a mistake. You might want a crate for when you're gone."

Kerry nodded rapidly. "I will."

"She's not like a toy or a game that you can put aside when you're tired or busy," Stephanie continued. "It's a real commitment. Your commitment. Not your sister's."

"I know," Kerry said. She looked at Lisa. "I'll take care of her. I promise."

"She's had all her shots and has been spayed. She's already been chipped in case she ever gets lost," Stephanie continued. "She's in good health now, but she's gone through some tough times, and she needs security and affection. I have to warn you," Stephanie added, "she's still in the chewing stage. You don't want to leave your shoes where she can get them. Chew sticks are advised."

Lisa started having doubts after the last comment but by then Susie's head was resting on Kerry's shoulder and the dog looked like she'd reached heaven.

"What is the fee?" Lisa asked.

Stephanie smiled. "We don't charge anything

if we find the right home, but I belong to a rescue group that accepts donations to help cover their costs. The name and address of the group will be on Susie's paperwork and it's completely voluntary. I'll never know whether you contribute or not."

Lisa looked down at Kerry. "What do you think, sis?" she asked, even though the answer was obvious.

"I want her. Please. Can I take her now?"

Lisa looked at Stephanie, who hesitated. "You'll need a collar and leash. Dog dishes. One for water, one for food. Dog food, of course. You can get that at the grocery store here in town. They have several good brands. You might want a dog bed. The general store has those, along with dog toys."

Lisa nodded, her mind a cash register as it started adding costs.

"Why don't we have lunch at Maude's?" Stephanie suggested. "We can talk about training Susie. Then you can pick up what you need before taking her home."

Lisa hadn't expected a new member of the family this fast. She'd intended to discuss the possibility first. She'd always been a planner, someone who looked at all aspects of an action before making a decision. But lately it seemed decisions were being made for her.

Then she saw the broad smile on Kerry's face

and nodded. Her sister obviously didn't want to leave the dog, and apparently Susie didn't want her to leave either as she pressed her body against Kerry's. She was claiming Kerry as much as Kerry was claiming the dog.

They walked several doors down to Maude's and went inside. Maude greeted Lisa like an old friend even though it was only the second time they'd met. She walked them to one of the few remaining booths and gave them menus.

Stephanie talked about Susie and what she'd observed since the dog had been with her, then asked Kerry about herself. "I heard you like horses, too."

"Oh, yes," Kerry said. "Mrs. Manning told Lisa she'd teach me to ride."

"What else do you like? In school, for instance, what's your favorite subject?"

"English and history."

"You'll have to go to our pageant Saturday night," Stephanie said. "It's all about the history here and the gold rush."

Kerry looked at Lisa. "Can we?

"Sure," Lisa said. "I'd like to see it, too."

Lisa listened to Stephanie and Kerry talk about Susie and the dos and don'ts of raising a puppy. She reminded herself that she needed to get home, check on her brother and read the files Dr. Bradley had given her. She planned to spend the entire day at the clinic tomorrow. There were a number of shots to administer to incoming first graders along with three scheduled annual physicals.

She looked up to see two men enter Maude's. One was Eve's husband, whom she'd met during her earlier visit here. The other man made her breath catch in her throat.

Lisa didn't know why exactly. It wasn't because he was cover-model handsome. But there was something about him that was strikingly different.

She'd heard the expression "hard face" but she never knew what it meant until now. His features seemed carved from granite: strong cheekbones, lips that were firm and unsmiling, a set jaw. There was a scar on his forehead near his hairline. He had the start of a beard, the kind that could look sloppy or surprisingly sexy.

His was the latter. His vivid blue eyes swept the room as if danger hovered in every corner, and he walked with a panther-like grace she associated with athletes.

His gaze lingered on her and she felt herself blushing. She forced herself to look away and take a sip of water. Her sister, thankfully, was listening intently to Stephanie.

She took a deep breath, then watched as the two men approached their booth. Josh Manning smiled at her. "Welcome. Good to see you again," he said to Lisa. "How's everything going?"

"Considering it's my first day and I'm already adding to my family, a little overwhelming," Lisa managed as her gaze was drawn to Josh's companion.

"Adding to your family?" Josh asked.

"A new puppy," she replied, concentrating on Eve's husband.

"Sounds like a good way to start your life here." Josh grinned, then turned to Stephanie. "I don't think you've met your husband's friend yet. This is Jubal Pierce. Jubal, meet Clint's wife, Stephanie, and Dr. Lisa Redding, our new doctor. Sitting next to Lisa must be her pretty sister, Kerry."

Kerry blushed at the compliment.

Jubal Pierce nodded at the introductions, nothing more, but his intense blue eyes seemed to look beyond her attempt at a polite smile right into her soul. She felt her stomach tighten and an odd confusion took over her mind. She didn't understand it. She'd met more traditionally handsome men. But none had ever rocked her ordinarily sensible world at first glance.

"Mr. Pierce," she acknowledged, praying that her face didn't reveal her inner turmoil.

He turned to Stephanie. "I understand now why Clint wanted to stay here." A shadow of a smile touched his lips, easing the rigid trails in his face.

Stephanie's face colored, and she looked startled. Then a smile started slow and spread across her face. "He's really happy you're here."

Jubal Pierce nodded and some of the hardness seemed to fade from his expression.

Jubal. It was an odd name but somehow it seemed to fit. His face and arms were deeply tanned and tiny lines branched out from those sea blue eyes. He looked as if he'd walked out of a western film.

She couldn't tell his age. Though there were touches of gray in his hair, his lean body radiated strength and tightly controlled energy like a wound-up spring. She wondered what a real smile would look like.

Instead, he seemed to peer straight through her, tearing down protective walls. As a doctor, she'd trained herself to suppress emotions. She tried to put that training in action and plaster a casual smile on her lips.

Josh saved her. "Here comes Maude to chase us toward our table." He smiled at Lisa. "I hope you like Covenant Falls."

"I'm sure we will," she said, hoping her voice sounded matter-of-fact.

The two men turned away and followed Maude to a table on the other side of the room but still in Lisa's direct line of sight.

She tried to relax and listen to Stephanie, but she was unsettled. Yes, *unsettled* was the word. Nothing stronger. Nothing mind-blowing.

Still, she didn't understand it. She'd met and dated better-looking guys before, but none had the stark masculine appeal Jubal Pierce radiated. The barest hint of a smile he'd given Stephanie made him even more fascinating. It was obvious he didn't use it much.

The simple fact was that he rattled her, and she didn't like it one bit. The man had military written all over him. Career military. She didn't know whether he was active or inactive, but she was wary of the type. She'd seen what guns and other weapons did to a human body and couldn't begin to imagine how it affected the person wielding them.

While she respected soldiers for what they did, she didn't want it around her and what was left of her family, especially Gordon, who'd talked about going into the service, even if she suspected it was an act of rebellion. He was capable of enlisting on his eighteenth birthday just to display his independence.

But then why had she been disappointed when Jubal Pierce walked away? Simple physical attraction, she told herself. Something she could easily control by staying away from him. She forced him from her mind, looked away and tried to concentrate on what Stephanie was saying.

"He's the fourth veteran to stay in Josh's cabin on the lake," Stephanie explained. "It's kind of a long story, but Josh inherited a cabin from a military buddy, and when he married Eve he passed it on to other vets who needed a way station for a few months. Jubal however, is just staying a few days to visit with my husband, Clint. They are longtime military friends." Stephanie then filled them in on the succession of veterans in the cabin and the resulting romances.

"That's…" Lisa was at a loss for words. It was just too weird to be true.

Stephanie nodded. "Eve says the cabin is magic."

"And you?"

"I don't believe in magic, but if someone told me I would fall in love with a sky jockey and risk junkie, I would've told them they were nuts," Stephanie admitted. "I nearly killed Clint the first time we met, and he laughed. I think I fell in love with him at that minute, though I gave him a rough time. I thought love was a weakness."

"And now?" Lisa asked.

"I discovered its strength. Clint's the only guy who let me be me, who respected me enough to let me solve a very big problem on my own—even if he insisted on hovering in the background while I did. And if that's not enough, he's a fine hand with a guitar."

Lisa watched Stephanie's face soften. Loneliness struck her like lightning. She'd been too consumed with meeting her goals to give any thought to a relationship. There had never been time for romance and there had never been real temptation.

And now she was twenty-eight and long past the giddy stage.

Why was she still seeing Jubal Pierce in her head?

She was relieved when Stephanie turned to Kerry and asked if she would like to volunteer at the clinic on weekends or after school. She was always in need of volunteers to socialize the rescues. Kerry could even bring Susie with her.

Kerry glowed. Lisa kicked herself for not realizing that her sister had probably been craving a purpose. She'd grown up fast, and Lisa hadn't noticed it.

"Can I, Lisa?" Kerry asked.

"Of course. I think it's a terrific idea."

"Awesome," Kerry said, then attacked her hamburger. She looked at Stephanie, who apparently was her new heroine. "Can I save some for Susie?"

"Don't get her in the habit of eating people food. Dog food is far healthier for her."

"Okay," Kerry agreed.

Lisa played with her cheeseburger. She tried not to look to her right, but her gaze wandered to the table where two men sat in deep conversation. She shifted all her attention back to Stephanie and Kerry. Her sister had apparently found a soul mate, and Lisa was tremendously grateful.

She breathed easier when the two men stood and left. She waited several moments, then turned to Stephanie. "We should go," she said. "I have to get to the clinic, and Kerry and I have to pick up those supplies if we're going to take Susie home."

THE NEW DOCTOR was far younger and prettier than any Jubal had seen before. Her hair was a rich dark brown, swept back from her face, the style emphasizing high cheekbones, thick lashes and expressive dark brown eyes.

When his gaze met hers, a sudden connection flashed between them, but he pulled away, and her eyes became guarded. This was obviously Gordon's sister.

Clint's wife surprised him even more. His friend had always gone for fancy, high-maintenance women. Stephanie Manning was attractive in a quiet, thoughtful way. Her thick copper hair was pulled back in a braid. Intelligent dark blue eyes appraised him before she gave him a big grin. His friend had done well.

For a moment, he envied Clint, who was obviously very much in love with his wife. Jubal had never been close to it. He'd had affairs, one that lasted a few months even, but both of them had known it was temporary. They liked each other tremendously, but she was very frank about not wanting to be a SEAL's wife with all the uncertainty that came with it. She didn't want that for her children, either.

"Kinda pretty," Josh said judicially.

"Huh?"

"Dr. Redding," Josh prompted him. "She's very attractive, and she doesn't look like a wicked sister, especially if she's letting Stephanie talk her into one of her rescues."

Jubal didn't answer, though he didn't think so, either.

"Maybe the kid won't show up. No more worries," Josh said.

Jubal sighed. "No such luck." He knew in his gut that, first, Lisa Manning was the kid's sister, and second, she would not be happy with his interference, and third, she would probably be furious he didn't come straight to her once he realized the connection.

"Dammit, it's none of my business," Jubal added. He knew what he should do. He should either drop the matter altogether or tell the sister what happened. That would be the responsible course of action. But the kid was crying out for help, even if he wasn't aware of it.

They finished eating in companionable silence. "I have to get to work," Josh said. "But I hope to see you at the pageant."

"The pageant?"

"The town sponsors a pageant about the founding of the town. The first performances were held nightly the first week of summer and then the second and fourth Saturdays since. The last performance this year is Saturday night. You might be interested because Clint's in it. And maybe it's something else your kid could do. Help move props."

"He's not *my* kid," Jubal insisted.

"In any event," Clint said, "it's a short walk and it's free. You might enjoy it."

Jubal couldn't imagine why.

"Clint is the star actually. He's singing most of the songs. Have you heard him?"

"Just some very raunchy songs. Nothing fit for a mixed audience."

"You'll see a whole new Clint on Saturday," Josh promised. "Definitely worth your while."

Jubal wasn't sure he wanted to see a new Clint. He liked his buddy just the way he'd been while raising hell in Kabul.

The bill came then and they argued about who was paying until Josh snatched it away. They stood just as Stephanie, Dr. Redding and her sister walked out the door. Jubal watched her go.

"She's very attractive," Josh commented.

"Yeah," Jubal agreed. She was the only woman to capture his attention since his return. But that was all it was. Momentary appreciation of a pretty woman. That was all it could be given his personal commitment to her brother and the fact that he was leaving soon.

CHAPTER SIX

WHEN JUBAL ARRIVED back at the cabin, he grabbed a beer and went outside. As far as he was concerned, he would always prefer the outdoors, regardless of the comforts offered inside.

He took a long pull from the bottle and pondered his dilemma. He had two personal rules for himself. Don't butt into other people's business and don't lie unless it's a military necessity. Lies always come back to bite you in the ass.

Now, he might have to violate both of those principles.

He glanced at his watch. A little before two.

Would the kid show? If he didn't, problem solved. He would do what he originally planned to do: leave the next day.

But if he did, what then? Things would become a lot more complicated.

Those expressive brown eyes that looked startled as his gaze met hers haunted him.

He never would have guessed the kid and the doctor were brother and sister. Her hair and eyes were dark, while Gordon's hair was blond and his eyes were blue. His younger sister had the same coloring. Odd.

The sun was getting warmer. He took off his shirt and leaned back in the chair...

"Hey, man."

The words woke him up. The kid stood next to him, staring at the scars on his chest. Dammit, he should have heard him approach. Jubal sat up and shrugged on his shirt.

Gordon held out a paper sack and Jubal looked inside. The sweats he'd given him were inside. Clean. Neatly folded.

The kid looked for approval. He didn't get it. "Ready to work?" Jubal said.

"You said you were military," Gordon said rather than answering.

"Used to be."

"Which one?"

"American, last I checked."

The kid look disgusted. "I mean branch."

"Does it matter?"

"I'm thinking about joining."

"Can't do that with a police record."

The kid shrugged. "I didn't do anything."

"Just wrong place at the wrong time?"

"Something like that."

"Bullshit. You put yourself there. Doesn't matter if someone else committed the crime."

"I don't need lectures," the kid said. "Get enough of those already." He paused, then asked in a more conciliatory tone, "Did you mean what you said about not telling anyone what happened last night, if I do some work for you?"

There was a plea in the kid's eyes, or maybe he was imagining it. But he saw himself thirty years ago when his mother took him from the father he loved. Probably not similar circumstances, but there was loss in the boy's eyes, pain Jubal recognized.

"Ever build anything?" he asked.

"Like what?" Gordon asked suspiciously.

"Anything."

The kid seemed to think for a minute. "A fort when I was fourteen."

"Was it any good?"

"Still there, last I checked." He smirked.

"Work on a car or a bicycle?"

"Maybe."

"Put something together? Read instructions?"

"I guess."

"Well, I think a bench would look real nice over that place you scorched on the dock."

"You can't even see it," the kid complained.

"There's enough to see someone started a fire there. Speaking of that, where's your partner in crime?"

"I don't know who you mean."

"The kid I saw last night. You know, the one who took off and left you holding...the evidence.

You don't seem any better at picking friends than you are at building a fire."

"I hardly knew him," Gordon mumbled.

Jubal raised an eyebrow. "Doesn't say much for your judgment, though, does it? Back to my question. You can read directions? Yes?"

"Yeah, but…"

"Anyway, I want a bench," Jubal said in a tone that intimidated most people. "I'll pay for the supplies, but you have to give me an acceptable design and build it."

"A design? I don't know anything about building furniture."

"It's not furniture. It's a bench. A rustic bench on the dock. I assume you can use a computer. Lots of do-it-yourself plans there. Bring me a couple."

"You gotta be kidding. I thought…" Gordon stopped midsentence.

"You thought you could mow a lawn once or twice?"

The kid's face told him that's exactly what he thought. "I don't have tools."

"I'll supply them once you bring me a worthy design and a list of materials you need."

The kid looked mutinous. Obviously, he was having an internal argument. He didn't want to do it, but he didn't want the fire reported and to have to suffer the consequences, either.

"You really a friend of the police chief?"

"He saved my life in Afghanistan. Piloted the chopper that rescued my team. That tends to bond people. We've been friends since. It's why I'm here." Jubal usually didn't talk about that but he wanted to define the relationship.

"For real?" the kid said.

"Yeah, for real," Jubal said.

Whatever defiance remained in the kid's face faded away. "I'll try," he said in a subdued voice.

"Never *try*," Jubal said. "You don't get anywhere by just trying. You *do* it."

"When?"

"Let's say Friday to see the plans and a list of materials needed to build it. I want several different plans," Jubal said.

The kid's eyes widened. "No way," he said.

"Hell, all you have to do is find something on the internet," Jubal said. "You thinking about going into the military? Well, you won't get a week to go on the internet and find a plan someone else designed." He stood. "Any other questions?"

The kid looked sucker-punched.

"Got a ride?" Jubal asked.

"I have a bike," the kid said.

"But not last night?"

"Someone picked me up in a car."

"Where did you find *that* loser?"

The kid winced. "Met him at the football

field. He dared me. Said all new kids had to prove themselves."

"And you were mad enough to do it?"

"My sister had no right to bring us here," the kid said angrily. "Chicago's our home."

"Just out of curiosity, what's so great about Chicago? Seems to me you're screwing up wherever you are."

The kid's face grew red. Jubal was pleased Gordon held his tongue in check.

"See you Friday," he said, dismissing the kid. "Two p.m."

Gordon stood there for a moment, obviously not quite sure what just happened. Then he mumbled something and left.

AFTER LISA RETURNED to the house from picking up the dog, along with several bags of dog food, toys, a dog bed, leash and canine paperwork, she started in on the pile of patient files.

It wasn't easy. The newest resident raced around the house, exploring, until both Kerry and Susie were banished to the yard. But the pure joy on Kerry's face lightened Lisa's heart. She hadn't seen that joy in a very long time.

If only she could see it on Gordon's face.

The phone rang. It was Janie at the clinic. "Can you catch a house call?" she said. "I know you don't start officially until tomorrow, but it's a six-year-old girl, and her mother is worried."

Lisa had already learned that Dr. Bradley made house calls, and she readily agreed. She drove to the clinic office and studied the child's records before heading out.

The mother, Amy Pritcher, was at the door when she arrived and led her into a bedroom. Teresa, her young patient, looked apprehensive when Lisa entered her room.

"Hi, there," Lisa said. "You must be Teresa. I'm Dr. Redding, and I'm going to make you feel better, okay?"

The girl nodded.

Lisa took her temperature and pulse, then examined her throat and ears. When she finished, she turned to the mother. "She has an infection in her left ear." Lisa prescribed ibuprofen and a heating pad. "If her temperature goes up, call me night or day, okay?" She gave Amy one of the sample bottles of ibuprofen she carried with her.

On the way out, the mother met her at the door with a tin box. Dr. Bradley had warned her that would probably happen with patients and advised her to accept the gifts to avoid hurt feelings.

Lisa accepted with thanks and felt an unexpected exhilaration. A success. A small success, but it was a transition, and it felt good. The little girl had looked at her with such hope and the mother with gratitude. Her first house call, and she enjoyed it.

She also liked Janie's grin as she reported on the house call.

"Not like a big hospital, is it?" the nurse asked.

"No, but I expect there are some difficult patients, as well."

"The veterans are the worst," Janie said. "They don't call unless they're critical. They think they're indestructible."

From the look of Eve's husband and the man she met today, Lisa didn't doubt it. She nudged the latter from her mind as she and Janie went over the billing procedures and their drug supply. When they finished, Janie sighed.

"I'm glad you're here, Doctor. We need you. Dr. Bradley needs you. The town needs you," Janie said.

There were no appointments and the two of them went over the records of the next day's patients.

We need you. It felt good to be needed. Of course, she'd been needed in the hospital, but then it had been more impersonal. Lisa glanced around her office. Hers. At least for a year. The comfortable-looking chairs in the waiting room and the nature prints on the wall gave the room warmth.

She looked at her watch. Nearly five. Her siblings would be hungry.

She called the number at their house. No answer. Then she tried Gordon's cell. To her surprise, he answered with a grumpy, "Yeah?"

"Are you home?"

"Yeah."

"Where's Kerry?"

"In the backyard with that dumb dog."

"It's not a dumb dog. Have you eaten anything?"

"No."

"You and Kerry haven't been to the park. I can get some takeout from Maude's and we'll have a picnic. Maybe you two can explore the community center."

A silence, then a reluctant, "All right."

She was stunned at his agreement but would happily accept small gifts. "What do you want from Maude's?"

"What do they have?"

He actually answered. Lisa was encouraged. "Most anything, I think."

"Cheeseburger and fries." Reluctance dripped from his voice.

Lisa ignored the tone. "Ask Kerry what she wants."

She heard a door slam then, and Kerry was on the phone. Lisa repeated her question.

"A salad with chicken," Kerry said. "A light dressing and an iced tea. Can I bring Susie?"

"I don't see why not. I'll pick you guys up at home in ten minutes."

After she hung up the phone, she called Maude's and placed the order.

Twenty minutes later, the three of them plus Susie arrived at the park, food and drinks in hand. The cheeseburger must have met Gordon's high standards because it disappeared in record time. Kerry shared a small bite of chicken with Susie. Lisa forced herself not to say anything. Not this time. Everything was going too well.

To her surprise, Gordon checked out the area around the community center. When he returned, she suggested they visit the center itself. Despite the fact it was nearly seven, there were several cars in the parking lot that apparently served both the center and park.

"Can I take Susie inside?" Kerry asked.

The dog barked at the sound of her name.

"I don't know," Lisa said. "I don't even know if it's open, but we'll find out. Maybe Gordon could look after her while we go in and ask."

"Ugh!" Gordon grumbled. But he took the leash. "We'll stay here," he said.

The community center door was unlocked, and Lisa and Kerry went inside. They found a large desk in the entry hall. Atop it sat a bell with a sign saying Ring Me. When Lisa did just that, a woman came down the stairs. Lisa noticed she wore a brace on her hand.

The woman reached the landing. "Hi. Welcome

to the center. I'm Andy Stuart. You must be the new doctor. I'm really glad you dropped by."

Lisa nodded. "I'm Lisa Redding, and this is my sister, Kerry. She was hoping she could explore the library but she wanted to know if she can bring her dog inside. She just adopted it."

"Sure," Andy said with a grin. "At times, there are more dogs in here than people." She turned to Kerry. "Hi, the library is to the left, along with a number of public computers. Business is slow since it's the weekend before school starts. Come on, I'll show you around."

"My brother's outside with the dog…" Lisa started, then stopped when she heard a loud yell from outside.

Lisa turned toward the door, but Kerry was faster and flung it open. Susie was racing across the park, the leash trailing behind her, and Gordon was running after her. The dog would stop and sniff something, then dash off again as Gordon approached. It was obviously a game to her.

"Susie!" Kerry cried, and ran after her brother. Her heart pounding, Lisa followed. Kerry couldn't take another loss. She passed Kerry and was almost up to Gordon when the dog reached the road that bordered the park. Susie turned and ran straight down the middle of it. Gordon was at least ten feet behind but wasn't catching up.

Through the corner of her eye, she saw a car start to turn onto the road just as the dog raced across the street, then ducked back again as Gordon nearly caught the leash.

Susie started back across the street again. The dog was so fast the driver of the car apparently didn't see her or Kerry, who was running to intercept Susie.

Lisa shouted and raced toward Kerry, but she knew she was too late. Then suddenly Lisa saw a tall figure in shorts and a T-shirt appear out of nowhere. He pushed Kerry out of the car's path and snatched the dog up.

The driver jammed on the brakes. The car skidded to a stop, but the bumper hit the runner and slammed him to the payment. The dog bounced out of his arms and ran to Kerry where she lay on the street.

Lisa reached Kerry and dropped to her knees. "Are you all right?"

"I'm okay. Susie…"

"She looks a lot better than you do," Lisa said as she checked Kerry over. As far as she could tell, Kerry had some open road burns on her forearms, but otherwise she seemed okay.

The little dog wriggled in Kerry's arms and licked her face. Lisa tried to slow her racing pulse. Then she turned to the runner, who was getting to his feet. *The man she'd met earlier today.* He was bleeding from several cuts.

Galloping Gulliver! It was an expletive she'd learned from her mother to use in lieu of a less acceptable one. It had been handed down from her mother's mother. It seemed perfect now.

"Thank you," she said, hoping her voice wasn't breaking. "And you're hurt!"

"No big deal," he said. "Superficial. Is Kerry okay?"

Lisa nodded, surprised he had remembered her sister's name. "Thanks to you. She has a few superficial injuries but nothing compared... I mean, to think what could have..." She sucked in her breath. She was shaking. She, who didn't think twice when she treated some of the worst wounds one could imagine, was not coping well when it came to her family.

The older woman stepped out of the car. "I'm so sorry," she said, a tremor in her voice. "There's not usually traffic on this road and I was thinking about something else."

"It wasn't your fault," Jubal Pierce said. "The dog ran in front of the car."

"But if you hadn't been there..." Tears were forming in the woman's eyes.

"I was, and no harm done," Jubal replied. His voice was gentle. Disconcerting coming from the brusque man with cool eyes and impressive muscles under his T-shirt.

"You must be the new veteran," the older woman said. "I'm June Byars. I live two houses down from your cabin." Then she turned to Lisa. "Are you sure your daughter is okay?"

"She's my sister. I'm Lisa Redding, the new doctor. I'm sure she'll be all right. And Mr. Pierce is right. It wasn't your fault. My dog ran in front of your car. If anything, I'm so sorry to have put you and Mr. Pierce at risk."

Her gaze returned to the bloodied man, who watched her with those darn compelling blue eyes. Blood oozed from a wide gash on his left knee along with other scrapes on his leg. His left hand, which apparently bore of the brunt of the fall, was also bleeding. She turned to him. "I have bandages and antibiotics in my car back at the community center. I can follow you home and take care of those cuts."

Amusement flickered in his eyes. "It's nothing. I'm perfectly able to take care of myself."

Lisa noticed then that Gordon had backed away. He looked as if he longed to be anywhere else. He must know a lecture would come later. And questions. How had Susie gotten loose?

She turned back to Jubal. "It may not make you feel better, but it would make *me* feel better if I looked at them."

He hesitated.

"Please," Kerry interceded as she stared in horror at the blood dripping on the ground. "I'm… so sorry." Gordon, on the other hand, had turned around and was headed back to the community center—slinking back was more like it.

Jubal looked at Kerry. Tears were forming in

her eyes. "All right, but I'll walk back. I don't want to stain your car. I'm in the last cabin on the road."

"You'll let me know if I can do anything," Mrs. Byars added anxiously.

No way was he going to take her up on that offer, Lisa sensed, but he gave the older woman a smile that would charm a rattlesnake and nodded. Then he turned and headed down the road.

Lisa took Susie's leash from Kerry. She wasn't going to get away again. *Stephanie didn't mention this part of dog ownership.*

Gordon was waiting for them at the car in the community center lot. "I'll walk back," he said.

"You won't wait for us?"

"Nothing *I* can do," he said, his gaze not meeting hers.

"You could have apologized," she said. "You let the dog go."

"Well, it's all okay now." He turned around and started toward town.

Lisa sighed. Nothing seemed to get through to him.

Andy had walked from the community center to where they stood. Lisa explained what happened.

"I'm a RN," Andy said. "I'll take care of your sister and watch the dog while you see to Mr. Pierce. We have a first aid kit here."

Lisa hesitated, then nodded. She went to her

car and drove down the street. She caught up with Jubal Pierce as he turned into a driveway and followed him to an attractive, rustic-looking cabin with a porch stretched across the front.

As she stepped out of the car and went to the trunk for her medical bag, she noticed he'd stopped at the steps and taken off his T-shirt. He tore it and wrapped the strips around his knee and hand to stop them from bleeding. He then opened the screen porch door and waited for her.

"Shouldn't you have stayed with your sister?" he asked.

It was an obvious attempt to get rid of her. She ignored it. "There's an RN at the community center. She's tending to Kerry." She took a deep breath as she looked at his bare chest. It was covered with old scars, as if he'd been whipped and burned. His eyes met hers. Challenged her to comment.

She didn't. "Bathroom?"

He opened the main door to the cabin and led the way down the hall to a bathroom.

"This isn't necessary," he said again as he held the door to the bathroom open. "I've had medic training. I can take care of this. If your sister hadn't asked…"

"Let's just say I need to satisfy myself." She eyed the bloodstained and torn t-shirt as he unwrapped it. "That's a goner. I'll replace it."

"No, you won't," he said flatly. "It was old. I

didn't want to bloody the floor and it was no loss."
He remained standing, obviously uncomfortable.

"Sit down," Lisa said in her best no-nonsense
voice.

To her surprise, he plopped down on the closed
commode seat. His sheepish expression touched
her heart. Oddly enough, he seemed to understand her need—and Kerry's—to do something
he obviously thought completely unnecessary.

Her gaze met his and for several seconds she
couldn't turn away. His eyes were impossibly blue
and intense. Her stomach tightened. She tried to
still the runaway attraction that was overruling
her brain, but she was too stunned by it.

He was lean but well-muscled and his arms and
legs were deeply tanned. He obviously worked
out. He'd been out on a run before…the near-
accident. He was all alpha male, the opposite of
what she'd thought to be her type.

His tanned, chiseled chest was marred by scars.
She'd seen bodies torn by gunfire and explosions
and sharp objects. While she noticed two obvious
bullet wound scars, there were also scars from
other sources. Burns. Cuts. Blows that probably
had resulted in broken bones. There were ridges
around his wrists. It was obvious he'd been tor-
tured.

"Not very pretty, are they?" he said casually.

"I've seen worse," she said, trying to keep her
voice steady and matter-of-fact.

He raised an eyebrow.

"You only have to be a resident in an emergency room in Chicago or any big city," she explained in a trained neutral voice. "There's little I haven't seen."

She forced herself to focus on the new wounds. There was a deep cut and other abrasions on his left knee, and more on his left hand. His left wrist was also swollen and he winced slightly when she felt around it. "I don't think there's a break, but it's probably sprained," she said. "I should do X-rays."

"It's not broken," he said with certainty. "I know the difference."

She didn't press the issue. She washed the open wounds with soap and water, then applied antiseptic cream and bandaged them. A lot of them were surface cuts. Not serious, but they could become infected. "I'm going to give you an antibiotic shot," she said. "As for your wrist, twenty minutes ice, then twenty minutes heat, then tape it. If it's not better in the morning, call me."

"Anything you say, Doc," he replied.

"Do you even have a heating pad?"

"Don't know. Haven't seen one."

"I'll bet Mrs. Byers does. I'll stop by her house and ask."

"No, ma'am," he said. "I'll just use a towel." He raised an eyebrow. "I'm pretty good at taking care of myself."

"Your body says otherwise."

He shrugged. "I'm alive."

"Not long, if you continue to do battle with large moving objects."

"It was for a good cause."

"Do you always go around saving dogs and kids?"

"Can't say I do. I usually stay away from both."

"Why's that?"

He looked directly into her eyes. "Emotions get you killed." It was said in that same matter-of-fact voice, but the tightening of his jaw emphasized the words.

"Are you still in the army?"

"Navy, Doc," he corrected, making it plain there was a huge difference. "No. We've separated, but I don't intend to stay in a rocking chair."

She couldn't imagine he would. He was all barely suppressed energy. Covenant Falls couldn't hold him long.

Go. Go while you can! her brain was screaming that warning to her, but she couldn't seem to move off her knees.

The room seemed to shrink, the air between them suddenly charged. She could almost smell the ozone. Her face flamed, and heat surged through her, fueling a raw hunger.

She was only too aware he was almost naked, that his body was too near to hers, his breath too close…

What was she doing?

He was a stranger. A patient. A man she had only met once before. A man who had obviously led a violent life. He was everything she'd fought against.

She was just lonely, that was all. She'd had no time for romance these past few years. Between the residency and her mother, she'd been too exhausted to think about sex, much less romance. When she wasn't on duty, she was sleeping, studying or trying to help at home.

"I have…to go." The words were forced out by some protective instinct. She hurriedly got to her feet, almost stumbling as she did.

He searched her face for a long moment—or was it a second that seemed longer? "Don't worry about me. I've had far worse after a day's training."

"W-well, then, I had better see about my sister." She was stuttering. She never stuttered. "Thanks again for helping Kerry. If you need anything, I'm at the clinic on Main Street."

"I'll be sure to call," he assured her solemnly, but there was a hint of mischief in his eyes, crinkles at their corners. He was obviously more amused than grateful for her attention.

If he hadn't just risked his life for her sister, she might have made a retort. Instead, she hurriedly replaced every item in her bag, then, as an afterthought, took out a roll of tape and another sample bottle of ibuprofen, putting them on the sink. "And use those."

"Yes, ma'am," he said.

Then with as much dignity as she could manage, Dr. Lisa Redding turned and walked out. She hoped he didn't notice that *her* legs weren't very steady.

JUBAL STOOD, FOLLOWED the doctor to the door and watched as she walked down the steps to her car and drove off.

He'd been close enough to catch a floral scent from her hair. Her hands had been efficient but gentle. Her face had held so much concern as she ministered to what he considered nothing more than minor irritations.

He had let her because her hands felt good. And because he hadn't wanted her to leave.

So now he knew for sure where the kid came from. And his dilemma was greater than ever. Before, he hadn't known Gordon's sister. Now that he knew, everything he did moving forward would be a lie of omission.

But he had, more or less, agreed not to say anything if the kid worked off the debt. Jubal had watched the boy back away tonight. Gordon was probably afraid that now Jubal knew who he was, he might well say something to his sister.

Lisa Redding certainly didn't look like someone the kid should fear. She had obviously been terrified for her sister and showed no blame toward the boy. She appeared to be a good doctor. Professional. But damn, there had been an instantaneous electricity that flashed between them, a moment of mutual attraction that was as strong as any he'd felt. She'd felt it, too, he'd wager. He had seen it in her eyes. He'd also seen the dismay.

He'd felt that, too. He was in no position to start a relationship, especially since his stay here was short. He was still suffering from night sweats and flashbacks. And couldn't even sleep in a bed.

And then there was a very basic conflict in their lives.

He'd been damned good at war. He had been among the best of the best and it had become his identity. Now that it was gone, he hadn't an idea in hell who he was or what to do.

Lisa Redding, on the other hand, was a healer who had a fine career ahead of her. She knew who she was and where she was going.

They were traveling in opposite directions. And why was he even considering anything other than a casual acquaintance? It was only his second day in Covenant Falls. What was it about this town that had transformed Clint from a hell-raising chopper jockey into a small-town police chief, and Josh Manning, a former Ranger, into a businessman with a wife and kid and a horde of animals? And why, dammit, couldn't he erase images of Lisa Redding from his head?

Something in the water? Whatever it was, it wasn't for him. The sooner he left, the better. Problem was his commitment to the kid.

Jubal changed from the stained running shorts to jeans and a clean T-shirt, then, ignoring the stiffness in his body from the fall, he headed out to climb the mountain trail. He made it past the lookout rock and continued until the path became uneven.

He knew he should head back down before it became too dark. Instead, he stared at the valley below. Beyond the town were fields, ranches, tiny dots that were probably grazing cattle. Peaceful, until the sun dipped toward the horizon and lit the sky with fire.

He suddenly felt lonely, an emotion he'd thought he had conquered. But then, he'd never been hit by a ton of bricks before, and that's what had happened when he looked into Lisa Redding's eyes and saw that she felt something, too. One of his more literate buddies once called it a *coup de foudre*, a blow of madness. Others simply called it a sock in the gut. He hated the whole idea. To him it had always sounded more like a loss of sanity. Or a fairy tale to explain a basic human need.

He reached the end of the path and walked back to the cabin. He went inside, made a sandwich, grabbed a beer and went out on the screened porch.

His cell phone rang, and he saw it was Clint. He almost ignored it, but hell, he was his guest. He punched the button and Clint's voice came on.

"You okay?" Clint asked. "I heard about the accident with the new doctor. I'd planned to take you to the Rusty Nail tonight, but I was delayed by a domestic call, and then you didn't answer the phone."

"I took a long walk up the mountain. I'm fine. Just some small scratches."

"Andy told me you saved the new doctor's sister."

"Highly exaggerated. The driver was going all of five miles an hour."

"Well, you're famous now. What about the Rusty Nail?"

"Can we make it tomorrow?"

"You're staying, then?"

"A few more days," Jubal answered cautiously.

"Terrific," Clint said. "And I won't ask why. I can take tomorrow off and show you around a bit more."

"And deprive the town of protection? I thought I would explore on my own, if that's okay."

"It is. I'll pick you up tomorrow evening at six unless we have a major crime wave." Clint hung up.

Jubal turned the cell off. He needed time alone after today. He hated being the center of attention. The last thing he wanted was to be "famous."

He watched as clouds moved in and took over the sky. Distant rolls of thunder moved closer. Lightning streaked across the darkness and lobbed arrows of fire toward the lake.

He watched it all, this theater of nature. He was usually content with his own company. The months of isolation in the jungle should've made him crave company, but they hadn't. He'd learned to cope with silence. He'd made up games, reread books in his mind and even wrote a few. He relived his childhood days at rodeos and talked to his father.

He stretched out in the chair and closed his eyes. The thunder was strangely comforting. Still, he couldn't quite banish a brown-haired, brown-eyed doctor from his thoughts.

CHAPTER SEVEN

GORDON WAS IN his room when Lisa and Kerry arrived home with Susie.

Kerry limped slightly but insisted she wasn't hurt. Lisa gave her an ibuprofen and suggested she go to bed.

Then she knocked on Gordon's door.

To her surprise, he opened it immediately. "Is Kerry all right?" he asked.

"Just shaken up a bit."

"I didn't mean to let the dog go," he said. "It saw a squirrel and took off, jerking the leash out of my hand." Then he hung his head and some of the defiance slipped away. "I should have held on tighter."

"You went after her," Lisa said. "I just wish you hadn't disappeared afterward. You could have met Mr. Pierce."

"Yeah, well, I felt in the way," Gordon said.

She nodded. "Don't forget you have an appointment tomorrow with the police chief. Nine a.m. I'm going to the clinic then. I'll walk with you. It's just across the street from the police station."

"You don't trust me," he accused.

"Should I? I remember you promised me you wouldn't meet with your so-called friends again in Chicago, then you tried to sneak out."

He shrugged, but his gaze met hers. "I *am* sorry about today," he said.

Dumbfounded, she stood there at the door. Then she nodded her acceptance of the apology before heading downstairs. That was the first positive reaction she'd heard from him since… it seemed like forever.

Maybe this was a good move, after all. Despite the great escape, Kerry was happy with Susie. She'd scolded the dog upon reaching their house, but it was probably meaningless, since she was kissing and hugging the dog at the same time.

Lisa counted the other good experiences. She had her first patient without a disaster. She'd met two interesting new friends in Stephanie and Eve.

She had also met a rather fine male specimen. She quickly erased that plus from her mental list. The last thing she needed in her life now was someone with as many scars on his body as Mr. Pierce had. She suspected from his gruff manner that not all of them were physical.

Besides, he wasn't her type. Not that she really had a type. She'd been too busy for much more than coffee dates these past few years. She wanted to establish her career first, and she still had several years to go. And then there was her family. Who would want an almost fourteen-year-old girl and the sullen seventeen-year-old boy that came with her? It was definitely best to stay away from him completely, even in her thoughts.

A crash of thunder echoed outside, followed by lightning that lit the backyard. It broke off her mental meandering. She went to check on Kerry. Her sister was reading in bed with Susie snuggled next to her. Lisa thought about saying something about germs, but she resisted. The doctor part of her said it probably wasn't a good idea. The sister part delighted in the first real look of pleasure she'd seen on Kerry's face in months.

Lisa returned to the medical charts she was reviewing, but instead of seeing print on pages, she saw Jubal Pierce's penetrating eyes as she bandaged some of his newest wounds. She suspected he'd been indulging her...

It was nearly midnight when she finished the last patient file. She checked again on Kerry. Still asleep. She picked up the dog, who protested with a small growl. Ignoring it, Lisa found the leash and took Susie out. It was raining, but it felt good to her. Cleansing. Susie quickly did her business, then headed back inside.

Lisa wiped the dog dry, then put her back in Kerry's room where she promptly jumped up on the bed and cuddled next to Kerry.

Exhausted, she went to her bedroom. It certainly had been a busy and interesting day. She'd treated her first patient, obtained her first dog, her sister had survived a near-serious accident. And then there was Jubal Pierce...

She grabbed a novel and went into her bedroom. Hopefully that would divert her from this afternoon—and from the man named Jubal.

JUBAL ROSE AFTER a sleepless night. The rain had kept him inside and the room had kept closing in on him.

He went out to the porch. It was not quite dawn. The sky was clearing and the air was warm. He decided to take a swim. He pulled on a pair of trunks, jogged down to the dock and dived into the lake.

The fact that his left wrist hurt like hell slowed him down, but he made it across the lake and back. By then the rising sun showered golden streams of light across the water. It should have been hopeful but instead he felt a cold emptiness. Maybe it was lack of purpose or being an outsider. It had been a long time since he was part of a team.

Or maybe it was the young woman whose concerned eyes and gentle touches had awakened an aching need in him. That need was still in him hours later, although he knew it could go nowhere.

A world of experience divided them. She

fought for life. He'd seen the worst men could do. As much as he told himself he was on the side of civilization, that he was one of good guys, he was haunted by too many dead and dying faces.

He should keep on schedule and leave tomorrow. The kid could manage without him. He waded to shore rather than lifting himself onto the dock. No sense in aggravating his wrist, even if the pain reminded him he was alive. He took a hot shower, hoping the rush of water would wash away unwanted memories and quiet a current need.

After showering, he applied ointment to his wounds and taped his wrist, then changed into an old T-shirt and sweatpants. After eating a breakfast of toast and cereal, he grabbed a bottle of water and headed out for his run.

He decided to expand it beyond the town. From his perch on the mountain yesterday, he'd noticed a road that appeared to only service outlying ranches and farms. He judged the first ranch to be about five, maybe six miles from the cabin. An easy run for him.

The sky was clear after last night's storm, the air fresh. He turned right at the community center, passed a school, then ran alongside the lake for four blocks before starting east toward the road he'd observed yesterday.

He passed several fenced properties, then stopped when he saw a grouping of horses taking their leisure under shady trees. On a whim, he stopped running and walked over to the fence and whistled. Several of the animals approached cautiously, and he ran his hand down the neck of a pinto.

Memories flooded back. He used to hang on paddocks during rodeo days. He was seven, and he thought traveling from one rodeo to the next with his father was the best life ever.

His mother hated it.

He recalled the constant arguments. The fights. The accusations. He would sneak out of the cheap motel room or rented trailer and run over to the arena where he'd find the horses. Not the wild broncs, but his father's horse and the other riders' horses. He pocketed sugar cubes from the diners where they ate and usually had several with him.

He remembered the first time his father had put him on a horse. "Kid's a natural rider," he'd crowed to anyone who'd listen. It remained the second proudest moment of his life.

Number one was the receiving the SEAL Trident. After seven months of pure hell, he'd emerged among the few who had survived the most rigorous military training of any service. The trident was his only tattoo. Nothing could ever top it. He only wished his father had lived to see it.

He shook off the memories and looked around. Beyond the horse pasture, cattle grazed in a separate area. The grass was a rich green, which meant the rancher probably had an irrigation system. A modest ranch house and several other buildings were located well back on the property. The road leading to it was barred by a locked gate.

Another horse, curious about the stranger, wandered over, nickered and stuck his head over the fence.

"Hey there," Jubal said. "You're a handsome fellow."

The horse tossed his head as if he understood. He was a buckskin, the same as Dusty, his father's cutting horse. A flashback sent him back to the dust-filled arenas and his father aboard a bucking bronc. He also remembered the hospital rooms when his father had been thrown…

He was suddenly aware of a pickup barreling down the driveway. At the same time, he heard the sound of a police siren coming from the direction of Covenant Falls.

The gate must have been electronic because it swung open as the pickup neared. A wiry man of somewhere near sixty stepped out, a shotgun in his hands. It was pointed at the ground, which was a hopeful sign.

"Just stay there, mister," the newcomer said.

Jubal wasn't about to refuse. He spread out his hands. "I'm not armed. I just stopped to see the horses."

The man squinted his eyes. "Who are you?"

"Name's Jubal Pierce. I'm staying in Covenant Falls."

"You one of those veterans?"

"I guess I am," Jubal said. "I was out running and saw the horses. They brought back some memories."

"You know horses?" The shotgun was in a more relaxed position now.

"A little."

"Ride much?" the rancher asked.

Jubal shrugged. "Not recently. Some as a really young kid, then briefly in Afghanistan."

"Afghanistan, huh? I would sure like to hear about that. Sorry about the shotgun. We've been having a rustling problem around here. Both cattle and horses. They usually strike at night, bring a truck, cut the fence and load them up in a matter of minutes. They only take a few, don't stay long enough to get caught. I have cameras along the fence line now and called the police when I saw someone loitering."

A patrol car arrived just then, and Clint stepped out and approached them. "You just can't seem to stay out of trouble, can you, Jubal?" he said with a grin.

"It's okay, Clint," the rancher said. "He just stopped to say howdy to my horses. Sorry about the false alarm."

"Glad you did. You can never be too careful, and I'm determined to get those bastards." He turned to Jubal. "Luke Daniels here raises some of the best quarter horses in Colorado. Luke, Jubal and I go way back. I was army. He's navy but despite that faulty judgment on his part you won't find a better man." Clint studied him, his gaze on Jubal's taped wrist and the bandage on his hand. "I thought you told me you weren't hurt."

"It's nothing. A mild sprain."

Clint looked at the rancher. "He won't tell you but he rescued the new doc's sister and dog yesterday. Pushed them out of the way of Mrs. Byars's oncoming car. Took the hit himself."

Jubal glared at him.

Clint ignored it and his eyes hardened as he turned to Luke. "Any more trouble out here?"

"Nope. But I'm ready if there is. Thanks for answering the call even though I'm outside the city limits."

Clint shrugged. "I have an agreement with the county. We help each other. Don't hesitate to call again if you see strangers prowling around."

"I wasn't prowling," Jubal said, defendeding himself.

Clint raised an eyebrow, turned and left.

The rancher looked back to Jubal. "Jacko, the horse you were touching? He doesn't let many people do that." He hesitated, then asked, "Ever ride a quarter horse?"

"When I was a small kid. My dad taught me

how to ride his personal horse, Dusty. Then my folks divorced and I moved to Baltimore when I was seven. My mother didn't want me to have anything to do with horses after that."

"What about Afghanistan?"

"They needed four of us to work with a tribe there to capture a Taliban leader. I sorta exaggerated my experience and had to learn fast when I got there. The horses were small and scrawny, but they could go forever without tiring."

Luke shook his head. "From what I hear, if you can ride those horses, you can probably ride anything."

Jubal shrugged.

"Want to ride Jacko?" Luke asked.

"Hell, yes," Jubal replied, and Luke grinned.

The rancher opened the gate between them and climbed in the pickup. "Get in."

It was a short ride to the barn. Fenced pastures were on both sides of the road, which led to a parking area and a riding ring that fronted a large barn. Beside it stood a modest ranch house.

Jubal followed Luke into the barn. Stalls lined both sides of the building and a large equipment room was in front. "Impressive," Jubal observed.

"Twenty-two stalls. We have sixteen of our own horses, and we board four more," Luke said with obvious pride. "We have an arena barn in back where we train them."

"Must keep you busy."

"Too busy. My kids were helping around here but they left this week for college. Now it's mostly my wife and me, and a stable hand who cleans out the stalls and does whatever else needs to be done. We also have some high school kids who come and help exercise the horses, but they'll be back in school next week and I'll be short-handed. Don't have time to do the training I need to do." He stopped at a tack area with a number of saddles sitting on sawhorses. "Western saddle?"

"Yeah."

"Can you saddle him with that wrist?"

"I can manage," Jubal said, ignoring the fact that his wrist was hurting like hell. He used his right hand to throw the blanket on Jacko, then the saddle, while Luke tacked the pinto that had followed them to the barn. He realized he had a problem in tightening the cinch with his injured hand. "Guess I do need a little help."

Luke nodded. He took the few steps to Jacko and tightened the cinch. "Here you go," he said.

"Where did Jacko get his name?" Jubal asked.

"My son."

"Is this his horse?"

"No. He's for sale, but I have to find the right buyer. I don't sell my horses to just anyone." Luke swung up into his horse's saddle.

Using both hands, Jubal did the same.

They walked their horses side by side. Jubal

noticed the rancher was sizing him up much as the trainers had back in SEAL training.

Luke talked about ranching and how difficult it was these days. "We can't hang on forever. Federal regulations are killing us, and it's too dang hard to find responsible help. Both my kids love horses and the ranch, but Boone is going into business agriculture and my daughter has her heart set on journalism. Like I said, both left for college last week. Won't be back until Thanksgiving."

Luke guided the way around his property, including two pastures for horses and a third for the cattle. "We've had to sell most of our cattle when we lost grazing rights. Now, I specialize in breeding Black Angus cattle and training and selling quarter horses, mostly for performance competitions. I have a champion stallion and some fine mares." He slowed his horse. "You have a damn good seat for someone who hasn't ridden much."

"My dad said I was born to the saddle, like him," Jubal said.

"What did he do?"

"Rodeo. Bronc riding mostly and calf roping, and steer roping."

"Hard business."

"He died from it," Jubal said. "Never did get that PRC championship buckle he wanted, but he made enough prize money to keep trying."

Luke nodded in understanding. "Ready for a faster gait?"

Jubal nodded and tightened his knees. Jacko obliged with an easy lope and Jubal's body quickly adjusted.

The breeze brushed Jubal's cheeks, the sun was warm, and Jubal felt freer—and happier—than he had since that last mission. He felt, strangely enough, as if he was exactly where he belonged.

Is that why his father stayed with the rodeo circuit for so long, even at the risk of his marriage and the loss of his son? For the first time, he understood.

Luke slowed and led the way to a clump of trees. When they reached it, he dismounted. Jubal did the same and followed him to a stream. "This is the lifeblood of the ranch," Luke said. "Without it we would be in trouble."

They walked over to a little rise overlooking the stream. "My great-great-grandfather came here in 1865 after the war," Luke added. "He fought in the Civil War for the north. Rebels came, too, but after some hostility, the Rebs and Yanks banded together against Indian raids and outlaws. Five generations of my family are buried here. I would hate to be the last one."

Jubal couldn't imagine having land that housed one family for a century and a half. Deep roots were something Jubal had always envied, always missed. It was one reason he'd joined the navy and become a SEAL. He'd wanted to belong to something that had meaning. When he'd left the navy, he'd felt anchorless.

As if he knew exactly what Jubal was thinking, Luke asked, "What about you? Where's home to you?"

"Don't really have one," he said. "Coronado Island was my home base for years and that came closer than anything else." He didn't add that home had been a shared apartment between missions.

"Coronado Island?" Luke repeated. "You a navy SEAL? I know they train there."

Jubal nodded reluctantly. "Retired a month ago." He didn't like talking about it, but Luke seemed like a straight shooter and he didn't want to lie to him.

"I spent four years in the navy," Luke said. "You might say I ran away from home before I realized everything I needed was here."

"So you came back."

"Not at first. My older brother was to inherit the ranch, and I wanted adventure. Found out I couldn't stay away from horses and returned home. Then Bob passed away—cancer—without children, and here I am." After a moment of companionable silence, he turned in the saddle to face Jubal. "Mind me asking what you're going to do now?"

"I came here to visit Clint for a few days. We

were friends in the service. Then I thought I would wander a bit."

"No family?"

"No. My mother and I never got along, and I didn't think much of my stepfather. I left for the navy two days after graduating from high school. After qualifying for the SEALs, I didn't think marriage went with the job."

"I was lucky," Luke said. "I met my wife at a horse show where she was a champion barrel racer. She trains horses, too, does most of the teaching here. She has more patience than I do. We also offer trail rides in conjunction with Josh's new inn. One of us has to go along with pleasure riders now that the kids are in college."

"Sounds like a good life."

"It is that, if I can keep it afloat."

They were nearing the barn. "What would it take?" Jubal asked.

"Another championship. We have two students who are very close to achieving that on horses we bred and trained. A win would promote our teaching and training programs as well as our horses. We need more land to expand our cattle herd and more employees than I can afford. Why don't you stay for lunch with us? Tracy's probably going nuts dealing with paperwork."

Jubal considered it. Gordon wasn't supposed to return until tomorrow afternoon. He didn't have much else going on until then.

After unsaddling the horses and cooling them off, they walked to the ranch house.

Tracy met them at the door. She was lean and tall, and as tanned from the sun as Luke was. She immediately made Jubal feel at home.

"Wondered what was keeping him so long," she said with a quick smile. "I have some stew I can heat up."

"Sounds good to me," Jubal said. "I've been living on sandwiches."

It *was* good. He ate every bite of his first bowl, then a second before consuming two slices of apple pie.

After lunch, the two men sat on the broad front porch.

Luke talked about his horses, then leaned forward in his chair as if he'd just made a decision.

"Look," he said. "From what you say, you're at loose ends now. You obviously like horses and have a way with them. I noticed it when you first stroked Jacko. He usually doesn't allow that. It's the reason he's still with us. He's not usually friendly to would-be buyers. Likes to nip them."

He paused. "What if I offered you a job? We need someone to exercise the horses. Tracy and I will teach you what you need to know. Can't pay much but you'd learn a hell of a lot about horses and riding." He paused. "What do you think?"

"You barely know me," Jubal said slowly as he absorbed the offer.

"I've done a lot of horse trading in my day. And I'm better than average at sizing up a person," Luke said. "You listen and learn fast. And you can't fake that natural connection with the horses."

"I wasn't planning to stay more than a few days or so," Jubal said slowly, although something like excitement built internally. It had been a long time since he'd enjoyed anything as much as that day's ride.

"No commitment needed," Luke said. "I would enjoy having you around and appreciate any help you can give us."

Jubal made an instant decision. "Done, then. When do I start?"

"When *can* you start?"

"In the morning," Jubal replied with an eagerness that startled even him. "Although I do have an appointment at two."

"Whatever time you can give me will be welcome. A warning, though. Horseback riding abuses a whole different set of muscles than running. You might be sore for a few days."

"I expect I will," Jubal said, but he inwardly smiled. Comparatively speaking, a few aches were nothing.

"And you'll need something heavier than sweat pants. Jeans are okay, but you really need heavier riding pants."

Jubal left soon after and started running back to the cabin. For the first time since his escape he truly looked forward to something.

CHAPTER EIGHT

"I DON'T WANT you to go in with me," Gordon said as Lisa and her brother reached the police station the morning after the encounter with the car.

"I won't stay," Lisa said. "I just want to meet him. He's the police chief and we'll be in contact with each other." The morning had been a nightmare with Gordon resisting going to the police station in the first place, let alone Lisa going with him.

This time, though, she wasn't giving in. She wanted to take measure of the man who could have an impact on her brother and his future.

"You didn't say anything about that earlier," Gordon said.

She didn't answer. She hadn't said anything because she hadn't wanted to get in an argument with him, especially not after his surprising apology last night.

They reached the station that occupied the left side of city hall. It was five minutes to nine o' clock. They'd walked, Gordon dragging his feet and complaining every step. So much for the brief cessation of hostilities.

An older woman sat at a desk in front of a computer. She looked up when they entered. "Hi, I'm Patti Newcomb. Dispatcher, secretary and all-around gofer," she said good-naturedly. "We're all glad to see you. We've been worried about Doc Bradley a long time."

"Thank you," Lisa said. "This is my brother, Gordon. He has an appointment."

Patti nodded. "The chief is expecting you." She motioned to a glassed-in office, and Lisa saw a man in his late thirties sitting at a large desk. "You can go on in. We don't stand on ceremony here."

"Thanks," Lisa said while Gordon stayed silent. She led the way to the office door, hesitated, then saw the man motion for them to come inside. He stood as they entered. "I'm Clint Morgan," he said. "You must be Gordon." He held out his hand to shake Gordon's.

Gordon looked surprised, then took it. The police chief did the same to Lisa. "Dr. Redding, we're happy you're here."

His handshake was firm, his dark eyes warm. She liked him immediately and she particularly appreciated the way he handled the greeting. Gordon had been acknowledged as a welcome visitor rather than a felon.

She couldn't help but notice Chief Morgan

had the same alert presence as Josh Manning and Jubal Pierce, but there was something easier about him, more open. She glanced around and noticed a model helicopter along with two photos on a cabinet. She recognized Stephanie in one. The other depicted a flight crew standing in front of a large helicopter. Clint Morgan stood in the middle.

"Were you a chopper pilot?" Gordon blurted after doing a similar survey of the office.

"I was," the police chief said.

"That's awesome," Gordon exclaimed.

"Sometimes," Chief Morgan corrected. "Sometimes not so much."

Lisa noticed Gordon had lost his reluctance, had even seemed to forget she was there. It was probably a good time to leave.

"I have to get to the clinic," she said. "Pleasure to meet you, Chief Morgan."

"It's Clint. Everyone calls me that, and I imagine we'll be working together at times. I'm also with the volunteer fire department."

"I hope not too often on a business level, then," she replied.

"Me, too, but I'm sure we'll see each other often for other reasons, as well. Such is Covenant Falls."

"I'm quickly learning that," she said. She left, satisfied to be leaving Gordon in his hands. He appeared to be someone Gordon would respect and listen to. She worried, though, about the heli-copter aspect and the way Gordon's eyes lit when he saw the model. She was belatedly grateful that he did not hang around Jubal Pierce's cabin last night.

She crossed the street to the clinic. Janie was already there. "Good morning, Doctor," she greeted her.

"Please call me Lisa. I looked at the appointment book yesterday and noticed we have a number of immunizations today."

"They will start coming in half an hour. I usually handle them myself," Janie said, "but I got the definite impression that people want to meet you."

"That's fine," Lisa said. "I want to meet them, too. And I love them at that age. I'm planning to specialize in pediatric surgery."

Janie looked startled. "What are you doing here, then?"

"Taking the year off," Lisa explained. She didn't know how much Janie knew, or how much anyone knew, but she might as well explain it now. She'd learned that nothing remained private very long. But she shortened the story considerably, skipping the part about Gordon's legal problems and stressing the fact she wanted to spend more time with them.

"Well, I'm grateful and the town is, too. It will give Dr. Bradley time to find a permanent replacement. If you weren't here, I'm sure he'd kill himself trying to do the impossible."

"I'm glad it seems to work out for both of us. Now if only I can convince my brother and sister…"

"I know it's a world away from a big city," Janie said. "But the sports here are terrific, and most of the kids are really great. There's always the bad apple, of course, but on the whole, we've been blessed."

"That's good to know." She prayed that Gordon wouldn't be that bad apple. She looked at her watch. "Is there anything we need?"

"We're out of suckers."

"Suckers?"

"We always give them out after a 'no tears' vaccination," she said, then added with a smile, "And we usually sneak one to those who do shed a tear or two."

"The old 'candy makes the medicine go down' trick?" Lisa said with a grin. "I'll run and get some at the general store while you man the office."

"I can do it," Janie said.

"I don't mind. I've been wanting to go over there. I'm told I can find nearly anything at the general store."

Janie nodded. "You can."

"And what kind of suckers?"

"The red suckers are the most popular."

Lisa was fascinated the moment she arrived at the general store. There seemed to be a little of everything inside. It even had an old-fashioned counter window loaded with packaged and individual candies.

A woman who looked to be in her forties approached from the back. She took one look at Lisa's white coat and grinned. "You must be the new doctor. I'm Heather. What can I do for you?"

"I need suckers for vaccinations," Lisa explained hurriedly. "I am the new doctor, Lisa Redding."

"Good to meet you," Heather said as she loaded a paper bag with a handful of suckers in various flavors. "Twenty enough?"

"More than enough," Lisa said, then realized she'd left her money at the office. "I'm sorry. I left my purse at the office. Is it okay if I pay you later?"

"Nonsense," Heather interrupted. "We always provide them free to Dr. Bradley. It's little enough we can do for the clinic and the kids." She handed the bag to Lisa. "We're just happy you're here."

Touched by the affection for the clinic, Lisa thanked her, then started for the door when she thought about Jubal Pierce and his bloody T-shirt.

"Do you have any T-shirts in—I think—extra large?"

"Sure. For your brother?"

"Ah…yes."

"I'll be back later to pick them up." She hurried back. This small-town thing wasn't bad at all. A friendly police chief, a welcoming mayor who offered horseback rides, free candy for small patients. The latter wasn't a big thing, but the openhearted gesture was overwhelming to her. Wouldn't happen in a big city.

The small waiting room was filling up when she arrived back. Four small people—she always thought of them that way rather than as children—waited with their mothers. She stooped down to their level. "Who wants a sucker?" she asked.

She was greeted with "I dos" except for a little girl who tried to hide.

Lisa nodded her head. "Good. Whoever goes first gets first choice of flavors."

"Me," said a girl with a ponytail and well-worn jeans that were too large.

"Good for you. I'm Dr. Lisa. What's your name?"

"Jenny," the child said shyly.

"Well, you certainly are a brave girl. I promise it won't hurt, okay?"

"Okay." Jenny didn't sound too sure, though.

Lisa stood and extended her hand to the harried-looking woman with Jenny. She had a toddler with her, as well. "I'm Dr. Redding," Lisa said. "Mrs...?"

She waited for the woman to identify herself. "Akin," the woman said. "Alice Akin."

Lisa remembered the name from looking over the files yesterday. Alice and Robert Akin. They had four children under eight. "Please come into my office," she said to mother and child.

Janie was inside with the prepared needles. Janie could give it, but Lisa wanted to do it this first day. She wanted that personal contact with the patients.

Jenny sat in a chair and Lisa crouched next to her. "What do you like to do best," she asked as she rubbed alcohol on the injection site.

"Draw."

"And what do you like to draw?" Lisa asked as she inserted the needle. Jenny's lips pursed as she tried to think of an answer. "Flowers," she finally said.

"Well, that's a fine thing to draw," Lisa said as she took the second needle and inserted it.

"That didn't hurt much," Jenny said, glancing down as Lisa swabbed the skin again and put a Wonder Woman bandage on it.

Lisa picked up the sack of suckers she'd put on her desk. "And now you can pick which sucker you want and take one for each of your brothers, too."

"Thank you, Doctor," Mrs. Akin said. "You've been very kind. What do I owe you?"

Janie had already coached Lisa on that aspect of the clinic. Many of the residents lived or had retired on a small income, but they didn't want charity. It was a particularly sensitive issue since children had to have shots to enter schools and it often meant no food on the table. Dr. Bradley charged them only a fraction of the usual fee.

Lisa approved.

After Mrs. Akin and Jenny left, she quickly immunized the other children without a problem. After Jenny emerged with a big smile, none of the others wanted to be less brave than the smallest among them.

The mothers and fathers were curious but friendly as they asked questions and answered a few of hers. They all wanted to know where she went to medical school and whether she would be staying.

Then it was nearly noon. No more appointments until two p.m., but Lisa planned to be back early to get ready for them. She had just enough time to get home, make lunch for Kerry and check on Gordon.

She dropped by the general store and selected two white T-shirts, then walked home. Kerry was teaching Susie how to sit. Or trying to. "Have you seen your brother?"

"He's in his room on his laptop."

Lisa knocked on his door and was surprised when Gordon opened it. His laptop was open. "The internet here sucks," he said.

She'd noticed the same thing. On that they could agree. "I know. Want some lunch?"

He nodded.

"How did it go this morning?" she asked.

"Okay."

"Chief Morgan seemed like a nice guy…"

Gordon shrugged. "He's okay."

"What did he say?"

"He wants me to check in every week." He shrugged again. "And he wants copies of my grades." He hesitated a moment, then added, "He said high school graduates can go directly to chopper pilot school and become warrant officers."

"I rather imagine they must have excellent grades and no juvenile record," she said, trying to keep her voice calm. Why on earth would the police chief encourage that?

"You said if I didn't get in trouble again my record would disappear," her brother retorted. "And I'm not stupid."

"No, you're not," she said. "Though you couldn't prove it with your most recent grades. I know you could do anything you want to do. You could be an engineer like Dad." She knew she shouldn't continue. Her opposition would only spur his interest in the military.

"You always know best, don't you?" he shot back. "Well, sometimes you don't. Maybe I don't want to be an engineer." He headed for the door.

"Where are you going?" she asked.

"I'm not going to rob a bank if that's what

you're thinking!" he said while opening the door. He slammed it behind him.

The pleasure of the morning faded. She fought to hold back tears. She couldn't seem to do anything right as far as Gordon was concerned.

She couldn't chase after him. She only had enough time to fix sandwiches and canned soup for Kerry and herself. She would do better that night. She would listen, really try to listen, to Gordon.

When they sat down to eat, Kerry didn't meet her gaze.

"Something wrong?" Lisa asked.

"Ah, well, Susie…she found one of your shoes."

"And…?"

"She kinda chewed it."

Lisa closed her eyes and prayed for patience. She didn't have that many shoes. Money had been really tight the last few years. "Which ones?" she finally asked.

"The blue ones. She ate the heel."

Her only good pair. But Lisa knew it wasn't the dog's fault, and it was a small price for the change in Kerry. The sadness in her eyes was gone. "I'll train myself to put shoes and other potentially tempting objects out of temptation's way. Okay?"

Relief flowed from Kerry, and Lisa wondered if her sister had feared her reaction. Had she really been that unapproachable?

"Dr. Morgan said she would help me train her," Kerry ventured. "I thought I would go over this afternoon and take Susie," Kerry said tentatively. "If it's okay with you."

"I think it's a terrific idea. You check with Dr. Morgan first, to see if she has time. I'll drive you over."

"We can walk," Kerry said. "I think Susie would like that."

"If you promise no more encounters with cars," Lisa said, pleased that Kerry felt comfortable enough to venture out on her own. "I'll call Mrs. Manning and ask about riding lessons this weekend."

"Oh, really?" Excitement radiated from Kerry. She was practically wriggling in her chair.

If only she could get half that excitement from Gordon. "That doesn't mean Eve won't be too busy, so don't get too excited, okay?" Lisa cautioned although her heart was warmed by Kerry's reaction.

"Okay," Kerry agreed. She looked down at Susie. "Did you hear that, Susie? We're going to the clinic today and maybe I'll ride a horse this weekend."

Susie barked in reply, and both Kerry and Lisa laughed.

"See? She understands," Kerry said. "She's a really smart dog."

Except when it comes to shoes. Lisa resisted mentioning the recent transgression. "I have to go. If you need anything, call me on the cell, okay?"

"Okay. I'll clean up and wash the dishes," Kerry offered.

The glow inside Lisa grew brighter. She glanced at her watch. She had about thirty minutes before her appointment. Maybe she would have time to run one of the T-shirts over to Jubal's cabin to replace the one he lost thanks to her errant dog.

Hopefully, he wouldn't be there. She would just leave it on his porch with a thank-you note and no more would be said about it. She didn't like owing anyone anything. The fact that she misled Heather at the general store nagged at her, but the woman surprised her when she'd asked if the shirts were for her brother.

She had become fully aware in the past few days of the Covenant Falls gossip machine and, fearing misunderstandings, she instinctively indicated both shirts were for Gordon.

It was dumb, but it was also done.

She reached the cabin. His car was parked in front which meant he was probably home. Instead of feeling relief, she was consumed with confusion. Was this what she really wanted?

No. It was a bad idea. Worse than that. A terrible idea.

She was turning around when she saw him

jogging into the driveway. He ran directly to the driver's side of her car. The T-shirt he was wearing was drenched with sweat, as were his pants. He hadn't shaved and, darn, but the scruff made him even more attractive. Dangerous.

She'd never been attracted to dangerous before.

He leaned into the window. "Dr. Redding. What can I do for you?"

"I wanted to see how you were recuperating," she said, hoping she wasn't babbling. "And I brought you a new T-shirt to replace…"

"That isn't necessary."

"I thought it was," she replied defensively. She handed him the new T-shirt beside her.

"Thank you," he said with a trace of amusement. He opened the door of the car, inviting her to come out.

"I have to get back," she said.

"Don't you want to inspect my wrist and other various injuries?"

She looked at all the fine lines defined by the shirt and pants sticking to his body and soaked in the masculine smell of him. Heat bubbled up inside her.

"You look healthy, and I have appointments. I mainly wanted to drop this off. There's a thank-you note, too." More babbling. She never babbled.

"Until next time, then," he said. He took his hand from the window, turned and jogged to the porch.

Lisa took a deep breath. *Get yourself together.* She turned on the engine and drove out to Lake Road.

CHAPTER NINE

LIGHT CREPT THROUGH the gauzy curtains to wake Lisa on Friday morning. She stretched and thought of the day ahead. So much had happened since they'd arrived on Tuesday, she hadn't had time to unpack except for essentials.

She looked at the clock. It was six a.m. on her fourth day in Covenant Falls and she'd been so busy. They'd been living out of suitcases. She'd emptied the small rental trailer, and Eve had sent a city employee to return it in Pueblo. But boxes still sat unopened.

She stood and went over to the window where she had a glorious view of white-tipped mountains.

It was a nice way to greet the day. Unfortunately, she hadn't fallen to sleep until the early morning hours. A tall man with piercing blue eyes kept haunting her thoughts. *Go away*, she commanded silently.

The dog barked, apparently wanting to go outside. She sighed. Susie was worth the trouble if she made Kerry happy, and even Gordon seemed to have mellowed a little since Susie's arrival. It might have been guilt, however, for letting Susie escape.

She went to the kitchen and made coffee. While it was brewing, she stepped outside into the back-yard and took a deep breath. It tasted sweet, and the silence was soothing. The mountains were gorgeous in the gleam of early-morning sun.

The door opened and Kerry and Susie joined her.

"I hope Susie didn't wake you," Kerry said. "She really needed to go outside."

"I hope not every morning at six."

"I don't think she's lived in a house before," Kerry said protectively. "She'll get better." Kerry looked anxious as if Lisa would snatch the dog and throw her out. Had she given her sister that impression? Did her siblings think she didn't care about them or what was important to them?

"I think you're exactly what Susie needs," Lisa said, and gave Kerry a hug and Susie an ear rub. "Why don't you take her for a walk and then we'll have breakfast together. Your brother will proba-bly sleep until noon."

"Are you going to be here today?" Kerry asked.

"I have two appointments this morning. "Then I have to register both of you at school. It starts Monday, you know." She'd already sent their tran-scripts ahead.

"Can I help Dr. Morgan at the clinic? She said she can use me anytime and I can bring Susie."

"Sounds like a great idea. Maybe she can give you some more tips for Susie."

Kerry grinned. "Okay." She turned to the dog. "Come on, Susie. We're going for a walk."

"Don't forget to clean up after her."

"Okay!"

"I'll make pancakes when you get back."

Kerry's smile turned to a big grin Pancakes were Kerry's and Gordon's favorite.

She went to the front door and watched as Kerry marched Susie down the street as if they owned it. She wished they had been able to get a dog in Chicago now that she saw how happy it made Kerry. Why hadn't she recognized her sister's needs then? Or Gordon's? She'd been too wrapped up in her own career and justified it by looking toward the future, hoping to send her siblings to good colleges when the time came.

She swallowed hard and vowed to be more aware of their needs.

If only Gordon could find something to make him happy. He'd lost more than Kerry had, in a way. He'd had such a close relationship with their parents. Kerry had been too young to remember much.

Lisa whipped up the batter for pancakes before going to Gordon's room. She knocked lightly. To her surprise, he answered the door.

"Want some pancakes?" she asked.

"Yeah."

"They'll be ready as soon as you get dressed."

He nodded and closed the door.

All she had to do was put the batter on a griddle. She set the table and poured orange juice into glasses. She'd finished her coffee when Gordon, then Kerry, came into the kitchen. In minutes, she had a heaping plate of pancakes, which, to Lisa's gratification, quickly disappeared.

"I'm taking Kerry to the falls later this afternoon," Lisa said. "They're really beautiful. Want to go with us? We can take a picnic," she added hopefully.

Gordon shook his head, his gaze never meeting hers. "I'm looking for a job."

Lisa was startled. "You're starting school on Monday."

He looked at her as if she were clueless. "Part-time," he said.

"Where are you looking?"

He shrugged. "Go by some stores. Ask if anyone is hiring."

It sounded good, but something was off. The change was too sudden. She decided to give him the benefit of the doubt. "That's great. What about going to the pageant tomorrow?"

Gordon shrugged again. "Who cares about some dumb pageant?"

"At least think about it. I hear the music is great and you've complained there's nothing to do here. You might even meet some kids who'll be at your school on Monday."

His gaze didn't meet hers and she felt a tremor of apprehension. He walked out of the kitchen and she heard his footsteps on the stairs.

At least it wasn't a no, she told herself. And a job hunt was definitely progress. Maybe the meeting with the town's police chief had accomplished what the Chicago police couldn't.

Lisa turned back to her sister who was stacking dishes in the sink. "Why don't we drive to the medical clinic together so you can see it? The vet's office is just a block away. I'll meet you there at noon. We can have lunch at Maude's and drive up to see the falls. Then we can go to the pageant tomorrow."

"What about Gordon?" Kerry asked anxiously.

"I'll call him when we get ready for lunch. He can join us. Or not." She had learned not to try to force him. "I'm going to go take a shower and get dressed."

"Lisa?" Kerry's voice was tentative.

"What?"

"I think I'm going to like it here."

"I'm glad. I'm really glad," Lisa said, and her heart did a little dance. At the same time, a new worry emerged. What if Kerry wouldn't want to leave Covenant Falls next year?

JUBAL WOKE AS the first stab of light rose over the horizon. He was surprised to discover it was almost dawn. He'd slept better than usual.

Maybe it was because he had a goal now. A short-term goal to be sure, but a goal nonetheless. He had something to look forward to.

He had a job of sorts, even if it was a temporary gig. An opportunity to ride, he reminded himself. Nothing more.

He did need something. A future that would quiet the restlessness in him, that would challenge both his mind and body. So far, nothing had interested him. Certainly not the security jobs he'd been offered. Protecting some politician or executive wasn't his idea of a challenging life.

Maybe Luke's offer *was* the answer. He didn't have to stay, but he could learn something about ranching. Yesterday had awakened the love of horses he'd once had, satisfying a yearning deep inside. But that meant he would stay here longer than he expected, and in a town this size, he and Dr. Redding would meet often, making their palpable connection something he'd have to confront after all.

To his puzzlement, she'd affected him in a way no woman had before. He hadn't been able to get her out of his mind since she'd knelt on the floor of his bathroom and tended to his various abrasions with such care and gentleness. Her eyes had widened slightly when she saw the scars on him but she hadn't seemed repulsed, nor did she ask questions. When she'd so earnestly finished, he'd wanted to pull her into his arms. But he knew she was off-limits. She was a healer with her life in front of her and he was an over-the-hill warrior with little future.

Of course, Gordon was another reason why he should run like hell. He could continue his quixotic plan for the kid and keep it from Lisa Redding, or he could tell her about her brother's playing with fire and the kid wouldn't trust anyone again. He was damned either way.

Maybe the kid wouldn't show up today. Maybe the near-accident had scared him off.

Damn it all. How could he have become so involved in so few days, he who made it a practice never to get involved in anyone's business other than his own?

He took a quick swim to cool off, not that it worked, then drove to Luke's ranch.

He found the rancher in the barn currying a stocky bay horse with muscular hind quarters.

Luke nodded in greeting and scrutinized his jeans and running shoes. "You're gonna need heavier pants and some riding boots," he said. "What size shoe you wear?"

"Eleven."

"There are several worn pairs of boots in the tack room. Find some that fit. The jeans will do today but you'll need something heavier for the long run. The general store in town should have what you need."

Jubal nodded and went into the tack room. He found a row of boots, sighted a pair that looked big enough and tried them on. They fit. He returned to Luke's side.

"I'm starting you with Sara Jane," Luke said. "She's a sweet-riding mare with a great disposition. Tracy will look after you and give you some pointers. Okay?"

A lanky young man dressed in worn jeans and boots emerged from the back of the barn.

"This is Tim, our stable hand. He looks after the stalls and equipment and generally helps out wherever needed. He's going to be helping me set up flags in the arena for one of our students."

Jubal shook hands with Tim. "Anything I can do to help?"

"Nope. I'd rather get you riding. Tracy will go through everything with you. She's expecting you at the ranch house. In addition to teaching, she keeps all the books. And," he added, "call her Tracy. She'll be mad as hell if you do the missus bit. Makes her feel old."

Jubal walked to the ranch house. The door opened before he got there and Tracy Daniels handed him a cup of coffee. "Hi," she said. "I had a bet with Luke over whether you'd turn up."

"Who won?"

"Luke. He usually does when it comes to people."

"I'll try not to disappoint, but I told him I haven't ridden much."

"I saw you ride yesterday. You have a good seat. You'll need a better one to stay on some of our quarter horses. Their movements are instinctive and quick. They have to be for roping and barrel racing and other performance competitions. They can toss some of the best riders. You can't let your attention wander."

He nodded, absorbing everything, grateful she was so frank. He gulped down the coffee in several swallows. He wanted to get started.

Tracy Daniels seemed in no hurry. "Luke said your father was on the rodeo circuit."

It felt like a question more than a comment. "Rode broncs, steer roping. Calf tie-down," he said. "He didn't ride bulls. He didn't like them and said they sure didn't like him."

She just nodded. "I can surely understand that. I've been at a lot of rodeos, and that's one event I don't like to watch." She led him out to the barn. "Luke suggested you start exercising the horses we use for teaching and trail rides. They're well trained, gentle and anxious to please. Most are for sale as pleasure horses. They get less attention and exercise because our emphasis is on breeding and training championship horses in the performance field—rodeos, horse shows, barrel and flag racing."

He felt he should warn her that he was temporary. "I told Luke I won't be here long. I'm just passing through."

"He told me that, too, but we rarely have commitments from ranch workers. Most are wanderers. You'll be a help as long as you're here." She led the way to the barn, down the row of stalls and stopped halfway. A bay reached her head over the top of the stall gate. Tracy said, "She's one of the teaching horses. Steady. Reliable. She has a great trot. We've had offers for her, but she's one Luke won't give up."

She led the mare out and gave the lead to Jubal while she took out another horse. "Luke said you might have a problem cinching the saddle for a few days. I'll help you there."

Jubal liked her. No nonsense. He nodded, determined that next time he would do it.

"Hate to admit it, huh?" she said.

"Yep."

"Well, don't. Everyone helps everyone else around here, and injuries are not uncommon. I sure wouldn't want the cinch to be too loose."

She walked the horses to the tack room. Jubal claimed the saddle he'd used the day before and did all but pull the cinch tight.

Tracy saddled another horse while Jubal talked to Sara Jane, who seemed to dance with eagerness. They both mounted and Tracy led the way to the outside training circle.

"You ever heard the expression 'stopping on a dime'?" Tracy asked.

"Sure."

"That's what a quarter horse does. It's the most important thing to remember. The quarter horse can be at a full gallop and come to a complete stop without warning. If you don't know that, you're going over the saddle to the ground. Their speed and agility make them the perfect cow pony, but it means the rider has to be alert every minute. They're also versatile, willing and generally good-natured," she said.

Dusty came to Jubal's mind. His father's horse had been all of that. He never knew what had happened to the horse when his father died, and it had bothered him for years.

"Okay, we're going to start with a sitting trot," Tracy said, interrupting the memory. "I know you did all this with Luke yesterday but I want to see how you handle the reins and your legs. Okay?"

"Sure."

She took him through the different gaits and variations, suggesting changes in the way he held the reins and used his legs.

Tracy was a good instructor. Minute by minute, Jubal grew more comfortable. More confident. After an hour of basics, they rode out of the circle toward the stream.

"Luke was right. You do have a natural seat," she said. "Let's start with a trot, then a canter."

An hour later, they turned back. "You have something that's hard to teach," Tracy said. "Sara Jane likes and trusts you. That's the secret. Earn a horse's trust and she will do her best for you.

"I think Luke showed you most of our acreage," she continued. "In exercising our horses, you can ride them anywhere inside the property, but it's best to start in the ring if it's a horse you haven't ridden yet. Let them get used to you, trust you."

They turned back. "We'll go and see how Luke's doing, then you'll be on your own," she said. "I'll race you back."

They took off. She won. As they reached the barn, Jubal saw an expensive sports car in the driveway.

They cooled the horses and put them back in the stalls. Tracy led the way through the barn to the back door, then into a large arena.

A rider was racing a horse around flags, making what looked like impossible turns. Luke had one foot on the railing separating them from the rider. An older man stood next to him watching the rider intently.

Tracy joined Luke at the fence but Jubal stayed several feet behind. He watched as the young rider knocked down a flag but kept going. The rider, a girl of about fifteen, finished and rode over to Luke. "He did everything I asked," she said. "I'm the one who messed up."

"You still made good time," Luke replied as he closed his watch. "It takes more than three rides to develop a relationship between rider and horse, but you did just fine."

He turned to the older man, who was apparently the girl's father. "They need some work, but I think Darby might be the horse for her," Luke said.

"Will they win?"

"Probably not at first, but he's a fine horse. If they work hard together they can go a long way."

"Will you continue to train her if I buy him?"

"Yes. We can also board him for you."

"What do you think, April?" the man said.

April had slipped from the horse and stood stroking his neck. "I love him already."

The man nodded to Luke and they shook hands. "Draw up the papers and have Stephanie give us a health certificate." His daughter gave the horse a big hug, then led Darby out of the arena and into the stable.

Jubal closed the gap to stand next to Tracy.

"He's a handsome horse," he said.

"And very even-tempered. We raised him from a colt and I've been training him. The sale will take care of the feed bill for a while," Tracy added. "The girl, April Morris, has been looking for a while. She came here two weeks ago on a referral and tried out several horses. She wanted her father to see her on this one."

"The sale is solid?" Jubal asked.

"I think so. I've talked to other horsemen who've had dealings with him, and they say his word is good. The frosting is she wants lessons and will board the horse with us. It's a win, win, win for us." She looked at his watch. "I remember you said you had to leave at noon. Have time to ride another horse solo?"

He definitely did.

An hour later and filled with an exhilaration he hadn't felt since his last successful mission, Jubal rode into the barn on a bay mare. He unsaddled the horse and cooled her off, then went to the ranch house.

Luke opened the door. "I can tell from your face it went well."

Jubal nodded. "She tried one of those quick turns Tracy warned me about. Thanks to her, I was ready. I have to get back," he said reluctantly. "When can I come again?"

"Let's make it Monday. We have lessons tomorrow and four of the horses will be on a trail ride."

"I'll be here Monday morning."

Luke nodded. "I'll have a list of horses that need riding."

"Thanks," Jubal said.

"We haven't talked about salary," Luke said.

"I think *I* should pay you."

"It was that much fun?" Luke asked. "Even so, I wouldn't feel right about it. We'll talk about it Monday. Are you going to the pageant tomorrow night?"

"Hadn't thought much about it."

"Sara Jane and Night Shadow have ride-on parts," Luke said.

"Then I guess I should go."

He said goodbye and walked out to his car. He was a little stiff but overall he felt better than he had in months.

He reminded himself that Covenant Falls was only a stopover. The cabin wasn't his, and he was taking the place of someone who might really need it.

But maybe he would stay one or two weeks, just long enough to learn new skills in an activity he really enjoyed, and finish his business with the kid.

CHAPTER TEN

JUBAL STOPPED AT the community center on his way home.

He parked his car and went inside. An attractive young woman was sitting at a desk in the entry hall, her eyes on a laptop screen. She glanced up and her smile was immediate. "You must be Jubal," she said.

"That obvious?"

"I'm Andy Stuart. I had the cabin before you. I thought about visiting, especially after your heroic bout with the car," she said with a grin. "But I was assured by Dr. Redding that you were fine and I resisted. I know how overwhelmed I felt when I came here. I just wanted to holler, 'Leave me alone.'"

"Ditto," he replied. "I thought a town called Covenant Falls would be restful. How wrong can a guy get?"

"Well, unfortunately, it'll probably get worse. You're a celebrity hero now. Mrs. Aubry is one of the town's favorite citizens," Andy continued. "Her son was killed in the service and she dotes on the veterans. She's been singing your praises all over town. You'll probably be showered with all kinds of cookies, brownies and pies."

"You've got to be kidding," was all Jubal could manage.

"Well, I might've exaggerated a little, but not much. I thought I should warn you."

"Kind of you."

She laughed. "We have to protect each other. Besides I like Clint, and Clint likes you and that means *I* like you. Even if you are navy."

"What's your role here?" he asked to get the topic off himself.

"Good question," she said. "I'm president of the chamber of commerce. Now, before you start wondering what a chamber of commerce does in tiny Covenant Falls, I'm also curator of the museum, chief librarian and, along with Clint, a computer coach and volunteer fireperson."

"That's quite an impressive résumé."

"Good to see you have a sense of humor," she said with a big grin.

"It kinda depends on whom I'm talking to."

"Come to the pageant tomorrow night, and hopefully you'll be more impressed."

He raised an eyebrow in question.

"I was dumb enough to suggest it and somehow I ended up being in charge, even to the extent of chasing camels down the street. There's a lesson here. Never volunteer for anything in this town."

"Why did you?"

"I really like the town's curmudgeon, Al Monroe. He was the former council president, and he was a challenge I needed...

"And then I fell in love with Nate, a veteran and lifelong resident of Covenant Falls. Nate and Josh hoped the pageant would bring people here. I needed a cause, and Covenant Falls gave me one. It worked. We get a crowd on Saturday nights, and it's good for the businesses here. We're getting tourists but we need a lot more. But you didn't come to hear about that. What can I do for you?"

"I'm looking for books on quarter horses and ranching if you have any."

"I'm pretty sure we do. I'll show you the section on agriculture. I placed ranching in there, as well. Quarter horses will be among the horse breeds in the animal section."

"Sounds logical to me."

She led him to the library. Old sofas and stuffed chairs were scattered around. Several children were sitting on the floor reading books.

Andy showed him the sections. "We're closing early because of the pageant," she said.

He found two books, one on quarter horses and another titled *Modern Ranching* dated thirty years earlier.

He took them both out to Andy. "How do I check them out?"

"You don't. It's the honor system."

"This is a weird town," he observed.

"It took me a few more days than you to discover that," she replied. "I suppose someone told you about the Monday night poker games?"

"They did. It was the carrot in Clint's invitation, and a few others have mentioned it since then."

The phone on the desk rang, and she picked it up. He gave her a wave, then left.

He reached the cabin a little after one and found a tin on the steps to the porch. He picked it up, opened it and found brownies. No note, but he suspected Mrs. Aubry. He was hungry after the long day and tried one. Then a second. He forced himself to put them away. He had been warned to expect such gifts. He hadn't expected them to be quite so good.

He headed for the bathroom. A layer of dust had caked on his body, and he smelled like horse. He took his second shower of the day, dressed in an ancient pair of jeans, grabbed one of the last beers and made a sandwich. Then he took both—and the book on quarter horses—outside and settled down in the lounge chair. He'd always been obsessive about preparing for any job or mission. He wanted to know everything that could go wrong because it usually did.

Whether he stayed here a week or longer, he'd made at least a short-term commitment to Luke and he wanted to be prepared.

He was through the first chapter and well into the second when his instincts kicked in, and he looked up to see the kid turn the corner of the cabin and approach him. He had a fat folder clutched in one hand.

Jubal put down the book and looked at his watch. It was ten minutes until two. Progress.

"You have something for me?" he asked.

Gordon shifted from one foot to the other and mumbled, "Thanks for not telling my sister the other night…"

"I probably should have." Jubal took the folder, opened it and slowly scanned the pages. Gordon had included three designs. Clipped to each one was a list of materials required. He'd even added a note to one design with a suggestion of ways to improve it.

What pleased Jubal was that only one design was a simple one. The other two had wide arm-rests and slanted backs. Both would be more difficult to build but would be more comfortable and better looking.

After a moment's silence, Gordon spoke up. "I figured a six-foot-long bench so two people could sit. You would need treated lumber for the bench and carriage bolts to fix it to the dock."

"That sounds about right," Jubal said. "What kind of lumber?"

"It's all there on the paper," the kid said rebelliously.

"I want you to tell me."

"Treated pine. Amount depends on which one of those benches you want."

"Which would you want?"

"None," Gordon muttered.

Jubal smiled. "Don't like the water?"

"Not that water."

So he remembered how cold it was. "It's really not bad," Jubal said.

"Maybe for crazy people," the kid mumbled.

Jubal ignored the comment but inwardly smiled. The boy hadn't lost his spirit. "You think you can build any of these?" he asked.

Gordon nodded. "We'll be even then?" he asked. "You won't tell Chief Morgan? Or my sister? About the fire?"

"Won't your sister wonder where you are or what you're doing?"

"I told her I was looking for a job. I'll tell her I found one."

"Slick," Jubal said, hating the fact he was becoming complicit in what was, at the very least, a deception. But he'd made a deal and the kid, thus far, had held up his end.

"It's the truth," the kid defended. "It *is* a job."

"I'll keep my part of the bargain if you build the bench and stay out of trouble."

Another rebellious look, but the kid held his tongue.

"When does school start?" Jubal asked.

"Monday."

"Then after school Monday, meet me here and I'll tell you what comes next."

Gordon started to turn away.

"Aren't you going to ask which one I want?" Jubal said.

"I figure you'll tell me when you're ready." He disappeared around the corner. Jubal looked at the plans again and realized the kid was a lot smarter than he wanted anyone to think.

When the phone rang, he recognized Clint's number. "I hear you're working for Luke," Clint said.

"For a short time."

"I didn't know you were that much into horses."

"I hate to tell you this, but there's probably a lot of things you don't know," Jubal replied.

Clint chuckled. "I saw the way your eyes fastened on that buckskin. But that's not why I called. What time do you want to go to the Rusty Nail tonight? Also, Josh is having a steak fry at his house tomorrow night before the pageant."

"Can I say no?" Jubal said.

"It would be rude," Clint said cheerfully. "And you *are* living in the cabin he owns. Hell, you might even enjoy it once you get used to the chaos."

"That's a real incentive," Jubal groused.

"Supper will be very simple, very informal, and Josh does grill a mean steak. Baked potatoes, salad and a pie from Maude's. Minimum fuss."

"What time?"

"Six p.m. The pageant is at eight so no one will linger."

It was the last thing he wanted to do. Particularly the pageant. He didn't like crowds, but Josh was his host and he'd liked him when they'd met.

"You've convinced me," Jubal agreed after a short silence.

"I'll pick you up at six." Clint hung up.

One thing about Covenant Falls, it wasn't boring. He'd thought it would be. He'd thought it would be relaxing. Spend a couple days with Clint up in the mountains, then leave in search of… what?

Instead, he felt tentacles begin to wind around him. The kid. Luke. Clint. The lady doc. And all that, God help him, was just in the first few days. No telling what would happen if he didn't run like hell.

He went into the bedroom and looked over his pitiful wardrobe. It consisted of jeans, more jeans, warm-ups and sweatpants. He remembered then that Luke had told him he needed riding pants and boots.

He looked at his watch. He just had time to drive to town and pick up some riding clothes and maybe a decent shirt for the steak fry tomorrow night.

IT SEEMED EVERYONE in Covenant Falls had a cold, rash or aches on Friday. Mainly, Lisa decided, they wanted to take her measure. She felt lucky to leave at six.

She picked up Kerry at the veterinarian's office. She tried to call Gordon on his cell but there was no answer. She made a note not to pay his bill next month.

She stopped by Maude's and ordered takeout salads for herself and Kerry. Gordon would have to do with what was in the fridge.

He sauntered inside a few minutes after they arrived at home with a folder in his hand.

"Would it be too difficult to answer the phone?" she asked.

"I got a job."

Nothing could have shocked her more. "Doing what?"

"I'm going to build a bench," he said.

"You don't…" She stopped before saying something she might regret. She amended the sentence. "For whom?"

The phone interrupted them. It was Eve inviting them for steak dinner the following night. "If you come half an hour earlier, we can introduce Kerry and Gordon to the horses." She added, "We'll be going to the pageant afterward."

"That sounds great. Kerry will be thrilled. We'll be there at five-thirty. Can I bring anything?"

"No. Everything is under control. Oh, and I heard you adopted one of Stephanie's rescues. Bring her if you want. She'll have plenty of canine company, and people take dogs to the pageant. I'm sure Josh will bring his. See you then." Eve hung up.

Gordon was looking at her. "Where will we be at five-thirty?"

"We've been invited to dinner at Mrs. Manning's."

"I don't know them. I'm not going."

"You *will* go, and you *will* be polite," Lisa said. "I've given you a lot of room but you *are* on probation, and I want a little cooperation. Frankly, I've had enough of your miserable attitude. So has Kerry. Now where is this job?"

"The guy in the cabin at the end of that road around the lake," he said reluctantly.

"Mr. Pierce?" She couldn't tame the surprise in her voice. "What are you going to do for him?"

"I told you. Building a bench on his dock."

"Why?"

"How should I know? Maybe because he wants one?" Gordon replied.

"I'm getting very tired of those smart remarks, too," Lisa said. "Why you?"

"Because I asked if I could do something," Gordon said sullenly. Anger flashed in his eyes. "And I knew I could do it. You don't think I can do anything right!"

"That's not true, Gordon. I've always known you're really smart. If anything, I find it frustrating to see you not using that brain."

"I'm using it now," he said. "And all you do is interrogate me like I'm public enemy number one." He took the stairs two at a time and slammed his door.

She followed him, and opened the door without knocking. "I want you to come tomorrow night and be polite, or I'm cutting your allowance in half. Indefinitely," she added for emphasis. She wondered about the wisdom of dragging an unwilling Gordon along, but it was time they had an understanding.

He stared at her defiantly for a minute. "I don't know why you want me around now," he said. "You were never there when Mom was sick and now you're trying to take her place. Well, you can't."

There they were. The unspoken words that had been buried under grief and resentment.

"I couldn't take her place," she said quietly. "I wouldn't even try. She wanted me to finish that residency. She wanted it more than anything. It was why she asked Aunt Kay to stay with you guys. I didn't…"

She stopped. Lisa had spent every moment she could with her mother, but she knew her siblings and her aunt had borne the brunt of watching the person they loved most slip slowly away.

Gordon had a bleak look in his eyes as he turned away. Her heart broke for him, but she knew from the bottom of her soul that if she didn't do something, she would lose him and he might lose himself.

"Gordon."

He turned around.

"Please go with us tomorrow night."

He shrugged in what she considered agreement.

"Thank you," she said softly, and turned away before he changed his mind.

CHAPTER ELEVEN

JUBAL WAS READY when Clint arrived in a police car Saturday night.

"You didn't say we would be going in a police car," Jubal said as he slid into the front seat.

"Makes you a bit nervous, does it?" Clint asked.

"You didn't drive it last night."

"I was drinking last night."

Indeed he had been, but not to the extent they once had. The Rusty Nail was everything Clint had said it was. It had been full, but a table in the corner had been reserved for them. A few people—all vets—had walked over and introduced themselves, but for the most part they had been left to reminisce about past meetings.

Jubal had found himself smiling, even laughing. It had been a good time, but he had no such hopes for tonight.

"It's your driving that makes me nervous. I seem to remember some interesting rides…"

"I'm the world's safest driver these days," Clint said with the grin Jubal remembered.

They drove by the park, which was bustling with activity. Picnic tables had been moved back, and what looked like a large structure on wheels was being moved in front of the lake.

"They're setting up for the pageant tonight," Clint said.

Jubal heard a woof from the backseat and looked behind the screen that separated the back from the front. "I see you've brought your police dog with you."

"Please don't make fun of Bart."

Another woof came from the back.

"Sorry. I didn't know he was sensitive."

"Well, he is," Clint said. "If you had a dog, you would know that. Now Stephanie has a few—"

"I'm thinking more about a horse," Jubal blurted, much to his own surprise.

"You gotta be kidding. I thought you were dead set on wandering. Can't wander with a horse."

"Don't know why not. All you need is a trailer." Jubal had absolutely no idea why he said that, either. Clint was right. The last thing he needed was a horse.

He tried to explain. Even to himself. "I'm enjoying the riding gig at Luke's place. I guess I just have horses on my mind."

Clint stole his gaze from the road for a second and glanced at Jubal. "Does that mean you're going to stay longer than you planned?"

"No…well, maybe a few days. I figure while

I'm here, I might as well learn something. And horses don't talk."

"Is that a hint?" Clint said as he turned into a driveway. Several cars were parked there, including a silver sedan with Illinois plates. Jubal felt a jolt of electricity run through him as he saw the back of a slim figure at the fence of the pasture. Lisa Redding was watching her sister, who was sitting atop a white horse. He spotted Stephanie standing next to the girl, talking to her.

The doctor had apparently heard the car approach, because she turned around and seemed startled to see Jubal as he exited the car. Apparently she hadn't known he was invited.

Clint noticed his surprise. "Eve likes all the newcomers to feel at home," he said.

Feeling trapped, Jubal walked over to the fence. "Dr. Redding," Jubal said.

"Mr. Pierce," she replied. "You seem to have recuperated nicely."

"It's Jubal," he corrected as their eyes met. Hers were such a rich, expressive dark brown, he felt torpedoed by the same powerful attraction he'd felt before.

She nodded. "And call me Lisa."

She looked like a Lisa. Like a portrait. Her dark hair was tied back with a blue ribbon. The sun overhead tinted the dark brown with copper. She wore a light blue blouse and dark blue pants that fit her perfectly. She used a light shade of lipstick and just a little blush on her cheeks, although it just as easily could've been the sun. She looked young and fresh and pretty and completely wrong for him.

He forced himself to look away and watch Stephanie hold the horse while Kerry Redding dismounted. They walked over to Clint and Jubal.

"Thank you again for what you did Wednesday," the girl said shyly. "For me and Susie."

"Where *is* the little culprit?" Jubal asked.

"Inside with Eve's dogs," Lisa said. "Where hopefully she can't get in trouble. How are your injuries?"

"Gone," he said.

"Yeah," Clint said. "I hear he's been going for long swims at all hours and riding horses."

The doctor looked at him quizzically. "Swimming with those cuts?"

"In that *cold* water?" Stephanie added.

"Hell, he's a SEAL. Can't keep them out of the water."

Jubal wanted to kick Clint where the sun didn't shine. He wasn't fond of the attention a SEAL sometimes received. In any event, it wasn't anyone's business.

Stephanie cast a sympathetic look at Jubal. "My husband has a big mouth, but the water is still freezing."

"A navy SEAL?" Kerry said in an excited voice. "Like on the news?"

"Ex–navy SEAL," Jubal said shortly, and glared at Clint.

Lisa broke in, changing the subject. "Kerry retains everything she sees and reads about. She's a walking encyclopedia."

Clint gave Jubal an apologetic look when another car arrived. Jubal recognized Andy from the community center. She didn't wait for the driver to get out before coming right over to them.

"I'm glad to see you both again," she said. She turned and introduced Jubal to the man who'd exited the car behind her. "Meet Nate Rowland. He's also a vet. Army. The Strykers. He's a partner with Josh at the inn."

Jubal and Nate shook hands, each sizing up the other. "I hope you play poker," Nate said.

Jubal nodded but his gaze went back to Lisa. She was frowning. Because of what Clint had said about being a SEAL?

"I smell charcoal burning," Clint said.

"And I have to help Eve," Stephanie said. She turned to Lisa. "Clint with the big mouth can take you and Jubal to the backyard. Can I get you a glass of wine or a beer?"

"Wine would be great," Lisa said. "Can I help?"

"Eve and I have this down to a science," Stephanie said. "Everything is ready but the steaks, and that's Josh's responsibility, anyway."

Clint and Bart led the way to the backyard. Jubal stood back to allow Andy, Lisa and her sister to go next, and he followed behind. He wanted to clock Clint. The last thing he'd wanted was to advertise what he'd been but no longer was.

As he turned the corner, he saw the kid—Gordon—hovering next to Josh, who was re-arranging hot coals while a huge plate of steaks waited on a nearby table. Josh's dog, Amos, and a young boy of eight or nine played with a ball.

"Lisa. I'm so glad you and your family could come," Josh said, then turned to Jubal. "You've met Amos. This guy next to him is Nick, dog whisperer and my best friend, as well as my step-son. Nick, this is Jubal Pierce, who is using the cabin."

The boy beamed. "Nice to meet you, Mr. Pierce."

"Among friends, I'm Jubal," Jubal said.

"Mom wouldn't approve of that," Nick said with dignity.

"Okay, then," he said. "I don't think I want to tussle with your mother."

"Good decision," Josh said.

Jubal noticed then that Gordon Redding had backed away, his eyes darting from his sister to Jubal. His face had paled.

Lisa turned to Jubal. "Gordon said you hired him to do some work for you," she said.

The kid's eyes begged him, even as his gaze slid toward Clint before returning to Jubal. It was obvious, at least to Jubal, that he was last person Gordon wanted to see here.

Jubal was trapped. He would either have to lie to Lisa, at least by omission, or he would be another adult who failed the kid. He recalled how he'd felt at that age years ago. Rebellious with few friends, and none he trusted.

He nodded. "He's going to build a bench for Josh's dock. Thought it might be a good way to thank my host." *Why in the hell did he add that and make the lie bigger?* "Gordon brought me some good designs."

"I didn't know that," Clint said. His eyes had turned watchful as if he sensed currents he didn't understand. Beneath Clint's good nature was a sharp, intuitive mind.

Jubal shrugged and dug even deeper. "I heard you built the dock. I thought I would do my part and add a bench, and then this young man was looking for a job just after I acquired one of my own…"

Lisa's steady gaze seemed to see right through him, but she didn't say anything. Neither did Josh, who started putting steaks on the grill. Stephanie emerged with a tray of drinks: glasses of wine for Andy and Lisa, beers for Josh and Nate and a soda for Clint. Jubal nearly choked at Clint's choice.

"I'm driving a police car," Clint explained. "And I'm singing in the pageant tonight. It wouldn't be seemly if I smelled like beer." Although his words were wry, Jubal felt his friend's gaze on him.

"I'm curious," Stephanie said. "Clint calls it nosy, but I was wondering about your name. Jubal. It's unusual."

"My father was born in Texas," Jubal explained, relieved that the subject was changed. "The first Pierce who settled there had served under General Jubal Early of the Confederacy. He named his first son Jubal and it became a family tradition. I'm about the fifth one."

"You grew up in Texas, then?" Stephanie persevered. "There's no accent."

"My parents divorced when I was seven. My mother took me to her family home out east. I grew up there."

He hoped his short reply would dissuade more questions.

"I hear you're doing some work for Luke Daniels," Stephanie said.

"I'm just going to exercise some of the older horses for him," he said. He glanced at Lisa. She had taken a seat but her gaze was on him. Listening. Letting Stephanie ask all the questions, but then maybe she wasn't interested enough to ask any herself.

He was talking too much, something he rarely did. It came partly because he felt at home with

Clint and Josh, and partly from a need to divert the conversation from Gordon.

"The steaks are done," Josh said, handing him a reprieve from attention. Josh handed the heavy platter to Jubal. "Can you take them in for me? I have to douse the fire. We have a real problem with forest fires around here."

"Follow me," Stephanie said. She led the way to the back door of the house, heading inside through the kitchen to a dining room with a large oak table in the center. There was a huge salad on the table, and a bowl full of wrapped potatoes with steam coming out of them alongside another bowl of rolls and four plates of butter.

"I debated about the seating arrangement," Eve said, joining them. "And decided to leave it all to fate. Each place has a number. I have a hat here with numbers in it. Draw the number and that is your place."

There was a dash for the hat by hungry people. Jubal and Gordon were the last two and Jubal found himself sitting at the end of the table between Nate and Lisa. Gordon was seated between Clint and Andy.

The food was so good there was no need for small talk. He watched Gordon eat in record time, but then boys did that no matter what problems they faced. He used to be like that. Not even a loaf of plain bread was safe.

He looked at Lisa. She was eating like a soldier. No picking for her. She met his glance, and the floor under him seemed to rock.

"I like the drawing system," she said softly enough he doubted anyone else would hear. "I was afraid that since we apparently are the only single adults here, they would try to match us. But it's nice to know they didn't."

"You were worried?"

She nodded. "Now we can relax. No expectations." She paused, then added, "When Gordon told me earlier that you hired him to build a bench. I...didn't know whether..." She stopped suddenly, and he realized that she thought Gordon was lying.

"He brought over three designs," Jubal said. "I liked one, and he's going to work on it next week." She just nodded, and he didn't know whether it was approval or not.

He hated lying to her, except he wasn't exactly lying. But it was closer than he liked. It went against everything he believed in, especially when it came to someone he liked, and he was liking her more every moment, which was stupid considering he had no intention of sticking around.

Clint, perhaps sensing the tension, turned to Lisa. "How do you like Covenant Falls?"

"I'm going through culture shock. I've never lived anywhere but in a big city where you take the bus or the L everywhere, but I like it. I love the falls."

"What's the L?" Nick asked.

"The rapid transit system," Lisa explained. "A lot of it is above ground."

"I've seen it in movies," Nick said. "Looks neat."

Eve glanced at her watch. "Everyone who has to be at the pageant area early should go now. Stephanie and I can clean up. Won't take long and we'll meet you there. Save us a couple of seats."

"Oh, and we're having a reception at the community center after the pageant to celebrate," Stephanie added. "Maude is bringing all kinds of delicious treats so we're not having dessert here. Everyone's invited."

Andy turned to Lisa. "Are you going to the pageant tonight?"

"Kerry and I are going." She looked at Gordon.

All eyes turned to Gordon, who squirmed slightly, and looked at Jubal. He nodded. Reluctantly.

"Gordon can ride with Andy and me," Nate said. "We have to be there early, and Gordon could help with the props. We need all the help we can get."

Gordon had the look of a trapped fox, but to Lisa's relief, he nodded.

"Why don't you and Kerry follow Jubal and me in your car?" Clint said to Lisa.

"I was going to help with the cleanup," Lisa said.

"Thanks for the offer," Eve said. "But it's not necessary. Stephanie and I have it down to a science."

"All right, then," Lisa agreed.

Once in the car, Clint kept his eyes on the road ahead. "What is it with you and Gordon Redding?"

"I don't know what you mean," Jubal said.

"He seemed nervous around you."

"Maybe it was *your* presence. The badge can be an unnerving sight."

"I also saw the way you looked at his sister."

Jubal shrugged. "She's attractive, but she's a forever type of woman and I'm definitely not a forever type of guy. I'm only going to be here two weeks if it's okay with Josh."

"I thought it was only days," Clint said with a wry grin.

"Doesn't matter. We don't have anything in common. She has a career. I have an old car and wandering ways."

"I've heard that before," Clint mumbled as they turned into more traffic than Jubal had seen yet in Covenant Falls.

When they reached the parking lot, Clint drove into a roped-off area behind the community center and they linked up again. Andy took Kerry to see the horses in their makeshift corral, and Nate took Gordon to the staging area. Clint accompanied Jubal and Lisa to the first two rows, which were roped off.

"First or second row?" Clint asked.

"They look reserved," Jubal observed.

"Yep. Reserved for newcomers, VIPS and friends of the cast. You qualify in all three categories," Clint said. "I assume you want the end seat on the second row for a quick getaway."

Jubal swore to make Clint's life miserable in some manner. He hated being the focal point of attention. He'd spent his entire adult life doing the opposite.

Clint disappeared and Jubal was alone with Lisa, left to inhale the subtle scent of flowers that rose from her hair.

He wasn't quite sure how he'd been maneuvered into coming to an event he never would've gone to on his own, let alone into sitting next to a woman who was everything he didn't need.

But, God help him, he did want her.

Lisa looked equally ill at ease. She glanced around at the people rapidly filling seats. "I don't believe this," she said.

He could agree with that. "Four hours ago this was a park," Jubal said. "Now I feel like I'm in a western movie."

"Magic?" Lisa replied, looking around at the darkening sky and a half moon casting its reflection in the lake. A cool breeze ruffled through her hair.

"More like organization and hard work," he replied.

"Ah, a cynic?"

"More like a realist," he replied.

But he had to admit to a certain amazement as he looked at the set. He was impressed by the fact that in the hours he'd been at Josh Manning's home, the picnic area beside the community center had been turned into a small trading post dominated by a two-story log facade. It was clever stagecraft, especially the study on the second floor. There was talent behind the sets, an ingenuity that impressed him. That he found it in a small town like Covenant Falls impressed him even more.

He glanced at Lisa. She, too, was a stranger here. He understood from what little Clint had said that she'd moved here from a major hospital in Chicago. There was some mystery as to why, but he suspected it had something to do with Gordon. If that was true, that made his own role in Gordon's life even more questionable.

What was it about Lisa that so attracted him? She was pretty, but he'd been with pretty women before and they hadn't affected him as Lisa did. After he'd returned to the States, his friends had tried to fix him up with every eligible woman in San Diego. None of them had come close to arousing any feelings in him, much less the strong attraction he felt with the woman next to him.

Maybe it was the thoughtful brown eyes that seemed to take everything in, the concern in her face as she looked at her brother, or the warm smile when she mentioned her newly acquired dog. Or maybe it was the quiet reserve. She was a watcher and a listener. He liked that.

The row they were in started to fill. Eve and Stephanie joined them, along with Kerry and Susie. "Gordon's going to help with the props," Stephanie said.

Susie, he noted, was not the only dog in attendance—both Clint and Josh had brought theirs. To his surprise, Susie happily settled at Kerry's feet.

Minutes later, the lights dimmed and a spotlight focused on Clint leaning against a fence with a guitar in his hands. Bart was with him.

Jubal saw an entirely different Clint than the one he'd known during their hell-raising days. It was obvious he was happy. It was in the music, in the looks he gave Stephanie, in the pride he took in his role in the town.

Clint was still the fun-loving, good-natured guy he'd always been but contentment oozed from him now; the danger-junkie was gone. Had it been that easy?

Could Jubal ever do that? Or would he forever be haunted by the past? What he'd been through in captivity had seared his soul. It was why he couldn't sleep. He dreaded the flashbacks, the nightmares, the fear he would wake up in captivity again. Or worse, have to relive those final moments with the friends he'd lost on that last mission.

He couldn't inflict that mess on another person.

He tried to concentrate on the play. It was good, really good for an amateur production. The music—both Clint and the choir—were excellent. He felt the founder's grief and triumphs. He began to better understand Clint and Josh's affection for the town.

The audience stood, and everyone around him was singing the state song of Colorado. He stood with them as they applauded. The pageant was over, and he'd missed the last few scenes.

"Clint is quite good, isn't he?" Lisa asked.

"I never realized how good," Jubal replied, his gaze resting on her for a few seconds. "I've heard him sing before, but never like that." He didn't add that she might not have appreciated some of Clint's earlier performances.

Eve came over and asked if he'd join them at a celebration in the community center.

It didn't sound like such a great idea. He looked at her and Josh and knew the other couples would be there; he would be paired with Lisa again. It was the last thing either of them needed.

"Thanks," he said, "but I think I should head back to the cabin."

Josh nodded, and Jubal knew he understood.

"Thanks for coming tonight," Josh said. "I know better than most how overwhelming Covenant Falls can be for a newcomer."

"The supper was great, and the pageant… I was impressed, and I have a new appreciation for Clint's voice. Just don't tell him that."

"I won't." Josh put out his hand. "Let me know if you need anything."

Jubal took it. It wasn't so much a formality as it was recognition of a bond, a private understanding that the others wouldn't get.

"Good night," Jubal said, then turned and joined the stream of people leaving the park.

Most of the audience had been families. Moms and dads were struggling to keep their children with them. Some were holding toddlers. He felt a poignant regret he hadn't known before. A sense of being totally alone in the middle of a crowd. Ironic. Even when he was alone in the huts and caves where he'd been imprisoned, he'd hung on to his training, to what and who he was. He'd believed then he'd one day resume his place as part of a team.

He no longer had that. Now, at thirty-eight, he watched the smiles and laughter, and families talking to families, and he felt hollow. He'd seen so many wrecked marriages from the time he was a toddler that he had little faith in love and marriage. Better for him to have short liaisons in which neither party got hurt nor children torn apart.

He reached the cabin, but he was too restless to try to sleep. The moon was bright enough that he could risk a trip up to the lookout on his neighboring mountain.

He walked slowly, carefully, until he reached his spot. Then he looked down. The floodlights were still on at the site of the pageant, and there were lights in the community center. A few small figures were moving around the park, although most of the chairs were already gone and the picnic area had been cleared. He probably should've stayed. Helped.

But he'd been eager to leave the mass of people and the curious looks sent his way.

The town was apart from him. But he appreciated what he'd heard about the man behind the story. It was a story of strength, kindness to a foe and finally, his love and defense of his Ute wife, which was a taboo at that time.

Was that what love did? Crossed barriers and boundaries and to hell with anyone who tried to interfere? He knew some SEAL wives who did that; he knew of others who couldn't stand the pressure. He didn't know how long he stayed on the mountain, but he waited until the floodlights went off, then the lights in the community center.

He started back to the cabin.

Lisa didn't understand the jab of disappointment she felt when Jubal Pierce left so abruptly.

She tried to tamp it down. She accompanied Kerry in putting Susie in the car for the short time they would be at the reception, making sure the windows were half down. It was cool enough for her to be comfortable. They then joined Eve and Stephanie in the community center. She thought it important to meet the people she would be treating.

The room to the right of the entry hall had been decorated. Two punch bowls and a coffee urn sat on a bar in the corner. Tables were covered with cupcakes and brownies as well as healthier snacks.

Kerry picked one small brownie and Lisa, still full from dinner, opted for coffee only.

"How did you like the pageant?" Stephanie asked Kerry.

"Very much. Mr. Morgan was great. So was the choir."

"It's last year's school choir with a few additional adults."

"Maybe I could join," Kerry said shyly.

"I don't know why not. The school has a great drama department, as well," Stephanie added. "With the exception of a few graduating seniors who have left town, they've all continued to perform with the pageant."

Lisa was introduced to a number of new people. She tried to mentally catalog the new faces, but her mind kept going back to Jubal Pierce and his abrupt departure.

Then Lisa saw Gordon and Nate enter together. "You have a good worker there," Nate told her.

Gordon straightened from his usual slouch. "Didn't do much," he mumbled.

"Don't believe him," Nate said. "He catches on quick and he moves fast."

Gordon? Her brother? "Thanks for taking him under your wing," Lisa said.

"I didn't need to. He saw something needed to be done. He did it."

This was a whole new Gordon they were discussing. She recalled how Gordon had been with Jubal. Both Nate and Jubal appeared to be strong male figures. That had been missing from Gordon's life since their father died.

Hope and fear both sprung in her. Hope that Gordon would find a mentor he could respect, and fear that he would find the wrong one. These guys were all ex-military, and that was not the future she wanted for Gordon.

But she recalled how good Jubal had been with Kerry after the accident on Lake Road. For a man who'd apparently been at war for nearly two decades, he was surprisingly good with young people and apparently more instinctive than she was. She'd seen the sidelong glances Gordon had given him at the Manning ranch. There was respect there, and maybe a little fear. At any rate, he seemed to have the positive impact on her brother she'd been unable to make herself.

It was unsettling. Even more unsettling was the way she felt when Jubal Piece was near. Tingly and warm and expectant.

After complimenting Clint and the others who'd been involved in the production, she gathered Kerry and Gordon to go home. Unexpectedly, Gordon came willingly.

It was nearly eleven when they pulled into the driveway. Kerry and Susie headed to bed. Gordon grabbed a glass of milk and started to follow his sister upstairs.

"Gordon?

He stopped.

"Enjoy working at the pageant?"

"It was okay."

"Okay" was good for Gordon. "You think you might like it here?" Lisa ventured. She wouldn't have asked it earlier, but tonight she saw an opening.

He shrugged, started upstairs, then hesitated. "Sorry I've been such a jerk," he said before taking the steps two at a time.

Shocked, she watched him disappear. Maybe miracles did happen. She locked the doors, turned off the lights in the kitchen and headed for her room. After pulling on her nightshirt, she looked out the window. There were reasons to be hopeful. Kerry seemed happier than she'd been since their mother died. There were cracks in Gordon's hostility. Small ones, to be sure, but cracks none-theless. He had a job of sorts. He worked with Nate without complaint. He'd even gobbled up a few desserts at the reception.

And then there was the clear sky and the moon that looked larger than it ever had in Chicago.

Could Jubal Pierce be looking at the same moon? Why was she even thinking of him? She barely knew the man, but the problem was, she couldn't stop. She'd heard opposites attract. Maybe so, but that didn't mean it was a good thing. Her parents complimented each other. They'd both liked to read, learn and work hard to make a safe home for their kids.

She'd always thought that if she ever mar-ried, she'd marry a fellow doctor. They would understand the demands of the profession. But she hadn't been in a hurry. She'd wait until the right guy came along. And if he didn't, that was okay, too.

What was it about Jubal Pierce, then, that at-tracted her? What made her want to know more about him? And, heaven help her, to feel his lips on hers?

She'd never been much of a sensual person. Now she wondered if it was because she'd never met anyone who aroused those kinds of feelings. She sure didn't want them aroused by someone so overwhelming, so unlike the person she'd dreamed of marrying someday.

She finally got back into bed. She'd had precious little sleep these past few days.

She did what she always did when she was too worried to sleep, and started counting medical books in her head.

CHAPTER TWELVE

AFTER HIS USUAL morning swim, Jubal arrived at Luke's ranch on Monday morning with a number of questions in mind.

He'd spent a quiet Sunday reading the books he'd picked up at the community center. He'd also used his laptop to research ranch properties in Colorado. The prices varied widely and he suspected it was what he'd always heard about real estate. Location. Location. Location. Did it have water? Good grazing? Close to a town or city?

He had questions now, even as he realized the kernel of interest was crazy. He knew next to nothing about ranching or horses. He had no idea how far his admittedly decent savings would go, but he also knew how fast it could all disappear in some momentary flight of fancy.

He patted the bag full of carrots next to him. He'd begged them from Maude yesterday when he'd stopped by for takeout.

As he drove up to Luke's ranch house, Jacko was in the pasture but then trotted over to the fence when Jubal exited his car.

Luke came out of the barn and met him at the gate. "I don't know what it is with you and that horse, but he's never been that eager to see anyone before. You can go ahead and take him first. There's five others I would like you to exercise today." He handed Josh a list. "They're my trail horses. Now that school's started, they won't get much riding."

Jubal scanned it. "You're actually paying me to do this?"

"Horses are naturally lazy. They need exercise to stay in good shape. And I wouldn't feel good not paying you."

"I'll make you another deal," Jubal said. "I spent Sunday reading about quarter horses and ranching and it got me thinking. How about instead of you paying me, you teach me about ranching and raising horses?"

Luke looked surprised. "You thinking about trying it?"

"I don't know. I used to dream about it as kid. At least the owning horses part. I'd be interested to hear what it takes."

"It's a deal, though I have to warn you— ranching isn't like it used to be. More government regulations every year, particularly on water rights. You wouldn't believe some of them."

"Can a rancher survive with just horses?"

"You have to love ranching and horses and

know you aren't gonna get rich," he said. "You need an instinct about horses, too—which have championship potential and how to best match stallions and mares. It's twenty-four hours a day, seven days a week with no holidays, and even then you may barely eke out a living. Does that answer your question?"

"Ever thought about quitting?"

"Hell, no," he said. "They'll have to drag me to the grave kicking and screaming all the way."

"About what I thought," Jubal said.

"We're still having a problem with rustling, though. One of the ranchers twenty miles down lost some horses the night of the pageant. Problem is they're registered. Can't sell them to a legitimate buyer, and no telling what will happen to them. God help me if I see them, there's going to be big trouble," he said.

"Clint knows about the latest theft?"

"Sure does. Ranchers around here are meeting at noon today. Start a nightly patrol of our own."

"If you need any help…"

"Thanks, I'll let you know." Luke seemed to hesitate, then added, "About your proposal, how about we talk again later this afternoon? I'm looking at a stallion this morning, then going to the ranchers' meeting at lunch."

"I can't today," Jubal replied regretfully. "I have to meet with a young man who's doing some work for me. I told him I would see him after school."

"Noon tomorrow, then. You can have lunch with Tracy and me. She probably knows more about the business end than I do."

Jubal nodded his approval.

"I'll leave you with the horses, then," Luke said. "Aim to spend an hour with each one. Tracy is in the house if you need her."

Jubal nodded and watched as Luke drove away. He gave Jacko a carrot and was rewarded by a nudge of the horse's head before leading him into the barn to be saddled. It was still difficult to fasten the cinch but he managed it. He swung up into the saddle and started out at a walk.

Jacko tugged at the bit. He wanted to go faster. Jubal's knees gave him permission to canter. The breeze felt good, and Jubal felt free for the first time since he was separated from the service. Until now, he'd still felt chained to the memories. It was why he swam each morning, did daily push-ups and tried to run at least six miles a day. As long as he did that, he was still Chief Petty Officer Jubal Pierce.

Jacko stretched into the canter. They rode along the fence line, then to the stream that ran through the property. Jubal took a deep breath, and drank in the exhilaration he felt.

He slowed Jacko and looked at his watch. He had to get back if he wanted to stay on schedule with the other horses on the list. He'd have to leave by three to meet Gordon. He finished at two and walked stiffly to the ranch house. He knocked and Tracy opened the door.

"I just wanted you to know I'm leaving soon. Anything I can do before I go?"

"Don't think so. I've been watching you on and off. You did well."

"You're a good teacher."

"I can teach some things. Can't teach that natural seat or affinity for horses."

"I'm indebted to you and your husband," Jubal said. "These last few days...they've meant a lot."

"Don't thank me," she said. "Luke and I figure we owe you guys in the military. Luke did his bit and came home whole, and I'm grateful. Since Josh, Clint and Andy moved here, we've been trying to figure out how we can do more for you guys. Turns out you're all doing more for this town than we could ever do for you."

Jubal hesitated. He felt he'd already asked too much.

"I know this young kid. He's building something for me, but he'll probably finish this week. Would it be okay if I bring him out here? See if he's interested?"

"Sure. Just let me know when. You can instruct him if you want. Either Luke or me will sit in at first."

"I'm not sure if he'll even want to…or if his sister will approve, but…"

Jubal wasn't usually at a loss for words. And he didn't know why he mentioned Lisa. But riding had been therapy for him. Maybe it could be for Gordon, as well.

"He's welcome if he does," Tracy said.

On the way back to the cabin, Jubal decided he had time to stop at Maude's before Gordon was due to arrive. Having skipped lunch, he was starving.

After Saturday night's dinner, Gordon was no longer "the kid." He was Gordon Redding, and he had a family that cared about him.

The thought reminded him that he really was in no position to withhold information from his sister.

As if that worry had conjured her up, she was the first person he saw when he entered Maude's. She was, in fact, the only person sitting in a booth.

He hadn't shaved that morning and he smelled like horse and sweat. He thought about going to the counter, but then she looked up from something she was reading, and their gazes met. He felt strangely awkward. He didn't want to impose. But he didn't want her to think he was purposely avoiding her.

Maude took the choice away from him. "Why

don't you sit with Dr. Redding?" she said. "She just ordered."

They were standing close enough for Lisa to hear. It would be churlish to refuse.

"I smell like horse," he protested.

"Many of my customers do," Maude replied with a grin and and led him the few steps to the booth. She placed the paper menu on the table in front of him. "Do you want to look at the menu or do you want the steak?" Maude asked.

"The steak," he said.

"I'll bring it with your salad," Maude told Lisa, and left before her customer could answer.

"I'm sorry," he started to say at the same time she uttered the same words. She started to laugh.

He chuckled.

"I've learned," she said, "never to say no to two people in this town. Maude and Eve."

"I can move," he said helpfully.

"Please don't. I'll feel guilty."

"I wouldn't want that," he said as his body relaxed into the seat.

"Why do you smell like horse?"

"I'm exercising horses at a ranch about six miles from here."

"I remember you said your father was in the rodeo."

He shrugged. "I haven't done much riding since I was a kid, but it seems it's something you really don't forget."

"I don't think it's that easy." She paused. "You said at dinner the other night that your family comes from Texas."

"My dad was born there."

"Was he a rancher?"

"His family lost the ranch before I was born, but my dad grew up riding." Jubal didn't like talking about it much, and he realized his tone had become clipped. He changed the subject. "Late lunch?"

She nodded. "Several poison ivy cases. Two annual physicals, three fevers and a few other odds and ends. I have four more appointments this afternoon."

"How does it compare with working in a large hospital?"

"Certainly a lot less hectic here," she said. "Takes some adjustment. But I suppose you've been experiencing that, too."

He simply nodded.

Maude arrived with an iced tea for him. Lisa already had one.

"So, Gordon is going to your place after school?" she confirmed after Maude disappeared.

"We're going to talk about the materials he needs to build the bench." He hesitated. "Is this all right with you?"

"It's fine. I was surprised when he first told me, though. How did you happen to get together?"

It was the question he'd been dreading. He'd

carefully avoided a direct lie. Now he couldn't. He could either tell her the truth about the fire or tell a lie that might not be forgiven. Or he could ruin any trust Gordon had left.

He shrugged. "He seemed at loose ends," he compromised. He saw from her eyes it was unsatisfactory. He expected a follow-up but it didn't come.

She looked him squarely in the eye. "Our father was killed in a small-plane crash when Gordon was ten. They were really close. Our mother died a little less than a year ago of cancer. He's had a hard time coping with that."

He sensed the reluctance in her measured words. It was obviously hard for her to share problems, particularly about her family, and he was virtually a stranger.

But he knew now she too felt the connection between them, even if neither of them could explain it. But basically she was telling him that her brother was vulnerable and don't mess with him.

"He fell in with a bad crowd," she continued in a low voice that wavered at times. "I think it gave him a sense of power, or maybe control, one that he hadn't felt for a long time. I thought moving would help but it seemed to have the opposite effect. I took away his control."

She paused to take a sip of her iced tea. "I don't know how you met. It worries me that he hasn't really told me. But I can tell that while he seems a little wary, he respects you."

Jubal didn't know what to say. His silence confirmed some of her supposition. But he saw the guilt in her eyes, the frustration of not being able to make things right.

He also understood the source of Gordon's anger now. He, too, had lost his father at a young age. In a way he'd lost his mother then, as well. He'd always blamed her for his father's death. If they'd been with him, it wouldn't have happened.

"He's a smart kid," he said after a moment's silence. "I talked to Nate yesterday. He said the kid is a born engineer, and from what I hear Nate's no slouch himself. When they worked with the props, Gordon had several ideas of how to move them easier. He's just been too busy resenting the world to use that brain."

"Thank you for caring," she said. She paused and added, "Just...don't let him down."

Maude came with their food then.

The steak was probably as good as always but he couldn't enjoy it. He was still withholding information that she had every right to have. And when she looked at him with those trusting eyes, he felt lower than a turtle's belly.

She ate half of her salad, then looked at her watch. "I have to get back," she said apologetically. "I'm late for an appointment." She looked around but Maude wasn't to be seen.

"You go on," he said. "I'll take care of the bill. You can pay me back later. Or not." He smiled.

She started to protest, then looked chagrined. "I will. I'm not good at accepting favors. Thank you again. Maybe you can come over for supper some night."

He nodded.

She slipped from the booth and hurried out.

Maude appeared suddenly, as if she'd been hovering nearby. "Was everything okay, Mr. Pierce? You want a box?"

He shook his head. "You are not subtle, Maude."

"I don't know what you mean, Mr. Pierce." She grinned and handed him the check.

GORDON APPEARED AT four-thirty on a bike. He looked part rebellious, part interested and part apprehensive.

"I decided I want the bench with the arms," Jubal said. "You think you can buy the materials you listed?"

"Me?" Gordon asked.

"You. You're a contractor now. You designed the bench. You're building it. You should supply the materials."

"I don't have any money," Gordon protested.

Jubal gave him an envelope. "There's a hundred and fifty dollars in there. Should be more than enough for the lumber and other materials. Try to get the price down. Don't worry about tools. There are some here and I can probably borrow whatever else you need."

"How will I bring everything back?"

"Ask to have them delivered."

Gordon stared at the money. "You trust me?"

"Shouldn't I?"

"Yeah. I guess. What about the change?"

"What do you think?"

"I'll bring it back," Gordon said.

"Good guess. That's an advance for materials. You owe me the labor." He looked at his watch. "You better go now so you can report back with time to spare. I expect your sister will want you home for supper."

Gordon looked shell-shocked. He got on his bike and peddled away.

He was back in forty minutes. "You got a ten percent discount, you being a veteran," he said. "The guy I talked to said he needed to order the treated wood. Should be here by Friday. I picked out some metal trimming, too. That okay?"

"It's your bench," Jubal said. "When it's finished, I'll tell you whether it's acceptable."

"You're a real hard-ass, aren't you?" Gordon asked.

Jubal just shrugged.

"Here's the rest of your money." Gordon held out a now tattered envelop.

"And you'll be here Saturday to work on it." It wasn't a question.

"Yeah."

IT WAS AFTER six before Lisa left the office. She hadn't had time to think about Jubal Pierce since she returned to a full waiting room. There had been several walk-ins along with her scheduled appointments. She suspected they were there to inspect the new doctor more than for the sniffles and rashes they reported.

She walked the several blocks home. It helped with the nervousness she felt. Today was the first day of school, and she wondered how Kerry and Gordon fared. Would they find friends? Like the teachers? Be challenged?

Kerry was on the sofa, reading a book with Susie curled up next to her. Obviously thinking it was her job to greet anyone who came to the door, the dog jumped down and ran over to Lisa.

Lisa stooped down, and the dog rolled over on her back waving all four feet in the air.

"She wants you to rub her belly," Kerry said.

Lisa complied, thinking it was nice to have at least one warm body happy to see her.

"How was school?"

"I liked it," she said. "The kids were nice. They think it's neat you're a doctor, and they want to know what it was like to live in Chicago. I talked to the music teacher about trying out for the choir.

She had me sing for her and said she definitely wanted me in it."

"I think that's terrific," Lisa said. "You do have a good voice. So did Mom. You must have inherited that from her."

"Yeah, maybe I did." All of a sudden, tears welled up in Kerry's eyes. "I miss her so much." Susie crept up in Kerry's lap and whined.

"I know you do," Lisa said. "I miss her, too."

Kerry's arms went around the dog. "I'm so glad we adopted Susie."

"I am, too."

"And I'm glad we moved here," Kerry added shyly.

"I'm happy to hear that."

"I know you did it for Gordon. I didn't like his friends. They scared me."

"Why didn't you tell me?"

"You were so busy…and he's my brother."

Lisa nodded. Guilt again. She knew Kerry didn't mean it that way, but she still felt it. She should have put off that last year of residency.

She looked at her watch. "I knew he was going to do something for Mr. Pierce's cabin today, but I expected him home by now."

Kerry shrugged. "I'm hungry."

"Me, too," Lisa said. "Want to help me make supper?"

"What are we having?"

"Why don't you make the salad and I'll make

Swiss steak and tomato gravy." It was quick and everyone liked it, including Gordon. At least he did when their mother used to make it.

Kerry nodded eagerly.

They were nearly finished when Gordon strolled in.

"Wash up," Lisa said. "Supper's almost ready."

Gordon merely nodded and went upstairs.

A small miracle. Apparently a Jubal miracle.

She knew she should be pleased. But she couldn't ignore the apprehension she felt.

They'd only been here a week, and one man had already made what felt like an oversize impact on her and her family. He'd told her Covenant Falls was just a way station for him. What if he left wreckage in his wake?

CHAPTER THIRTEEN

IT WAS NEARLY seven when the kid left. He wasn't sure exactly how it happened, but Jubal had become far more involved in Covenant Falls than he'd intended. Gordon and his sister. Luke and the ranch. A renewed friendship with Clint. That reminded him of the poker game tonight. He'd told Clint he would try to come. Now he regretted it, but Clint was a friend. The least he could do was go this one time.

He looked at himself in the mirror and realized he hadn't shaved that morning, although he'd taken a shower after lunch at Maude's. The days-old bristle made him look like a biker.

He took the time to shave, wishing he'd done so this morning before running into Lisa. Not that it should matter. In fact, it was probably for the best.

Jubal walked to the community center for the veteran's poker game. It was late, and there were a lot of vehicles in the parking lot, many of them pickups.

Once inside the center, he followed the noise to the right room. He would have known the occupants were all vets, even though they appeared to range in age from midtwenties to sixties. There was an alertness, a confidence and an ease that he recognized. He mentally counted twenty-one people and three dogs, Andy's Joseph, Clint's Bart and Josh's Amos.

Andy was the only woman present. Clint and Josh stood nearby as the other men introduced themselves and named their branch of service. He was one of two navy guys. Most of the rest were army with a couple of air force vets thrown in.

A beer was thrust in his hand, and he helped himself to some chips and dip before joining one of three tables for poker.

Jubal felt instantly at ease. No one asked questions. No one mentioned SEALs. It was just navy. Conversation centered around the pageant, two recent queries about opening businesses in Covenant Falls, including a budget motel and a combination bakery/gift shop/bookstore. The latter was proposed by one of visitors to the pageant who was also interested in buying a lakeside home.

Several of the vets seized on Josh's idea to develop an outdoor adventure business.

"Would you have enough business to sustain it?" Jubal asked.

"Not in the beginning," Josh admitted as he dealt cards. "But it surprised the heck out of me how many people will drive even a hundred miles to see the pageant."

"Yeah, and now with Josh and Nate's inn and several bed-and-breakfast places, we have to convince 'em to stick around for a few days," chimed another vet. "We need the tourism."

"Andy is getting queries about activities," Nate said. "Josh has been able to arrange some trips up to the abandoned gold camps with this old miner Clint befriended. And Luke's not the only rancher offering trail rides, but they need some coordination and publicity."

Josh took up the conversation. "Maybe the answer is a cooperative effort. No one person has the time or money to start an ongoing program. But if a group of us, each with different skills..." He left the sentence dangling, his eyebrows raised.

Jubal kept his mouth shut and listened. He would be gone before they got organized. He didn't have a dog in this fight and didn't want one.

It wasn't a bad idea, though. Visitors might be intrigued by an all-veteran/ex-soldier wilderness company. Might even feel more secure, as well.

Several vets heard the conversation and drifted over to the table.

"Could be a fairly inexpensive business to operate if a group got together," one said. "Most of us have boats and camping equipment. It wouldn't be a full-time job for anyone but could bring in extra income."

The others nodded. "Something to think about," someone added.

The game resumed. Jubal won a few hands, lost a few hands and was up about seven dollars when the game broke up.

He walked back to the cabin, still thinking about the conversation. He couldn't seem to shake it. There was risk associated with any group going into business together, but these were veterans who were used to working as a team.

None of his business, he reminded himself again as he went out to the lawn chair. Bed still didn't welcome him, and he started to wonder if he'd ever be entirely comfortable with four walls around him again.

LISA HAD THOUGHT there might be slow days in a small-town practice.

How wrong could she have been?

She was busy ten hours a day her second week in Covenant Falls. On Monday, she had a nine-year-old with a broken leg from a bike accident. It was a compound fracture and because she didn't have the operating facilities, she could only stabilize it and send him to Pueblo.

Then on Tuesday, there was a patient who'd had a heart attack and had to be medevaced out. The following afternoon, a teenager collapsed on the way home from school. He had severe swelling on his face, lips and throat, and by the time he'd been taken to the clinic, his blood pressure had fallen precipitously.

His name was Dan Waters, and mercifully, a motorist had seen him go down and drove him to the clinic.

Her nurse immediately hunted down the family while Lisa gave him an epinephrine injection and found what looked like a bee or wasp sting.

He improved quickly, although he was shaken. Weak. She asked whether he'd ever had a reaction before.

"No, ma'am," he said. He tried to sit up as his mother charged into the office.

"He'll have to always have a kit with epinephrine nearby," Lisa said. "He's very allergic and the next sting could be deadly."

After he left, the waiting room was full of patients waiting to see her.

She finally left the office at six p.m., but she felt good about the day. The boy could have died without the injection. It wasn't Chicago, but she might've saved a life, and the satisfaction was there.

She was prepared to take her brother and sister to Maude's, but to her surprise, Kerry had meat sauce simmering on the stove and a pot of boiling water ready for spaghetti.

Kerry shrugged when Lisa started to thank her. "I heard what happened to Dan Waters and thought you might be late."

"Have you met him?"

"Just did this morning. He's in the choir."

"Seems like he's going to be okay. Is Gordon home?"

"As usual, he's in his room," Kerry replied with another shrug.

Lisa went to her room and changed into comfortable clothes, then went to knock on Gordon's door. "You there?" He opened it. She was surprised to see what looked like a textbook on his bed.

"Homework already?"

He just shrugged. "Algebra. Chief Morgan said I had to keep my grades up."

"You saw him today, then."

"I just said I did."

Not exactly, but she would accept it. She wanted to ask more questions, especially about his project for Jubal Pierce, but she worried if she did he would completely close up. The fact he was studying without being prompted was progress. "Supper will be ready in about fifteen minutes."

He simply nodded.

Gordon's cell phone rang forty minutes later as they finished supper. She saw him check the number, then ignore it. After supper, Gordon and Kerry watched television for an hour, then Gordon said he was going for a walk. Kerry wanted to go with him, but he rudely rebuffed her. "Do you have to go everywhere with me?" he asked.

Kerry gave him an indignant look and marched off to her room.

Lisa knew her feelings were hurt. They were wounded easily these days. She went up to Kerry's room and opened the door.

"Let's get some ice cream and go to the park," she suggested. "Or do you have homework?"

"Just a reading assignment. I already finished it."

"Good. We'll take Susie with us. She probably needs the exercise."

A cool breeze relaxed Lisa as they walked to Maude's, ordered two cups of chocolate ice cream with fudge and wandered down Main Street toward the park. It was a gentle evening. A light breeze. A parchment half moon rising.

A car full of teenage boys went by with one leaning out, yelling something to Kerry.

"Who was that?"

"A boy from school," Kerry said. "I don't like him, but he hangs around Gordon."

"Why don't you like him?"

"Susan says he's trouble. She's in my classes and the choir. She was in the pageant, too."

"What's the boy's name?"

"Earl," Kerry said. "Earl White. Susan says his father's a truck driver and is never at home. "He kinda gives me the creeps. Like…" She stopped.

"Like what?"

"I don't know. I just don't like him…"

Lisa didn't like the sound of that, but Kerry was clearly uncomfortable and didn't want to say more. They reached the community center, and Lisa was amazed at how quickly the area behind it had become a park again.

They had just finished their ice cream when she saw Jubal Pierce running down Lake Road toward the park.

Susie started barking and straining against her leash.

Lisa's breath caught in her throat. He was dressed in sweats but there was power in every stride he made. He'd looked up when Susie barked. She saw him hesitate, then come running toward them.

"Hi," he said. He reached down and scratched behind Susie's ears. "No more flights for freedom?"

"No," Lisa said. "I think she learned her lesson."

She feared she was staring at him like a besotted teen. He really was, as the kids said, super hot. "Do you run every day?" she asked to break the spell.

"I try."

"And swim?"

He gave her a rueful smile. "There really isn't any privacy here, is there?"

"I'm discovering the same thing," she said, then glanced down at Susie, who was climbing all over his running shoes. "It's the opposite of Chicago, where you don't know the neighbor two houses down."

"Not used to a small town, either?"

"I've never lived anywhere but Chicago. I attended college and medical school there even. Culture shock."

He straightened, nodded. "Have a nice evening," he said, and took off before she could say anything else.

"He seems nice," Kerry said.

He'd seemed nice, if quiet, to Lisa, too, but his abrupt departure made her wonder if she'd said or done something wrong.

"I think we had better get home," Lisa said. "I have paperwork to do."

Most of the stores were closed and traffic had dwindled to the occasional car as they walked back. An alien world to her. And apparently for Jubal Pierce. It was the only thing they had in common except, perhaps, for Gordon, but she didn't feel good about that.

Gordon's job for him was temporary. A bench shouldn't take long to complete. Then her brother would be caught up with school and, hopefully, school activities. She tried to convince herself of that as they reached their home.

THE WEEK FLEW by for Jubal. He spent most of his time at Luke's ranch, improving his riding, learning more about what it took to raise horses and the pitfalls of running a ranch. There were a lot of them.

But each day he spent with the horses was sheer pleasure. It had been a long time since he'd felt anything like it. The more comfortable he became in the saddle, the more he wanted horses to be part of his life. For some reason, he felt at home in the saddle, as if it connected him with the boy who had been torn away from the father he worshipped.

But he knew the risks were high. He could lose everything he'd saved. A disease, a failure to breed winning horses or just plain bad business decisions could wipe him out. Luke did not dance around the problems.

At the end of the day on Thursday, Luke drew him to a large stall where a mare stamped nervously. "Ever see a birth?"

"Can't say I have."

"Melody's about ready to foal. Want to stay and watch?"

"Yeah, but how do you know?" Jubal asked.

"See the muscles around her tail head that have kind of slumped in and hollowed?"

Jubal nodded.

"They're relaxing so they can handle the stretch when the foal comes out. And her udder's bagged up. She's dripping colostrum. She's sweating some and keeps walking around her stall. She's in labor, but that doesn't mean she'll foal in the next twenty minutes, or the next twelve hours, for that matter. They'll wait until your back is turned, then drop it. Or wait 'til the middle of the worst storm of the year to foal. Crazy mares. You sure you want to wait?"

"Yeah, I do. Is Stephanie on call?"

"She knows about it and will be available if there's a problem, but most of the time there's no need for a vet. My wife and I have birthed a lot of colts and fillies. It never ceases to awe me."

"What can I do?"

"Need to lay the straw in the birthing stall and get her moved while she'll still come with us."

"Why straw?"

"Cleaner, for one thing, and doesn't stick all over or get up the foal's nose like wood shavings."

Jubal worked with Luke's ranch hand, Tim, to add to the straw at the bottom of the stall. Luke then led the mare into the stall. Without warning, the mare kicked her left hind leg straight out, barely missing Luke, then turned her head and bit at her side.

"She's feeling the contractions. We're pretty close. We'll stay here with her tonight," Luke said. "Pull up a bale of hay and settle down in the aisle. Foaling usually occurs between ten p.m. and four a.m. It's instinctive. In the wild, that means they have a few hours of darkness before the foal has to be up and running with the herd.

Most of the time, they don't need help but there's always the possibility of a breech birth. Then we have to reach in her and turn the foal. We don't have but twenty minutes for the whole thing. No time for a vet to drive out from town."

They talked softly for an hour, then Luke ran his hands over the mare's rump and nodded. "She's stopped eating and that's an indicator of impending delivery."

Jubal watched as Luke wrapped the mare's tail, then dimmed the lights. Labor started at midnight. Luke's wife arrived to stand in the aisle and watch over the top of the stall.

By two a.m., the placental sac broke, releasing a gush of fluid. Then the mare was on her side and began to strain. A foal slid out, still in the sac.

"Yeah, we're good," Luke whispered. "Two front feet and one nose." He reached down and pulled the placenta away from the baby's face.

Jubal leaned over and looked right into the baby's wide, dark eyes and watched brown ears wiggle back and forth.

"Stay back, Melody is getting up," Luke said.

"That fast?" Jubal jumped back into the aisle as the mare gave a giant heave and surged to her feet. A moment later she turned, nickered gently and began to lick her baby. The pinto baby, which looked just like its mama, was already pushing to stand.

"Sometimes," Luke said, "we have to help

them up and guide them to the teat, but this baby seems to be doing it all on his own. We can watch from outside the stall."

To Jubal, it was a miracle. Life beginning. He'd seen so much life ending, often in terrible ways.

"It's a colt," Luke said with satisfaction, "And an easy birth. Mama did all the work."

"It was..." Jubal stopped, unable to express the feelings that were surging through him. The colt and mother together touched him as nothing else had.

He felt a hand on his shoulder. "I know," Luke said softly. "It never fails to amaze me. Every new birth is still a miracle, even after seeing so many. It's one of the bonuses of this business."

It was near dawn when Tracy left to make breakfast. Tim left for home. Jubal and Luke cleaned the stall, replacing the soiled straw with some that was fresh and dry. The colt was contentedly nursing and the mom kept looking anxiously at her new arrival. Jubal thought he saw pride in her eyes.

"They'll go out alone, just the two of them in the mare's paddock for a week or so. Let the others get used to talking to them over the fence," Luke said, then glanced at Jubal. "You want to name him?"

Jubal swallowed hard. An odd tug pulled on his heart. And a rare indecisiveness. He knew a lot about survival and weapons and killing. Not

so much about something so new and innocent…
a wonder, really.

"Can I think about it?" he asked.

"Yeah. No worry."

An hour later with a large breakfast under his
belt, Jubal drove home.

The moon was visible even as dawn spread
a golden light across the horizon. For the first
time he could remember, Jubal was at peace in
his world.

CHAPTER FOURTEEN

THE COVENANT FALLS Medical Clinic opened at nine on Saturday morning and closed a little after noon.

"An easy morning," Lisa said as Janie checked out the last patient. It had consisted of colds, a deep cut, a sprained ankle and prescription renewals.

Janie had given her a list of low-income patients with chronic diseases. She was discovering that finding ways to cut costs for her patients was part of her job. After talking to the town's pharmacist about ways to minimize their costs, she made a note to call pharmaceutical reps on Monday and ask for free samples.

It was treating the whole patient that she enjoyed most about the practice. Many of them told stories about Dr. Bradley and how he'd delivered them and even their mother or father. They all loved him.

Her cell rang as she locked the door. "Hi." Eve's cheerful voice came over the phone. "You haven't been to Josh's inn yet and we'd like to take you to dinner there tonight. It's short notice, but there's an excellent Western group playing tonight. Several of its members were in the pageant chorus. I know you enjoyed it and thought you would like this, as well. Josh has booked them before and he's always had great reviews."

Lisa hesitated. She wasn't sure whether the invitation included Gordon and Kerry.

"I thought you might enjoy an evening without worrying whether the kids are enjoying it," Eve added as though reading her thoughts.

"You noticed that the other night?"

"I've noticed my son doesn't enjoy the inn as much as he enjoys dinner at home. He feels he has to be on his best behavior."

Eve was right. Gordon and Kerry had said very little at the dinner at Eve's house, and yes, she would enjoy seeing the inn. She was fascinated with the Camel Trail Inn sign and the legend.

She paused, thinking. She could make a hamburger casserole for Kerry and Gordon. It was one of their favorite meals, and she would promise to do whatever they wanted tomorrow. Tonight, they'd be fine for a few hours without her. After all, Gordon was seventeen and Kerry nearly fourteen.

And the idea of an all adult dinner was attractive.

"I would love that," she said. "Thank you."

"Oh, and dress is nothing fancy. Maybe country chic, if that makes any sense."

Lisa wasn't quite sure what that was, but she guessed a simple skirt and blouse would do. "Okay," she said.

"Good. I'll make reservations. Josh and I will pick you up at a quarter to seven.

After Lisa hung up, she went home and found a note from Kerry. She had taken Susie over to Stephanie's clinic to volunteer. Maybe, Lisa thought, her sister was a budding veterinarian.

That meant she had the afternoon off. Gordon had grabbed two slices of toast and left for Jubal Pierce's cabin shortly after seven this morning.

She knew she should be relieved Gordon was being conscientious about the job, but she still had the feeling he was hiding something from her. He certainly had become adept at doing that in Chicago, and she hadn't truly trusted him since.

But what could it be?

Maybe she was seeing problems where there were none. Last year had been so traumatic for all of them. She'd let everyone down—her mother, her aunt, the kids, herself… If she'd been around more, if she'd waited another year to finish the residency, well, then she would have been home when needed. It was the reason she didn't confront her brother now. She didn't feel she had the moral authority. Gordon certainly didn't feel she did.

And that brought her back to Jubal Pierce. Unfortunately, he occupied too many of her thoughts and, when he did, warmth surged through her in a most disturbing way.

She mentally cataloged what she knew about him, which was precious little. He had no family; at least, that was her impression. He'd said his grandparents were Texans and that his father had been in the rodeo. Nothing about his mother. She didn't know whether he'd ever been married.

What she did know was disconcerting. He was a veteran and had been wounded, probably several times over if his body was any indication.

He was uncommonly fit. She knew of his runs and early-morning swims and had seen that hard muscled body. He was every inch a warrior.

After seeing that tattoo, she'd looked it up on her computer. It was the SEAL Trident. She'd read enough to know they were among the most skilled and fierce fighters. She also knew they operated in teams that were as close as any family. What had happened to his?

What fascinated her was the gentleness he'd displayed with her sister and the dog, and the odd connection he had with Gordon. And this morning she learned from Janie that he was now working for a rancher and had helped birth a colt.

Nothing, obviously, was a secret in Covenant Falls.

The fact that he apparently had a job on a ranch meant he would likely be staying longer than he'd originally intended. She'd understood he would be here only a few days and hadn't overly worried about his influence on Gordon. Or the attraction that had flared between them.

Darn it, but he was intriguing. Complicated. And the last person she needed in her life.

Or Gordon's. If Jubal Pierce became a hero to him, a role model, she'd guess the odds of Gordon enlisting in ten months would go up.

She didn't want to lose another family member. She couldn't.

So why didn't she put a stop to things? Why let Jubal linger in her mind?

Darn it, she wouldn't any longer. A long soaking bath sounded good, especially if she was going out for the evening. Bath oil and a candle sounded even better but she didn't have any. A trip to the general store was in order. She might even buy something new to wear tonight.

And she would forget about Jubal Pierce.

GORDON REDDING ARRIVED at Jubal's cabin at seven-thirty Saturday morning.

Jubal had been awake for hours, although he'd actually slept in the bed after a short rain shower chased him from the lounge chair.

He rose at dawn, ran several miles, then plunged into the lake for a swim. Then he settled down in the chair on the porch with his book on ranching. He knew Gordon would show. He had something to prove.

Gordon parked his bike, glanced at the porch, then went up the steps and opened the door. "I'm here."

"I'm not blind," Jubal said. "I borrowed the tools you should need. They are in the box next to the lumber. If you need anything more, tell me. If not, you can get started."

"You're not going to...?" Gordon stopped.

"Help? Supervise? No. Remember, you're the contractor. I'm going to sit here, drink my coffee and read a book."

The kid shook his head and walked to the boards, picked up two and carried them down the drive. Jubal watched as the boy carried everything out to the dock, then went back to his book.

He heard hammering on and off. An hour went by, then another. He told himself not to interfere. It would ruin the mission. Gordon had to do it himself. If you tear something down, you have to rebuild it.

At noon, he made a couple of sandwiches and grabbed two sodas. He started down the path when he saw Gordon talking to someone. He immediately recognized the boy from the night he arrived. He was the one that had apparently been a lookout but had run instead.

Jubal resisted the temptation to go out there and knock the kid in the water as he had Gordon. But he waited. He knew there was an argument. It was in Gordon's stance. The new kid suddenly took a swing at Gordon, who ducked. Gordon then charged his opponent and they both went into the water.

Jubal didn't wait another second. He dropped the food and ran to the dock, only to see Gordon pull the other kid out of the water and dump him on the dry ground. He stared at Jubal defiantly.

The other kid took off running toward an old Buick parked in the circle at the end of Lake Road. Jubal could have caught up with the boy but he was more concerned with Gordon at the moment. Besides, he had the boy's face memorized now and he planned to ask Clint about him.

"You handle yourself pretty well," he said. "Go inside the house. You can borrow those same sweats you wore before. I'll put your clothes in the dryer."

"What about the bench?"

Jubal looked at it. It was nearly finished, and it looked damn good. It hadn't been anchored, and there were no arms yet, but the bench seat was angled for comfort. It looked sturdy. Hell, he might even use it.

"Doesn't look like it'll take you long to finish. Looks like a good job. What did that coward want, anyway?"

"Nothin'," Gordon said. He obviously wasn't going to admit anything.

Jubal shrugged. "Okay, but I'll keep an eye out for him."

Gordon followed him to the cabin, changed clothes, then ate two sandwiches like he hadn't eaten in days. "I heard you've been working at a ranch," he said when he finished.

"Part-time."

"You like it?" Gordon said.

"Yeah, I do."

"You said your dad was in the rodeo. That must've been neat."

"It was, as long as it lasted," Jubal replied.

"You think I could go to the ranch with you sometime?"

"Your sister would have to approve."

"She let Kerry ride at Mrs. Manning's house."

"But your sister was there."

Interest seemed to die in Gordon's eyes. The kid obviously felt rebuffed and Jubal didn't want that. He liked him more every time he saw him. He had a chip the size of a boulder on his shoulder but he was a hard worker and smarter than he wanted anyone to think.

Jubal related to that, particularly the boulder.

The kid went back to work.

Back off, Jubal told himself. After the bench was finished, Gordon would no longer be his business. He would be doing a disservice to both of them if he encouraged any kind of friendship. The kid was obviously hungering for a father figure, and Jubal sure as hell wasn't one, not to mention he still didn't plan to stay around long.

His phone rang and he picked it up. "It's Josh. How would you like to come to the inn for dinner tonight? We have a damn good restaurant there and entertainment to boot. Can you join us?"

Jubal liked Maude's, but he was curious. Josh had apparently carved out a new life for himself. He seemed content. Jubal wanted to know his path. "Sounds good. What time?"

"Seven."

"I'll be there. Thanks."

Three hours later, Gordon returned to the cabin with the box full of tools. "I'm finished, unless you want me to paint it."

Jubal followed the kid to the dock and inspected the bench. He sat down on it and damn if it wasn't comfortable.

Gordon looked anxious. "I can paint it."

"I don't think it needs it. Consider your debt paid after you take the wood trimmings to the cottage."

Gordon picked up the bits and pieces of wood and headed back to the cabin.

"Ever build anything before?" Jubal asked as they reached the cabin.

"Just that kid's fort I told you about."

"What about with your dad?"

"A bicycle. A train set. Stuff like that." For a moment, he looked lost.

"Tough break."

"Yeah. Well, I gotta go."

Jubal reached in his pocket, took out a twenty and handed it to Gordon.

"What's this for?" Gordon asked.

"Call it a bonus."

Gordon looked surprised but took it. "You need anything else done?" he asked.

"Not at the moment."

"About the ranch," Gordon said tentatively. "Maybe I could learn to ride…?" He paused, then grinned. "I got twenty dollars to pay."

"If your sister agrees, I'll check with the rancher." Jubal tried not to smile. He was well pleased that Luke had already agreed, but he'd wanted the idea to come from Gordon.

Gordon hesitated. Shifted on his feet. "Thanks, Mr. Pierce," he said.

"No more fires," Jubal replied.

Gordon nodded. "No more fires," the boy confirmed before going to his bike and pedaling away.

Two hours later, Jubal shaved and dressed for dinner. An inn required something more than sweatpants or jeans. He had one decent pair of pants and he added a long-sleeved shirt. No tie. Hell, he didn't even own a tie.

He rolled up the sleeves of the shirt and looked at the clock. It was six-thirty.

He wanted a drink. Unfortunately, he was out of both beer and anything stronger. He sighed, half wishing he'd refused. He really just wanted to enjoy his victory today. Privately. He had been right about Gordon. The fact that the kid had lost his father at around the same age Jubal lost his made him feel even more confident in the work they'd done together.

At fifteen minutes to seven, he left the cabin.

LISA WAS LOOKING forward to going to the inn. She'd heard about it from Janie and several other patients who had asked how she liked Covenant Falls. Everyone loved Maude's, but they also mentioned the inn as something special. She made her casserole and tried to call Gordon to find out when he would arrive, but he hadn't answered. He'd said he would be working at Jubal Pierce's cabin, but he hadn't specified how long he'd be gone.

She thought about driving over there but that would be saying she didn't trust him. She told herself she had to give him some space. At least trouble seemed to be limited in Covenant Falls.

The front door slammed and Gordon strolled into the room.

His face was sunburned, and his clothes a mess.

"I'm glad you're home," she said. "I've been invited to dinner tonight with the Mannings. Can you stay home and look after Kerry? I have a hamburger casserole ready to go in the oven."

"Okay," he said.

The answer surprised her, but she wasn't about to question gifts. "Thanks," she said. "Did you finish what you were doing at Mr. Pierce's cabin?"

"Yeah. Mr. Pierce said I did a good job."

Lisa heard a pride that had been missing for a long time. She remembered before their mother got sick when he would rush home with some project or another that had won an award. He'd always had a knack for putting things together. "That's great," she said.

"He's working at a horse ranch outside town," Gordon said.

"I heard."

"They raise quarter horses," Gordon added.

Lisa didn't like the direction the conversation was taking. She waited for the bomb to drop.

"He said maybe I could get some lessons there," Gordon continued.

Ah, there it was.

"Eve said she and Stephanie will teach you," Lisa tried. "You're both invited tomorrow for lessons."

She saw the stubborn look come into his face. "I don't think so," he said.

"We'll talk about riding later. Okay?" She worried about a virtual stranger having influence over him. Why would someone like Jubal, a former SEAL, take such a strong interest in Gordon?

And to be truthful, she feared the reaction the

man aroused in her. Maybe *that* was influencing her.

"I can pay for it myself," Gordon said defiantly, then headed for the stairs without another word.

Lisa watched him go. She was losing him again. He obviously did not like her having a say in what he did. He wanted to learn with Jubal because it was his idea. And a bit of hero worship, maybe? If Gordon wanted a role model, why couldn't he pick a doctor or teacher? Or a builder like Nate?

She was grateful Kerry was outside, wearing Susie out, or maybe it was the other way around. She went upstairs and changed into a dark brown full skirt and lacy beige top she'd brought from Chicago. She added a coral necklace that had been a gift from her mother and piled her hair up into a twist in back.

After putting the casserole in the oven, she was ready to go at a quarter to seven. Kerry and Susie were curled up on the sofa, Kerry with a book and Susie snuggled up with a new toy. Lisa snapped a photo with her cell. She wished she had one of Gordon when he first came inside with his sunburned face and rare smile. It has disappeared too quickly.

"Have a good time, Lisa," Kerry said.

"You sure you don't mind?"

"No. You deserve it."

Lisa put her hand on Kerry's shoulder and gave her a hug. "Thanks."

Just then she heard a vehicle turn into the drive. She went outside. Eve was in the driver's seat.

"Hi," Eve said. "Josh went ahead to check on some things."

Lisa stepped into the passenger's seat and minutes later Eve drove up to the Camel Trail Inn.

She'd admired the outside before and loved the camel on the sign, but the inside lobby had a "wow" factor beyond her expectations. Paintings of mountain scenes decorated the wood-paneled interior. A huge rock fireplace dominated one wall. Eve led her through the lobby into a dining room that was lit by what looked like gaslights but must be electric. It looked like a late-1800s eatery with rich paneling and heavy tables, each with a vase of fresh flowers at the center. The room was both charming and warm.

She recognized some locals. She could also identify the tourists. It was obviously a special spot for the locals and they dressed for it. The tourists were mostly still in shorts and jeans.

Her heart skipped a beat when she saw Jubal sitting with Andy, Josh and Nate at a table set for six. The men stood as she and Eve approached. Jubal looked as surprised as she felt when her group neared the table.

"This is Josh's and Nate's treat," Eve said softly.

"I hope you don't mind if we included Jubal, but the guys wanted to show off the inn."

She did mind. She minded because of the way he made her pulse race. But he looked great in slacks and a blue shirt that made his eyes resemble the color of an evening sky.

They all sat and a young lady wearing jeans and a western shirt immediately approached to hand them menus, greeting them cheerfully.

Lisa tried to lose herself in the menu but found it hard to concentrate with Jubal immediately across from her. "I highly recommend the rainbow trout or one of the steaks," Eve said. "The trout comes from the mountain streams around here. Josh can't always get it."

Lisa ordered the rainbow trout as did Eve and Andy. The men all opted for the steaks.

Eve kept the conversation going, regaling them with town legends. Lisa recalled from the pageant that the town founder bought camels from the army to carry supplies to miners over mountain trails.

"Stephanie wanted to recreate the story in the pageant and rented two real camels," Eve said. "Unfortunately they got loose and galloped down Main Street just before the opening day.

"They were terrifying everyone, with Andy in chase," Nate said, looking at Andy with so much love in his eyes it made Lisa ache.

Eve took up the story. "Andy sent two befuddled police officers to get some bananas at the general store and coaxed the camels back by feeding them. Took every banana the grocer had."

"They were then Stephanie's responsibility," Eve continued. "She'd rented them as a joke. But then she had to take care of them during the rest of the week and they were very wayward camels."

"Where *is* Stephanie?" Lisa asked.

"In addition to being our vet, she's a search and rescue volunteer with her dog, Sherry," Josh said. "Just before six, she was called out on a search and rescue mission about a hundred miles from here," Nate said. "An elderly woman and her dog have been missing for six or seven days. No one knew they were lost until her car was spotted on a rarely-used road. After checking the registration, they found a family member. Apparently she doesn't always inform someone when she goes on a hiking expedition."

"And Clint is out patrolling," Josh added. "There's been some rustling in the area recently. All three of the cars are out this weekend."

Lisa's head was spinning. Runaway camels, cattle rustling and lost people. So much for peaceful Covenant Falls.

She glanced at Jubal. He'd said very little, but he was listening. His jaw seemed to tighten when Nate mentioned the rustling, and his eyes hardened.

Their gazes met. She was stunned by the pure need that skittered along her nerve endings and settled in the pit of her stomach. A powerful craving seemed to take over her body. She saw something in his eyes flicker and could tell he felt it, too. She fervently hoped no one else had noticed her…momentary distraction. Except it wasn't momentary. It had been there from the instant she'd first seen him.

The food came along with two bottles of wine, one white and one red. Lisa nibbled at the trout. She suspected it was very good, but her stomach was doing weird things. She tried to keep her eyes on the food, but they kept wandering to Jubal, who apparently wasn't similarly affected. He was downing the steak as if he'd never had one before. She gulped down her glass of wine.

Jubal looked up then, and to her utter surprise, he winked at her. Then his expression went blank again so quickly she wondered whether she'd imagined it. He was always so…stoic. Yes, surely she'd imagined it.

Dessert came at the same time a small band appeared in the corner of the room and started playing. The members varied in age and she recognized several from the pageant. There was a small dance floor, and by the third song, couples were dancing, including Nate and Andy.

To her surprise, Jubal stood. "Doctor?"

It would be rude to say no. But the simple fact was she didn't want to, anyway. He took her hand, and electricity shot up it. Then he put his arms around her. She was tall, but she felt tiny next to him. He was a good dancer, graceful and easy to follow, he seemed to do everything well.

Lisa looked up. He was looking down with a warmth that startled her. She wanted to lean against him, but that would mean surrendering to feelings she knew were only fleeting. They *had* to be; he had no place in her life.

But then why did she feel this intensity—this raw naked need—when she was with him? Their gazes met. Held. She saw the same want in him that was making her body ache.

They stayed on the floor for two more numbers before he returned her to the table. They walked back to their table, and their hands fell apart, but the warmth remained.

A few days. She'd known him for only a few days, she reminded herself as Josh took care of the bill.

The six of them walked out together. The sky had turned cloudy and Lisa felt the moisture in the air.

"I can take Dr. Redding home," Jubal said. "Her house is closer to the cabin."

"That okay, Lisa?" Eve said.

Oh, no! Lisa nodded and walked blindly to Jubal's car.

CHAPTER FIFTEEN

WHY THE HELL did he make that offer?

He hadn't meant to. It was the worst possible thing he could do.

The more he saw of her, the more he liked her. Was attracted to her. And this was definitely one relationship that couldn't go far. They were on completely different roads in their lives and going in opposite directions.

But when her body had fit so neatly into his while dancing, and he'd looked down at those expressive dark eyes, he felt a need he'd never experienced before. The problem was that it wasn't just physical; it was something even stronger, more irresistible.

Even more confounding was that he saw it in her eyes, as well.

As much as he tried to tell himself to run like hell, he couldn't. His good sense surrendered to stronger emotions, and he suggested driving her home. He was surprised when she'd agreed, although it made sense. The Mannings lived in a different direction.

It was only a short ride to her house. No danger here.

But once in the car, he realized he was wrong. He had been very aware of the flowery fragrance of her hair when they danced but now, inside his car, it was intoxicating—or maybe it was Lisa herself. Her smile was dazzling.

He counted the reasons he should drive her straight home, accompany her to the door and say good night in a calm, impersonal way.

He reached seven before he asked, "Would you like to see the bench Gordon built?"

She hesitated. She was probably counting the reasons she should say no. Instead, she took a deep breath and said, "Yes."

He changed direction and drove toward the cabin. It was past ten, and he'd learned that little stirred after ten in Covenant Falls. The community center's lights were off. There were no cars in the parking lot. Most of the lights in the cottages lining Lake Road were off.

It was a dark night, too. Clouds blacked out the moon. The breeze had freshened and it was cooler than any night since he'd been in Covenant Falls. Jubal knew a storm was brewing. He parked on the road and faced the headlights toward the deck. Then he left the car and hurried around to her side. She'd opened the door and had one foot out when he reached her.

He stretched out his hand. She hesitated, then

took it. It seemed natural. Even right. His fingers closed around hers and he led her out on the dock to the bench.

It was large enough for two adults.

"Should I try it?" she asked skeptically.

"I did."

She sat gingerly, then leaned against the slanted back. "It's comfortable."

He sat down next to her. "Your brother picked out the design and the wood and built it entirely on his own. I didn't say a word."

"Why?" she asked.

"Why what?" he replied, though he knew exactly what she meant. He should tell her the truth right now if he wanted any kind of relationship with her, even a brief one.

"He just came to you, and you said you wanted a bench built?"

"Something like that," he said. The kid did come to his cabin, and he did say he wanted a bench. But he was leaving a lot out.

"Why didn't *you* build it? You don't look like the sedentary type who'd sit there and watch someone else work," she observed with humor in her voice.

"He needed a job. I didn't."

She eyed him suspiciously. He realized she felt something didn't ring quite true but she couldn't quite figure out what. Had he shown too much pride in what Gordon had accomplished?

To his relief, she changed the subject. "Do you really swim in the lake every day? I hear it's freezing."

"Ah, the Covenant Falls rumor factory," he said dryly. "But yes, I do. It wakes me up."

"I could think of easier ways. Like a cup of hot coffee."

"I want to know I can still do it," he replied honestly. "It makes me feel alive. Wakens all my senses."

"And you need to feel alive?"

"Doesn't everyone?"

"Maybe not to the extreme of swimming in an ice cold lake every night."

He stood and looked out at the lake. She was far too intuitive. But his captivity wasn't something he could talk about.

She was silent for a moment, then asked the question that apparently had been bothering her. "If you are just going to stay a short while, why did you hire a kid you didn't know and turn him loose on something you probably won't use?"

He shrugged. "Do you know about this cabin?" he asked.

"A little."

"I'm the fourth vet to use it. Everyone has left it, or the town, a little better. Clint repaired and extended the dock. The bench was my contribution, small as it may be."

She looked at him, and he thought she wasn't

completely satisfied, but she nodded. "So what comes next?"

"My plan was to stay a few days."

"It's been more than a week," she observed.

"I've sorta become involved in a few things," he said.

"You're staying for a while, then?"

"Yeah," he said. "A while."

"Gordon likes you."

An uncomfortable comment. And Jubal had no answer without deepening the lie or betraying Gordon.

"I've tried and tried to get through to him and you've done it in a few days," Lisa continued. "How did you do that?" He heard pain in her question.

He shrugged. "I don't know if I have. I just gave him a temporary job."

"He said you were working for a rancher, that he wanted to learn to ride there." She was direct. And a damn good interrogator. The military could use her.

He shrugged. "I told him he would have to ask you."

Her tone softened. "Thank you for helping him. I didn't mean to question you. I've just been worried…"

"I wouldn't hurt him."

"You won't be here long," she said frankly. "I don't want him to lose someone else." She hesitated, then said slowly, "You know our father died when he was young?"

Jubal wasn't going to lie about that. He nodded.

"I thought you might, that he may have told you," she said. "He was so proud when he came home today. He was tired and his clothes were a mess but there was a light in his eyes that's been missing."

She hesitated, then slowly, cautiously, continued. "After Dad died, Gordon tried to become the man of the house. He looked after Kerry and our mother, or at least Mom let him think he did. Then she got sick, too. Cancer. And I wasn't there. I was in my residency. It was what Mom wanted, but I should've returned home. Put it off. I didn't. Our aunt came to help out.

"Mom got worse, and I couldn't do anything about it. Gordon blamed me for not being there, for not saving her, for doctors not saving her…"

He felt the pain in her. It ran deep and wide. How many times had he felt guilt when he couldn't save one of his team? He still felt it. He probably would feel it until the day he died. He would see a smile and think of Scott, or hear raucous laughter and be back with Hound Dog…

"*You* lost both parents, too," he said.

"But I was an adult. I didn't spend my teen years looking after a dying mother."

"I can't imagine how tough it was," Jubal said. "But he's a very bright kid."

"When he wants to be," she replied. "But after Mom died, his grades dropped dramatically. He got involved with some gang members in Chicago. He was trying to get some kind of control over his life, and he thought they were offering it. I hoped getting him away from the city would help, but he doesn't trust me."

"He probably thinks you'll leave him, too. He's afraid to care."

She looked at him and her face softened. "You know about that, don't you?"

Had he been so obvious?

A drop of rain fell. Then another. Then the sky seemed to open and rain poured down. Not just a few drops. A deluge. He grabbed her hand and they ran for the car as the sky opened. Once inside, she started to laugh and a chuckle started deep inside him. Then he leaned toward her. His fingers touched her cheek and wiped the drops away.

"Coffee?" he asked. "Until it stops raining quite as hard?"

She hesitated. "I should get home and check on Kerry and Gordon."

He didn't say anything. Waited. He wasn't sure what he wanted her answer to be.

"Maybe a quick one," she agreed.

He nodded, turned on the ignition and eased the car into the driveway, getting as close to the

porch as possible. He then reached in the backseat and pulled out a jean jacket.

"Here," he said. "Put it over your head and
we'll make a run for it."

He saw her glance at her shoes and the now
muddy ground outside. "Stay there," he ordered.
He got out of the car and went to her side. He
opened the door, put the jacket on her, then without saying anything picked her up and carried her
to the porch before setting her down.

They were both dripping as he opened the
door. "I'll get some towels," he said, "then make
that coffee…"

THE RAIN HAD come so fast and hard Lisa was
soaking wet all over.

She wiped the wetness off her face and arms
and looked around. The room looked comfortable, more than comfortable, and it was military
clean and tidy. The only item out of place was a
book on the floor next to a big easy chair.

She went over and looked at it. *Ranching in
Colorado.* Not what she expected. But then what
had she expected? Murder? Action adventure?
Why did she want to pigeonhole him? Because
it would be easier to dismiss him as just a big
macho guy?

She went to a wall of windows and looked out.
The rain was still coming down. Hard. She should
be home. She was stunned at herself. Not only

for letting him carry her inside—not that she had
had a choice—but for agreeing to stay.

For coffee only. Truth was, though, that she
hadn't wanted to leave, either. There had been
something about him when he spoke of Gordon,
a wistfulness that made her think he really cared
about her brother. He'd wanted to show her the
bench. There'd been pride in his praise of it. He
seemed to understand her brother better than she
did.

Jubal returned to the room wearing a dry shirt
and jeans and carrying a large towel and blue
shirt with him. He wrapped it around her. "Want
to change? I can put your blouse in the dryer. It
won't take long."

She mentally added *efficient* to the number of
qualities she was admiring in him today.

She looked at the shirt. It was large and long,
a soft cotton. But it meant staying at least thirty
minutes. *Thirty minutes. No.*

She nodded.

He handed her the shirt. "There are more clean
towels in the bathroom. Down the hall and to the
left. I'll start the coffee."

Lisa thanked him and headed to the bathroom.
It was as neat as the rest of the cabin. Everything
in its proper place. There was a big towel neatly
folded on the counter. She wiped the rain from
her face, then tried to dry her hair. It was falling
from the neat twist and she tried to repair it as

best she could before giving up. She wanted to touch up her lipstick, but then remembered her purse was still in the car. Along with her shoes.

She took off her blouse and put on the big cotton shirt. It was clearly well-worn.

Soft. Clean, but it had a masculine scent to it. She looked at herself in the mirror. The shirt reached halfway down the skirt. She was barefoot. Not one of her best looks.

She went into the other room and Jubal met her with a steaming cup of coffee. He'd started a fire in the fireplace that was licking the edge of a log. "Thirty minutes and your blouse will be dry. Okay?"

His dark hair was damp and crinkly and his jaw already had the slightest hint of a beard. He looked rugged and competent, which was extremely appealing. Yet, their earlier conversation had revealed a vulnerability she hadn't expected.

"Thank you," she said as she accepted the coffee.

"You're welcome," he replied solemnly, but she thought she detected a smile in his eyes.

"Not just for the coffee. Not only."

He gave her an inquisitive look. "Then what?"

"I've never been carried before."

"Someone's been missing out," he said with a crooked smile that went beyond charming, maybe because she couldn't remember seeing a real smile on his face before. Polite ones, yes. But a spontaneous one? No. Way.

It was the latter that made her senses go crazy. She could resist macho alone. She was discovering she couldn't resist macho mixed with the other qualities she found in him.

He'd accomplished something she hadn't. Gordon hadn't slouched into the house this afternoon. He'd even agreed to stay home with Kerry. He was changing for the better.

But those things didn't address her two main concerns with a friendship between Jubal and her brother. Jubal had made it clear he was just passing through, and she was even more worried that he might inspire Gordon to go into the service.

She had to address the latter.

"Gordon's talked about joining the army," she said slowly.

"That would be a bad thing?"

"I've seen the scars on you," she said, then swallowed hard. "A college classmate of mine was killed in Afghanistan. I don't want Gordon anywhere near war. I've lost too many members of my family already."

"He's asked a few questions. I haven't encouraged him, nor will I."

"He likes you. You're a hero to him. I don't think it's a good idea for you two…"

There. She'd said it. Almost.

But he understood. She saw it in his face, the

way it tightened. He nodded. "You want me to stay away from him."

"Or maybe discourage him from—"

"Should I distance myself from you, too?" His voice was suddenly cool.

She couldn't answer that. She should. He was going to be here a short time. She was returning to Chicago in less than a year, even if he stayed. They had nothing in common. There was no future, and she was a forever type of woman. But she couldn't say the words.

He led her over to the sofa and she felt herself stiffening even as she sat next to him. Next to the sexiest man she'd ever met and he was looking at her with the most penetrating and striking blue eyes she'd ever seen. But suddenly there was a huge chasm between them.

"How does it feel living in a small town after Chicago?" His voice was controlled, with none of the teasing she'd heard earlier. It was almost as if a big stop sign had been constructed. To her dismay, she wanted to tear it down. She felt a deep loss and she knew it was her fault. Small talk was agonizing now.

"I like it more than I thought I would," she said, trying to keep her voice impersonal even as she wanted to take her earlier words back.

She desperately wanted to leave but her blouse hadn't had time to dry. She tried to keep her voice steady as she replied, "I like having more time with patients and getting to know them. I like not having to worry about Kerry and Gordon getting mixed up with bad kids."

"There are bad kids in small towns, too," he said.

"Yes, but at least everyone knows who they are."

"Why medicine?" he asked, swiftly changing topics. He was obviously trying to relax her.

"I never wanted to do anything else," she said. "I used to request nurse and doctor toys for Christmas. I didn't want dolls except to use as patients. I always liked the hospital dramas growing up. I thought it was neat to make people well. And I love kids. I was planning to specialize in pediatric surgery."

"Was?"

"I was just about to start a fellowship when Gordon..." She stopped. It wasn't a story she wanted to share.

He sipped his coffee. She thought he'd press further, but then he may have already sensed the reason.

He reached over and took her hand, his fingers entwining with hers. His hand was warm and she responded by curling her fingers around his. It seemed so natural...so right.

"You've had a lot to shoulder these past few years, haven't you?"

"So have Gordon and Kerry. I want them to be

kids again and I'm so afraid they've lost some of their best years to grief."

"And what about Lisa?" he asked. "Hasn't she missed a lot, too? Hasn't she lost parents, too? When is the last time you've had a day just for yourself? When you haven't worried about your family or a patient? When you haven't tried to meet everyone's expectations of you?"

Lisa was stunned. He didn't try to tell her it would be all right. Or that she'd made the right decision or was making one now. He seemed completely nonjudgmental and accepting. The sensitivity belied every conception she had about soldiers.

His hand let hers go and he wrapped his arm around her shoulders. The fire was glowing now, the flames just beginning to snap.

He felt so good next to her. "Tell me about you," she said. "You haven't said much about your family."

There was a silence. "You know some of it. Not much more to tell," he said. "The day after my grandfather lost the family ranch, he shot himself. My grandmother had died several years earlier from pneumonia.

"My dad was eighteen when he lost his father. No money for college, but he didn't want that. He was a cowboy through and through. He started on the rodeo circuit. He wouldn't ride bulls. But he rode broncs. They were just as wild and ill-tempered as the bulls, but most didn't try to kill you like the bulls would."

Jubal's arm tightened around her and she felt the tension in him. "He was twenty-one when he met my mother. She attended a rodeo visiting a cousin. It was love at first sight, at least for my father. I think it was more rebellion on my mother's part. Anyway, they eloped and I came pretty fast after that.

"They traveled from rodeo to rodeo," Jubal continued. "I grew up in a trailer, and my best friend was Dad's horse, Dusty. Dad taught me to ride. I thought he was the best rider ever, although he never won a championship. He earned just enough money to take us to the next rodeo."

Lisa was transfixed by the story. His voice had deepened and his eyes were indecipherable. "When I turned seven, my mother had had enough. The big money pot was always around the corner. She packed us up and headed to her family's home in Maryland. My dad was killed by a bronc a year later."

Lisa understood a lot then, although she knew there was still much left unsaid. She could tell from his voice that he'd idolized his father and yet she sympathized with the mother.

She knew now why he related to Gordon. They had both lost fathers at a young age and it left marks on both of them. Similar to how Gordon partly blamed her for their mother's death, Jubal had obviously blamed his mother.

"I'm so sorry," she said. Then because she had to know, she asked an intrusive question. "Did you forgive your mother?"

"A kid doesn't understand, so it's hard to forgive," he said. "Maybe I would have if she hadn't married someone who disliked me on sight. We were at war until the day I graduated from high school and joined the navy. My mother died three years later."

She touched his face. It was so strong. Too strong to be handsome. But there was a vulnerability there, too. She heard hurt and regret in his voice even if he hadn't admitted to it.

"I should go," she said, afraid to stay longer.

"Yeah, I guess you probably should."

He stood and his hand pulled her up, too. He ran his fingers along her cheek, then he leaned down and kissed her lightly.

"You're very pretty," he said after.

She flushed. She'd never felt pretty. She'd never been wildly popular. Her only friends in high school and college were mostly nerds like her, and then in med school she was too busy with her studies and family to pay much attention to her appearance.

"I'll get your blouse," he said, apparently feeling her discomfort.

Jubal was back a minute later with her blouse.

It was supposed to be wash and wear, but it was still damp and wrinkled. She took it to the bedroom and reluctantly exchanged his soft shirt for her blouse. Her hair was a disaster, and she tried to tuck in tendrils that had fallen from the twist.

She truly hoped no one would be awake when she reached home. She glanced at her watch. Eleven-forty. Almost pumpkin time.

And she'd had her kiss, albeit a light and friendly one. Exactly what she'd originally wanted—to not get too involved.

So why did she feel so disappointed?

He was waiting at the door, her shoes in his hand. "I got your shoes," he said. "The rain stopped," he said lightly. How could he be so casual when her heart was still pounding hard? "A typical late-summer storm."

She stepped into her shoes and they walked out on the porch. A small piece of the moon was visible between clouds. The air was fresh, washed clean by the rain.

He took her hand and lifted her again to carry her over the mud. He did it so effortlessly she felt light as a feather. When she was in the seat, he leaned over. "Just to let you know, I was really tempted to turn that kiss into a world-class winner, but I didn't want to scare you away."

She was speechless when he stepped into the driver's seat. "You're not staying here long," she reminded him.

"Nope," he replied, and started driving, leaving her to ponder about that world-class winner kiss she'd missed.

CHAPTER SIXTEEN

LISA HAD HOPED everyone would be asleep when she arrived home just before midnight, but the light was on in the living room and the door was unlocked. She wasn't sure how she felt about that. She'd been told locking the door wasn't necessary in Covenant Falls, but having always lived in a big city, the need to lock doors was an automatic reflex.

She looked back. Jubal was still there, waiting for her to go safely inside. Apparently he didn't subscribe to the rather loose safety standards of Covenant Falls, either.

She closed the door quietly behind her. Automatically locked it.

Then she started for her bedroom when Susie started barking upstairs. She winced, saying a quiet prayer. She really didn't want to answer questions from inquiring minds tonight. Apparently the dog had good hearing.

She arrived at the door of her bedroom when she heard Kerry's voice at the top of the stairs. "Lisa?"

Lisa couldn't ignore her. She went to the bottom of the steps. "Hi, kiddo. Everything's fine. I just got caught in the rainstorm and was delayed. Go back to bed."

Instead, Kerry came down the stairs and her eyes regarded her anxiously. "I was a bit worried."

Thank God Gordon slept like a log. Unfortunately, Kerry didn't and usually read until late.

"The rain," Lisa said again. "It was a downpour."

"What happened to your blouse?

Lisa looked down at her still-damp and wrinkly shirt. Once Kerry got a question in her head, she didn't stop until she was satisfied with the answer.

"Mr. Pierce took me over to see the bench your brother built. While we were looking at it, the skies opened up and I got soaked. We waited until it stopped raining so hard."

"At his cabin?" Kerry had a gleam in her eyes.

"Yes, and he was a perfect gentleman." In her thoughts, she almost added a 'dammit.'

"Do you like him?"

"I do, but not the way you probably mean." *Liar.*

"He's handsome in a rugged way," Kerry observed.

"We're just acquaintances. He's only going to be here a short while, and we're going back to Chicago."

"Do we have to?"

The question shocked Lisa. Kerry had been as adamant as her brother about not leaving Chicago.

"I thought you liked Chicago, your friends, your school."

"I really like the choir here, and Mrs. Ames, the choir teacher. I already made a few friends. I have a dog and a job, well, kinda. And Mrs. Manning is teaching me to ride. I love her horse, Beauty." She paused before asking, "You didn't forget I have a lesson tomorrow, right?"

"I wouldn't forget that," Lisa said, relieved that the subject had changed. What young girl didn't want to ride horses? She had as a child, but Chicago hadn't offered affordable equine opportunities. She was thrilled Kerry had one now.

The old bubbly Kerry was back after being on hiatus for the last eighteen months. *What would happen when they returned to Chicago?*

"Maybe you're not ready to go back to bed, but I am," she said. "Oh, how's Gordon?"

"He was studying, but his light is out now." *Miracles. Did Jubal have anything to do with it?*

"Okay, well, good night," Lisa said.

"Good night." Kerry scooped up Susie and ran back up the steps.

Lisa went into the kitchen. It was clean, no dishes in the sink. She looked in the fridge, and leftovers had been put in containers. She poured herself a glass of water, went into the main floor bathroom and looked in the mirror. As Kerry had noted, her shirt was a wrinkled mess and her skirt was still damp and clinging to her legs. Her lipstick was entirely gone. Tendrils had fallen from the twist in back and tumbled along her cheekbones.

She winced, took the pins out and let it fall past her shoulders so she could brush it. Then she examined herself critically. Her hair was too straight, her brown eyes too serious, her cheekbones too prominent and her mouth too wide.

She'd never had a fire and storm romance. She always thought she would know when someone was right, and if it didn't happen she could live with that. She'd never expected all the bells in her to ring, especially with a man so completely different from anyone she'd known, with a background she couldn't understand and a future even he didn't see. It was crazy.

She crawled into bed, still trying to analyze her feelings the way she analyzed a medical problem. It didn't work, because nothing made sense.

JUBAL WOKE DRENCHED in sweat.

The sheet that had been covering him was twisted into knots as if he'd been fighting it.

He had.

His body was rigid from trying to escape the chains binding him to a wall. He heard them coming. He knew what had happened from the wailing outside. The terrorist he was supposed to heal had died. *The door opens and the blows fall*...

The room swam into focus. Not a bare hut in Africa. A streak of sunlight made it through the shutters in the room. He hadn't closed them last night.

His body was shaking, remembering the pain. Or was it all in his mind? He looked at the bed and knew he had thrashed around. Had he moaned, too? The nightmare, the visions, were all too real. He knew all about PTSD, how it would sneak up on him and hit when he least expected it.

It was the first full night he'd slept inside the cabin. Even then it had been more like a series of short naps than a real night of rest. He'd had those nightmares in San Diego, too, as he'd served out his last few months as a SEAL. He had been debriefed and studied, tested and retested. Every moment of his captivity and escape was explored and documented to be used in training. He'd relived those years over and over again. The mistakes. The failures. He'd hated it, but he knew it might be useful someday to another SEAL.

Another reason to avoid the pretty doctor. How could he ever go to bed with her not knowing if he would wake thinking she was the enemy?

And yet, he'd brought her to the cabin like that. So much for his self-discipline. It had saved him during those dark two years. It failed him last night.

Error number one: he never should've asked her to see the bench. He'd wanted her to see what Gordon had built. He'd wanted her to have the same pride in her brother that he did.

Error number two: he never should've taken her inside the cabin. He should have tried to squash the attraction that had grown stronger since they'd first met rather than feed it like dry wood to a fire.

At least he'd pulled back before making it worse. And then he'd spoiled that effort by blurting out what he really wanted to do. *Idiot!* No way could he continue playing with fire without one or both of them getting badly burned. The simple fact was that they had nothing in common outside that attraction. He'd sensed she wasn't totally comfortable with the military, and that had been his life. And she'd made it clear she was here one year before returning to the big city and a career that had taken her years to reach. There was no room in that picture for him.

Having made that determination, he made coffee, dressed in his trunks and went out to the lake. He needed the frigid water this morning to cool off.

Still, as he stroked out to the middle of the lake, he couldn't forget how adorable she'd looked in his shirt, or the wondering expression on her face as he'd kissed her.

He swam faster, telling himself he'd be wise to leave today. He'd done what he could for Gordon. He should end it now.

If it wasn't for Luke, he would. In return for lessons, he'd committed to staying an indeterminate time. He was pretty sure that meant longer than a few days. The pull of ranch life was strong. It was the only occupation that had interested him, and he realized he was clutching to it in desperation. After nearly twenty years as a SEAL, fruitless wandering did not actually appeal to him.

The little colt had cinched the deal. He still needed a name. He had no idea what to call him.

He bet Lisa would.

He swam back to shore, took a hot shower and pulled on his oldest pair of jeans and an old plaid shirt. He drank a large cup of coffee, ate three pieces of toast and drank a large glass of orange juice, then grabbed his keys. It was early, but he was pretty sure Luke would be watering and feeding the horses.

Luke was outside. So was the mare with her foal. In the sun, the baby had the same rich markings as his mama. He was actually trotting around with her in the corral, staying close as she kept turning her head to make sure he was there.

"Glad to see you," Luke said.

"Making up for yesterday, if that's okay."

"Sure. You're more than welcome anytime. Can't stay away, huh?"

Jubal looked at the colt. "Not from him. He's out in the big wide world already?"

"He's an eager little guy. He's got great breeding. A championship on his sire's side."

"I didn't expect him to be running so quickly."

"Hell, he was running yesterday. Horses are a prey animal," Luke said.

The mare came over to the fence and the foal followed. Luke took an apple quarter and gave it to her. "Good job," he said, and ran his hand down the mare's neck. The mare chomped on the apple.

"Gets to you, doesn't it?" Luke said. "As I said the other night, this is what makes all the long hours and financial risks worthwhile. You watch them grow, become confident."

The foal's big chocolate eyes regarded Jubal curiously, like it was thinking "maybe I should know you." He took a tentative step forward, then stopped when his mother nudged him back to her side.

"Could he remember me from the night he was born?"

"I doubt it. He's probably just curious."

"What's his schedule now?"

"Leave him with his mama at first. Accustom him to the herd across the fence, then when everyone calms down, move both mare and colt in with the others. We'll start imprinting today by putting a foal halter on him and letting him know we're friends. Ground training starts in about a year and a half, and real riding a year later."

Jubal was mentally counting the years before there could be a profit.

"If you want to sell early, you can put promising youngsters with good confirmation and top-notch breeding into one of the big auction sales as yearlings. You keep the best to train and sell yourself when they start bringing in some ribbons and prize money.

He looked at Jubal. "It takes several decades to build a horse ranch from scratch. The other option is to buy a going ranch with a good reputation and hire good trainers. We make it because we've built a reputation. Tracy is a former barrel racing champion so she's in demand as a trainer and coach."

Jubal watched the colt for several more minutes, then said, "I'd better get started."

"Why don't you start with Jacko. I think he missed you yesterday. He's been stomping around in his stall. As I said, I can't leave my horses out at night, not with this rustling going on."

"Has there been any more instances?"

"Not in the last few days, but we've alerted all the ranches within a hundred-mile radius. Bastards," he muttered.

"Mind if I bring the new doctor's brother to see the little guy?"

"Bring the whole family if you wish. I met Dr. Redding at the reception after the pageant, and I've heard good things about her." He gestured toward to the foal. "Come up with a name yet?"

"Not yet," Jubal said.

"Well, you'd better hurry up and give him a name or Nameless is how he'll go down in the registry."

Jubal grinned. "I'll do better than that. Promise." He went inside the barn and found Jacko.

He gave him the expected carrot, watched as he munched it, then led the buckskin to the washrack, saddled and bridled him. "You and me, kid," he said as he swung up in the saddle.

Seven hours later, he headed to the cabin. He'd had lunch with Luke and Tracy, then went back to riding. There would be some new horses added to his list tomorrow. Luke said he was ready for them.

Graduation of a sort. Accomplishment. He hadn't realized how much he'd needed that...

He thought about calling Lisa regarding visiting the ranch, then reconsidered. He really should stay away from her. He'd barely been able to keep his hands off her the previous night. It had taken every ounce of self-control not to deepen the kiss.

He was way out of her class. He'd kicked around in some of the worst places in the world and had seen things no human being should see. He had nightmares and sometimes woke up screaming. He'd almost seriously hurt a woman he'd slept with in San Diego. He'd thought she was the enemy.

Lisa was a healer. He had no doubt she'd seen terrible wounds in her career, but that wasn't the same as causing them.

No, it was better to stay away, and stay away from Gordon, as well.

Better for all three of them.

CHAPTER SEVENTEEN

AFTER GETTING FAR closer to Lisa on Saturday night than was good for either of them, Jubal spent the next week throwing all his time and energy into Luke's ranch and learning more about the business.

He needed the distraction and stayed until well past seven or eight every night with the exception of Monday when he and Luke both attended the poker game.

The foal had grown more adventuresome every day. He seemed to recognize Jubal now, and he and his mother, Melody, cantered over to the fence when they saw him. He always arrived with pockets of carrots or apples, and Melody lost no time nuzzling his pocket for a treat.

"He's a spirited little guy," he said when Luke appeared at his side.

"Yep. And he still needs a name."

"I know," Jubal said. "I'm still thinking about it."

"You're spoiling her, you know," Luke said as Jubal gave the mare half a carrot.

"I guess I am," Jubal said. "She's a great mother."

"She is that." He paused, then asked, "You mentioned the other day that the new doc and her kids might like to see the foal. I met them at Maude's last night and invited them to drop by tomorrow."

Jubal just nodded.

"You said the boy might want lessons?"

"He might."

"Why don't you give them? You're capable of it and it would be good experience."

That was the last thing he needed. He resisted. "I'm not qualified."

"Tracy can sit in," Luke said, persisting. "I could use another instructor for beginners. Tracy has a full load of experienced riders."

Jubal felt he had no choice, not after everything Luke had done for him. He didn't think, however, that Lisa would be happy. "If it's okay with them," he qualified.

It wouldn't be. He knew that. He wished he'd never mentioned the ranch to Gordon or mentioned Lisa to Luke.

He'd done everything he could this past week to avoid both Lisa and her brother. She'd made it clear on Saturday night that she worried about his influence over her brother. And Jubal worried about any involvement between Lisa and himself. He'd just barely stopped himself from deepening that kiss Saturday night, and dammit, she'd seldom left his thoughts since.

He realized the attraction was deeper and more complex than any he'd felt in a long time. Usually once a pretty face attracted him, there would be a few dates, a few passionate nights, and then he'd be off on another mission. He'd never made promises, nor wanted to make them. Maybe because he remembered those fights between his parents, how much his mother hated the waiting, the danger, the lack of a real home.

So he immersed himself in Luke's ranch.

In the past week, he'd learned to do nearly everything that needed to be done around the stable area, including grooming and cleaning the tack and stalls. He knew each horse now and which were difficult. He was there when Stephanie visited the new mother and baby, gave the foal its first shots and took blood tests. He went with Luke to buy feed in a bigger town fifty miles away.

He'd stayed late Tuesday and Wednesday talking to Luke about ranching, and Luke invited other ranchers over Wednesday night, as well. It was a good distraction. Not just from Lisa, but also from the fact that he was no longer a SEAL. He'd never liked being inactive, which was one reason he still swam every morning and ran every night. But he needed more than exercise; he needed a goal.

He didn't delude himself. If he did decide to try ranching, it would take months, maybe a year or more, to do the research and get the financing. It would be more years before he could build anything that would turn a profit.

Luke gave Jubal the list of horses for the day. "Start with Rob Roy," he said. "He hasn't had any exercise in the past few days. He's a cutting horse, can make a turn on a dime, so be sure to pay attention. Tracy will be around if you need anything."

Jubal nodded.

Luke walked back to his pickup and headed for a meeting he had in town. Jubal knew Rob Roy, had fed him several times and given him treats. He approached him with a carrot, and the short stocky bay seemed appreciative, even more so when Jubal walked him out to the tack area and saddled him. He sensed the horse's eagerness. Since the rustling problem, they'd been in the barn at night rather than allowed to wander.

He started out slow, walking the bay around the ring, loosening him up. After fifteen minutes, Jubal had adjusted to the horse's gait and quick movement. He opened the gate and rode Rob Roy into the large open pasture.

He kept him to a trot until he was sure of his control, then allowed him to stretch into a gallop. It was like riding the wind.

It felt like that was where he belonged. He recalled the rodeo, the dust and the crowds and the pride when his father placed. What he remembered most was being lifted onto Dusty's back and riding around the corral as he was applauded by his father's friends, a feeling unmatched until he'd earned the SEAL Trident.

As they approached the stream, he slowed to a trot. He was beginning to anticipate the horse's movements and relaxed slightly as they started back.

Lisa popped back in his head. He kept hearing the fear in her voice when she talked about Gordon, the spark of passion in her eyes when he'd kissed her, the melding of their bodies for just a few seconds.

For five days, he'd fought the impulse to call her. At the same time, he felt guiltly about not calling Gordon regarding the riding lessons he'd asked about. But Lisa made it pretty clear she didn't approve and he wanted to respect that.

Inexplicably, it had stung deeply. It also made him the bad guy with Gordon because he couldn't tell the kid why without furthering the rift between sister and brother.

And now, due to his own earlier careless words, Luke had done what Jubal had tried so hard not to do...

Rob Roy made a sudden turn. Jubal was ejected from the saddle right over the bay's head. The landing hurt like hell and it took a moment to realize what had happened, but he was thankful for the hard hat Luke insisted he wear at all times. He explored his body. No open wounds. No breaks. But he knew he would have a mass of bruises the next day.

Rob Roy immediately returned to him, nudged him as if in apology or maybe it was more like "pay attention after this." Jubal stood and painfully mounted, knowing he would be even sorer in the morning. It had been his fault and a good lesson. He'd become too confident and allowed his mind to wander to the next day, to seeing Gordon and his sister.

When he returned to the stable, Luke was returning in the pickup.

He stepped down, walked over to Jubal and his gaze roamed over Jubal's grass-stained clothes.

"Have a little tumble?" the rancher observed.

Jubal knew he looked sheepish. "Rob Roy made some of those little turns you warned me about."

"You aren't the first and won't be the last. You aren't a horseman until you take your first fall," Luke said.

Despite growing discomfort throughout his body, Jubal liked the sound of "horseman."

"How long have you had him?"

"Six months. I took him as a favor for someone who retired from the cattle business. I'm trying to find the right buyer for him."

"I hope you warn whoever it is."

"I will," Luke said. He hesitated, then added, "I hope you don't take it wrong, Jubal, but I talked to Al Monroe today. He's president of the bank and has insurance and real estate interests."

Jubal nodded cautiously. "I believe I met him at the pageant."

"I went to see him about some insurance business. I told him about your situation, as well. Said you might be interested in some ranch land. He suggested you come see him."

"I'm not ready for that..."

"I know," Luke said. "And I told him that. But before you get too interested, you might want to talk to him anyway."

Jubal hesitated. "Trying to get rid of me?"

"Hell, no, you're the best worker I've ever had and I don't even pay you. You're a natural with horses. I can't believe you haven't done more riding, although I suspect your experience overseas taught you a lot. Still, I don't know when I've seen anyone learn as quickly as you have. Especially without grumbling."

"You just haven't heard it," Jubal said.

Luke grinned. "I hope you stick around the area." He handed Jubal a business card. "Al comes across as a hard-ass, but don't take it personally. There's a heart in there somewhere."

Jubal just nodded, wondering whether he

wasn't being carried too far, too fast, on a wave of need. "Thanks."

Luke looked at the bruises already coloring Luke's left arm. "Why don't you take off, get some rest after your fall?"

"No, thanks." Jubal smiled.

Luke just shrugged and left.

Jubal was hungry when he finished the list five hours later. It seemed every bone in his body ached. He didn't have much food left at the cabin and he didn't want to run into anyone or answer any questions in town. Most of all he didn't want to see Lisa or Gordon.

He decided to try the Rusty Nail. He figured the owners wouldn't object to his less-than-respectable appearance, and it was unlikely he'd run into the Reddings. He'd washed thoroughly in the barn before leaving, but his clothes were stained and smelled like horse.

Out of habit, he took a table in the corner where he could see the rest of the room. In a matter of seconds, a pretty waitress approached him. "You must be the new vet." She smiled. "Sorry I missed you the other night, but I've heard the guys talk about you. Jubal, isn't it?"

He should have been surprised, but he wasn't. He was learning how fast information flowed in Covenant Falls. He nodded.

"Welcome," she said. "I'm Nancy. What can I get you?"

"One of those great burgers and onion rings. I'm starved."

"And what to drink?"

"A local beer. You pick it."

"Gotcha."

The beer was there almost as fast as the words left his mouth. It came in an ice cold bottle just like Jubal preferred. He looked around. The bar was half full but most of the occupants were couples, and he felt the odd man out. He didn't understand why it bothered him. He usually preferred to be alone rather than part of a group, especially since his discharge.

His first empty beer was replaced by a second, and came along with his hamburger, which tasted as good as advertised. Tastier than Maude's, but that might've just been the ropes of grilled onions on top.

Nancy was right about the onion rings, too.

He left a large tip on the table when he finished, a little after six, then drove to the cabin, looking forward to a hot shower and what? Another evening alone...

It had also been more difficult than he'd imagined to stay away from Lisa. There was no mistaking her response to him. She felt the same explosive attraction he did. It was in the kiss, in the way she rested in his arm, in her gaze. But she definitely was not the woman for him for more reasons than he could count...

He tried to erase her from his mind and concentrate on what Luke had said about the banker. To have any kind of discussion, Jubal knew he should put together a list of assets, though a horse ranch probably wasn't a banker's first choice as a sound investment, anyway, even if he had a substantial down payment.

He mentally counted his assets. He'd received a large check for two years of back pay when returning to the States. He had banked his three hundred thousand in two re-up bonuses, and over the years he'd usually saved half of his monthly paycheck. He managed most of his own finances rather than using a broker, putting half into CDs when the rates were high, and when they expired and the rates went down, he bought blue chip stocks that had dividends.

Over the years he'd done well. But he knew how fast it could disappear buying land and horses.

When he reached the cabin, Jubal saw Gordon. He was sitting on the bench he'd built.

Jubal stopped the car on the road and walked over, to Gordon, joining him on the bench.

"You were going to see about horseback riding lessons," Gordon said, looking straight ahead.

"Did you sister say it was okay?"

"She didn't say no."

"She just wasn't overly enthusiastic?" Jubal asked.

Gordon didn't answer. But disillusionment was in his eyes. Another adult had disappointed him.

Jubal wanted to tell him that the problem might well be solved, that Lisa planned to bring them to the ranch. Once there, he was sure Luke could talk her into lessons.

"Can't *you* say something?"

He'd already been told, more or less, to back off, but he couldn't say that, either.

"Luke Daniels, who owns the ranch, ran into her today and invited the three of you to come see the new foal. I expect when you get home, she'll tell you about it."

"For real?"

"For real."

"And I can ride?"

"Yeah."

"Did you have anything to do with it?"

"It was Luke's idea. He's a good guy. You'll like him."

"You think Lisa will do it?"

"I think you should let her bring it up herself." Jubal didn't like being duplicitous, especially with people he liked. He changed direction. "The foal is only a week old but he's galloping almost as fast as his mom." Truth was, he'd been wanting to ask Lisa all week whether she'd like to see the foal. How many times had he picked up the phone and put it back down? He wondered if Luke sensed that.

"How's school?" he asked after a silence.

Gordon shrugged.

"Go out for any sports?"

"Teams are pretty much set."

"What about track? You have the body for it. It's an individual sport."

"Is that what you did?"

"Yeah."

"Why?"

"I knew I wanted to go into the military."

"Why?"

"I was angry," he admitted.

"Why?"

"You need to expand your vocabulary."

"You're avoiding the question," Gordon charged.

"Yeah, I am. Ever thought about being a lawyer?" Jubal asked.

"I did want to be an engineer," Gordon said.

"You don't now?"

"I don't know. I got into some…trouble."

"That shouldn't stop you if you get your act together. I think you would make a good engineer."

"Why?"

"There's that vocabulary problem again. But I'll answer. I gave you a project. You selected plans, made changes and did a damn good job putting it together."

"Why did you do that? Why didn't you call the cops when you found me on the deck?"

"I didn't want to."

Gordon's lips turned up in a grin. "I don't get you."

"Why don't you go home?" he said. "Your sister might be worried about you."

"You really think she'll let me ride?"

"Yeah. She cares about you. A lot. From what I understand she gave up a lot for you and your sister, but mainly you."

Gordon looked at him for a long moment. "I guess."

"No guessing. And you might think about telling her about the first night you were here."

Gordon blanched. "She'll ground me forever."

"I don't think so. I think she'll respect you."

Gordon shook his head. "I've been reading about the SEALs," he said, changing the subject. "They're pretty awesome."

Jubal didn't reply.

"How long were you a SEAL?"

"Nearly twenty years."

"You ever kill a terrorist?"

"We can't talk about it," Jubal said. "Even if I could, I wouldn't. You're far better off as an engineer."

Gordon stood up. "I guess I better go."

Jubal watched him go. He feared his message hadn't gotten through.

CHAPTER EIGHTEEN

LISA FINISHED HER last appointment at noon on Saturday. She told Janie she could go. She locked the clinic and walked the few blocks home.

She'd told Luke Daniels they would try to drop by around noon if that was okay. Kerry was thrilled and was waiting at the door when Lisa arrived. Gordon was in the kitchen eating a sandwich, but he'd dressed in a new pair of jeans and an actual shirt instead of his favorite worn T-shirt, which was his usual Saturday uniform.

Lisa ate a quick sandwich, too, but Kerry was too excited to eat. They were going to an actual horse ranch. She loved Beauty, the horse she was riding at the Mannings' house but she looked forward to seeing the foal.

Lisa finished the sandwich, then changed into jeans and a light blue denim shirt.

It was less than ten minutes later when they arrived at the ranch. The gate was open and she drove up to the ranch house. There were five other cars there, as well, including one she recognized as Jubal Pierce's.

To the right of the house was a large barn with another large building behind it. An outdoor riding ring was to the left. There were several fenced-off pastures. She immediately focused on one that had a horse with a foal running and jumping behind it.

She recognized Luke Daniels as he emerged from the barn with another man. Jubal! He carried a riding hat in gloved hands and wore riding pants and plain leather boots. The sleeves of his blue shirt were rolled up to expose deeply tanned arms. She didn't remember them being that tanned. As the two men came near, she noticed Jubal's eyes looked even bluer than she remembered.

He took her breath away.

Somehow, she moved forward, pasting a smile on her face. "Mr. Daniels," she said. "Thanks for inviting us. You remember Gordon and Kerry?"

"Sure do. Come over and meet the newest resident of Covenant Falls Stables. He led them to the fence of the closest pasture. The mare trotted over, the foal by her side. Jubal handed Kerry a carrot to give to the mare. Lisa's sister stepped up on the lower cross bar of the fence, leaned over and offered the treat.

The mare took it, and the foal looked up at her. Pure joy shone in Kerry's eyes.

"Too soon for the little one," Luke said. "He'll still be nursing for a while."

"It's a colt?" Kerry asked.

Luke nodded. "And he's all boy."

"He's so cute. What's his name?"

"Ask Mr. Pierce," Luke said. "He helped bring him into the world."

Jubal raised an eyebrow. "I brought in the hay," he corrected. Lisa noticed he didn't provide the name.

"He was on foal watch," Luke said.

She had a hard time imagining him sitting still for hours to watch a foal being born. He seemed to be all barely restrained energy. But she knew how miraculous it was to watch a healthy baby being delivered. It never ceased to amaze her. Had it affected him the same way?

She wished she knew what he thought, but she, who was usually so good at reading patients, couldn't read him at all. He'd been quiet at the supper at Eve's when she first arrived and again the night of the pageant, and yet, she'd sensed he was absorbing everything—the words, the people, the interaction. Since then, he'd revealed very limited information about himself, his past and his thoughts, even during their time at the cabin.

She knew more about him through the changes she'd seen in Gordon, and that was more intuition than actual knowledge of what had gone on between them. She only knew Gordon seemed to be on an upswing.

But now she saw yet another side of Jubal. The

mare had gone straight to him, not to her actual owner, Luke Daniels, and allowed her foal to nuzzle Jubal's hand while protecting her baby from the others.

Even more telling, he'd worked for Luke just a short time and yet the man treated him like an equal rather than a hired hand. He seemed perfectly at home on the ranch, more at home than she'd seen him before.

He was an enigma to her. An enigma that fascinated, attracted and aroused her.

And scared the hell out of her.

He moved aside, giving her half of a carrot. "Want to make a friend?" he asked.

Lisa took it and offered it to the mare, who gently pulled it from her hand before scarfing it down. "How many carrots do you have in your pockets?" Lisa asked.

"A bunch. The grocery store is running out," Jubal said with a grin. "They ensure a warm welcome."

He seemed uncharacteristically unguarded and relaxed. She was stunned by his smile, its magnetism and the pure need that pulsed along her nerves and settled in her stomach.

Luke broke in. "My wife is giving a barrel racing lesson in the arena out back. Would you like to watch?"

"I would!" Kerry said.

"Good. Why don't you two come with me,

and maybe Jubal can introduce Gordon to the horses—if that's okay with you, Doctor. Jubal can show him how to tack up a horse and ride him around the ring."

Lisa wasn't sure that was the best idea, but she looked from Kerry's eager face to Gordon's pleading one and agreed. Luke led them through the barn, introducing them to the few stabled horses. "Most are in the pastures," he explained.

The name of each horse was inserted in a slot in the door. The stabled horses poked their heads out to see who was visiting, and Kerry made a point of saying hello to each one. Lisa noticed her sister seemed torn between lingering with the horses and watching the practice session. But then they were outside, taking a short path to the large building behind the stables.

Inside was a large ring. Three barrels were arranged in a cloverleaf formation, and a girl about Kerry's age riding a gray horse was talking to Tracy, whom Lisa had met earlier that week at Maude's. She noticed several others nearby, watching, as well.

After a discussion, the rider rode to the entrance of the ring, turned and raced around the barrels at what seemed an incredible speed. The whole thing was over in seconds.

"In barrel racing," Luke said, "the fastest time wins. It's not judged on style, only the clock, but the riders have to maneuver at high speeds. Precise control is imperative."

They watched for another twenty minutes, then Luke suggested they check on Gordon.

"Can I stay and watch?" Kerry begged.

Lisa looked at Luke, who nodded. "Sure. No problem. They'll probably be here another thirty minutes."

Luke led Lisa back through the barn and out the front doors. When they emerged, Lisa saw Gordon wearing a riding hat, sitting astride a dark brown horse in the riding ring.

Jubal attached a long rope to the horse's halter and stood in the middle of the ring while giving commands to Gordon. "Walk. Stop. Slow trot. Halt."

Then he told Gordon to take his hands of the reins and repeated the same commands.

"That's to help him learn to balance," Luke said as he watched beside her. "Your brother has a good seat."

Lisa knew nothing about riding. She'd watched as Eve had worked with Kerry but she never expected Gordon to be interested, as well, not until he raised the subject, and even then she thought it had more to do with Jubal than the actual riding.

She was beginning to understand the connection Jubal had with Gordon. One of the biggest things missing from his life was a strong male presence. He probably couldn't pick a stronger one than Jubal Pierce. Apprehension ran through her. The last thing he needed was to find one and lose him.

She'd hoped the police chief would've been that model. She had liked Clint immediately, and he lived here. Permanently. He had the open, friendly personality that she thought would appeal to her brother. Instead, he'd picked a quiet loner. Like himself.

Lisa continued to watch them. She didn't know if Jubal had taught before, but he was good at it. Patient. Calm. Encouraging. He took the rope off, and Gordon controlled the reins. At Jubal's command, he went from a walk to a slow trot. Back to a walk. Halted. Started again. When Gordon wanted to go faster, Jubal said no. To her surprise, Gordon didn't argue.

The lesson ended, and Jubal walked over to her. "Do you have time for him to cool off the horse and groom him? It's part of the process he should learn."

She nodded, trying not to wonder how it would feel to be in those muscled arms for more than a few seconds. "Kerry's still watching the barrel rider."

"Why don't we go inside and get something cool to drink?" Jubal asked. She nodded as he led the way into a room loaded with saddles and other riding equipment. He went to a small fridge and took out two bottles of water and handed one to her. It was ice cold.

He took a long pull from the bottle, then splashed some on his face. She watched as water dribbled down his lips. There was something elementally masculine about the picture that made her knees weak.

She decided not to be dainty and did the same. It felt good on her face as well as her throat.

He grinned. "Good?"

He looked as if he belonged here. Surrounded by salddles and bits and halters. His shirt stuck to his chest and he might as well have a sign: I am Man.

It scared her, and fascinated her and enchanted her.

He reached over and wiped a drip of water from her chin with a finger. It was both provocative and…caring.

The door opened and Luke entered. "Jubal," he started, then looked from Jubal to her and back again.

"Maybe I should come back later…"

Lisa knew her face was probably scarlet, but she squeezed between Luke and the door. "I wanted some water," she said, "and saw the trophies. They are really impressive." She was babbling.

"Most of those belong to Tracy," Luke said.

Jubal moved then. "I have to get back to Gordon," he said and disappeared out the door.

Lisa was left standing there, and she suspected her face was strawberry red. She hated losing control, but she had been doing a lot of that lately. She stepped back to the open door. "Thanks for asking us over today. I would like to pay for Gordon's lesson."

"No way. You're an invited guest," Luke said.

"What if he wants to continue them?"

"Is it okay if Jubal teaches him?"

No, she screamed internally. Outlwardly she tried to keep her cool. "Has he had any experience?" She didn't doubt Jubal's ability, not after watching him with Gordon, but she hoped to tempt out another kernel of information.

"Not teaching, but he's just a damn good rider and great with the horses. I'll be there with him because I want him as an instructor. I want to keep him as long as possible."

How long would that be? He would be galloping in and out of their lives. Could she knowingly subject her brother to that?

"There wouldn't be any charge," he added.

"I couldn't allow that," she said.

"It's Jubal's time, and hell, I'm not paying him anything."

"You're not?" She couldn't stop the question bursting from her lips.

"He won't take a salary. He just wants to learn

about ranching. He puts in a good fifty to sixty hours a week, too. Heck of a good man."

Lisa was stunned. She shouldn't be. Nothing about Jubal should surprise her now. "I still wouldn't feel right," she said. "Why don't I throw in free medical care if you need it?"

"Done," he said. "I'm relieved you're here. We have injuries now and then. A fall, a horse stepping on someone's foot. Concussions. Doc Bradley was great. Always available."

"I'm trying to do the same, but he has a lot of experience on me."

"Saw him yesterday. He says you're doing real good."

That's good to hear."

"Want to go see how your brother's doing?"

They walked to the front of the stable where Gordon was using a thick bristled brush on the horse he'd been riding. The horse seemed to approve, reaching her head around and nickering softly. Jubal sat on a bale of hay. He gave her that slow, crooked smile that made her heart beat a little faster. "He's doing good. He would make a good groom," he added with a grin.

She sat on the bale next to him. "Not exactly the future I planned for him." She paused, then asked, "Would you tell me if he didn't do well?"

"Yeah," he said. "I would."

She believed him. "Thank you," she said softly.

"I like him," he said simply.

She hadn't. She loved Gordon but she hadn't liked him much recently.

The silent admission saddened her. She should have tried harder to understand what he was going through.

Gordon finished cooling his mount. He looked sweaty and sunburned and happy. "We'd better collect your sister and go home," Lisa said. She turned to Jubal. "I suspect we're taking up too much of your time." She paused and then the words came out before she could stop them. "Would you like to come over for dinner tonight?"

"Yes," he said simply. Something else she appreciated about him. His directness.

She looked at her watch. It was already four. "Seven okay?"

He nodded.

She gathered her brother and sister and headed out. On the ride home, Kerry was telling Gordon about the barrel rider and how she wanted to be one. Lisa thought of the expensive-looking horse in the arena and hoped not.

She wondered what the heck she'd been thinking when she'd invited Jubal over for supper. She didn't even have much food at home. Maybe spaghetti with meat sauce. She usually kept ground beef around and she had spaghetti. She would just have to make it. No adult beverages, either... What had she been thinking?

She was thinking she wanted to see him and she certainly owed him after what he'd done for Gordon.

In any event, the deed was done.

As soon as they arrived at home, she looked in the cupboard and found several cans of tomatoes and the spices she'd need. She dumped them in the frying pan, along with chopped onions and some ground round, then put it on to simmer. No adult beverages, but she had chocolate cupcakes brought by one of her patients. They had been one of many such gifts during the past two weeks. A benefit and a curse as she felt her jeans grow tighter.

She took a moment to assess progress. Her sister was setting the table. Her brother was putting his stuff in his bedroom. Who were these well-behaved kids and what had they done with her siblings?

After the sauce was bubbling and a salad was made, she took a shower, then worried about what to wear. She finally just changed her shirt and put her jeans back on. No big deal. The supper was just a thank-you, nothing more. Or so she kept telling herself.

He arrived at seven on the dot. She wasn't surprised. Punctuality had probably been drilled into him during years in the military.

His hair was still damp from either a shower or swimming, and he was clean-shaven. He gave her that quirky one-sided smile as he handed her a bottle. Wine. Thank heavens. She took a deep breath. She'd never experienced this kind of internal confusion before—the rapid beating of her heart, the sudden rush of heat in the pit of her stomach.

She clutched the bottle. "I hope you like spaghetti."

"It's one of my favorites," he said.

Thankfully, Kerry appeared then. "Hello, Mr. Pierce."

"Hello, Kerry," he said with a disarming smile. "Did you like the ranch?"

"I loved the foal. Have you named him yet?"

"Nope. I want to pick just the right one, since it's the first horse I've ever named. Any suggestions?"

He was so easy with Kerry and Gordon. Lisa was good with other people's children, not so much with her own siblings. "I'll open the wine," she said.

He followed her to the kitchen. "Nice house."

"The town provided it," she said. "Most of the furnishings belong to the owner. We left ours in Chicago." It was a reminder that she was only here for a year.

"That must have been tough, leaving everything behind."

"There were as many bad memories as good

ones," she replied as she rummaged in a drawer. "I know I brought a corkscrew."

"Don't need one," he said. "It has a screw top. The guy at liquor store vouched for it. I'm not that good at choosing wine so I just asked for a nice red. I remember that's what you had at supper Saturday night."

She couldn't help but laugh. His blunt honesty always startled her. No man she'd known before would admit they knew nothing about wine. Well, she didn't, either.

"I like wine with screw tops," she admitted. "They keep better."

She put spaghetti in the boiling water and stirred the sauce. Steam rose from the pans. Seemed to hover between them.

She felt the temperature in her blood rise, as well. She looked up and was lost in the intensity of those blue eyes. The silence stretched tautly between them. She wanted to ask so much. But now was not the time or place, and he didn't make conversation easy. He always seemed to keep much of himself off-limits.

"Lisa?" Her sister broke the tension as she came into the kitchen.

Jubal stood back.

Lisa turned off the stove element.

"Can I do anything to help?" Kerry asked.

"You can strain the spaghetti," she said, trying to keep her voice steady. Natural. She feared there was a quaver in it.

She hoped Kerry's presence might cool the temperature in the room. It didn't. Every time she glanced at him, she felt as if she'd been reduced to putty. Dammit.

She managed to get everything together: the spaghetti on the platter, the sauce poured on top, the salad finished. She wished she had some hot bread, but there wasn't any. Kerry poured herself a glass of milk and Gordon helped himself to the iced tea she'd made yesterday.

To her surprise, Gordon carried the conversation. He wanted to know about SEAL training. Was it as bad as he'd heard? Was it true that only one in a hundred applicants made it through? How could someone go through nearly a week with only an hour's sleep?

Lisa felt her fear grow with every question. It competed with the constant somersaults in her stomach, or maybe magnified them. The two males ate is if they'd never had a meal, but she could hardly get a bite down. She finished her glass of wine and Jubal poured her another.

She served the cupcakes, drank the wine. It was refilled. Kerry looked at her with a question in her eyes. Lisa rarely drank more than two glasses but she felt like the proverbial cat on the hot tin roof. The more he sat there, talking more comfortably to her siblings than he had to her, the more an uninhibited need blossomed inside her. It warred against the fear she felt over Gordon's interest in the military, leaving her feeling overwhelmed.

When they finished, Kerry offered to clean up and Gordon said he had to study. Jubal followed her to the living room.

"I should go," he said. "It was a great dinner."

They walked together to the door.

He stepped outside and his hand guided her out with him.

"Do you ever get up early on Sunday morning?" he asked.

They were standing on the front porch. In front of neighbors and God and maybe even her siblings, who were probably looking out the window.

She nodded.

"There's a path near my cabin that leads up the mountain. The sunrise is spectacular from there. I'll have some coffee."

She shouldn't. She knew she shouldn't. She nodded.

"Six a.m.?"

She nodded again.

He gave her that half smile. "Good. Thanks for supper. It was great." Then he turned and walked rapidly to his car.

CHAPTER NINETEEN

THE NIGHT WAS GENTLE. The moon almost full. The stars plentiful. Wispy lacelike clouds floated in and out between them. Jubal never tired of a peaceful night sky.

Storms were different. Thunder and lightning ignited memories. Faces appeared. Dead friends. Dead enemies. He tried to stay inside then. Reading. Watching television. Anything but war movies or violent shoot-'em-ups. He had gone to sleep watching television several times and jerked awake at the sound of gunfire. He'd searched frantically for a weapon.

Clint said his dog helped. So did Josh and Andy. But he felt it would be a crutch. He feared crutches as much as he feared nightmares.

Was he using Luke's ranch as a crutch?

And Lisa? He couldn't remember ever being so attracted on an emotional basis as well as a physical one. But maybe he was just reaching for a life jacket. He drifted off at some point because he woke when the first edge of dawn was visible.

He got up, went inside and made enough coffee to have a cup and fill a thermos.

If she came...

He put on trunks and jogged out to the deck. It was still thirty minutes before six and the air was cool. He dove in the frigid water, which jolted every one of his senses.

Twenty minutes later he was thoroughly awake. After a steaming shower, he'd just finished dressing in jeans and a pullover sweatshirt when he heard a car in the driveway.

He hadn't known whether she would appear or not, but he should have. She had said she would. He imagined she always did what she'd planned or agreed to do. She had grit. Had to, to fight her way through medical school and residency and then abruptly change her life to help her brother.

He grabbed the thermos and went out to meet her.

"Hi," he said as she stepped out of the car. She looked great in a blue pullover sweatshirt and a pair of jeans. She'd braided her hair and pinned it at her back. Her cheeks were flushed, her dark brown eyes full of life.

"Your hair is wet," she said. "Did you take a swim already?"

"It's a habit," he said, then looked at her basket. "What's inside?"

"Every patient who comes to my office seems to feel obligated to bring a cake or pie or other pastry. Kerry and Gordon love it. This happens to be half of a coffee cake that Mrs. Jenkins brought me."

Without more words, he took the basket in one hand and her hand in the other and led her to the path. It was Sunday morning, and he'd noted that Covenant Falls was slow to rise. He doubted anyone saw them.

They made it to the viewpoint at just the right moment. A few clouds suffused the first light into different layers of gold and crimson. An eagle circled above pines that rose high and perfumed the air. Jubal thought it the perfect morning, or maybe it was the company.

They sat on the ground and he poured coffee into the top of the thermos and handed it to her.

The lake looked peaceful, the town like a toy village. He pointed out Luke's ranch.

"Now I know why you come up here," she said. "It's beautiful."

"Have you been to the falls?" he asked.

"Yes. Eve took me and I took Kerry. They're beautiful."

"Too bad. I was about to offer a picnic in appreciation for dinner last night."

"No need. You gave Gordon a free horseback lesson."

"That's my job."

"Not entirely, I think. You love it, don't you?"

"Every minute," he admitted.

She was more at ease than he'd seen her. And she was incredibly appealing. Her smile was quick rather than cautious and those wide brown eyes viewed the valley below with lively interest. He had an overwhelming urge to touch, to hold, to share. He leaned down and kissed her. Heat started at the point where his skin touched hers, then flooded through the rest of his body.

The kiss started light but suddenly became explosive. What was meant to be exploratory turned hungry. Their lips melded in an eager contest. He stopped thinking as the kiss deepened, and their arms found each other.

He broke off, looked down at her, at the earnest face that so charmed him and the expressive eyes that asked many more questions than he could answer. She made him feel alive after months, years, of stuffing feelings in a mental closet.

"I want to experience that world-class kiss you spoke of," she said, surprising him. It probably shouldn't. She was a strong, decisive woman.

"I think maybe this isn't the place," he said. "I'm beginning to think Covenant Falls has eyes and ears everywhere."

"Does anyone even come up here other than that eagle circling around?"

"He could be curious about human mating habits," he quipped, then wondered about the appropriateness of the comment. It was something he would have said to his buddies.

But she laughed, and he loved the sound. He hadn't heard it nearly enough. "Are you trying to avoid living up to the expectation you created?" she asked.

"Is that a challenge?"

"I think it might be," she said with a grin.

"Then I think we should go to the cabin."

"Won't people see us then?"

"Maybe. If anyone is awake. Do Kerry and Gordon know where you are?"

"No. They're never up before nine on Sunday. Kerry stays up late reading, and Gordon stays up late playing games on his phone. I left a note saying I was going out for breakfast."

He stood and offered her his hand...

LISA'S GLANCE SLID down to his hand. Strong and capable. Like everything else about him. She took it, allowing him to lift her as if she weighed no more than a feather. His height seemed to dwarf her as she looked up at him.

The air sizzled between them. A tingling started in the small of her back, working its way upward. It had been there since the first time she'd seen him, but she'd tried to suppress it. There seemed no future in it, and she was practical if nothing else. Why start something that could only end badly?

But that caution didn't matter now. Nothing was real at the moment but Jubal Pierce, the searching look in his eyes, the warmth of his presence, the glow she felt inside when she was with him.

She'd never felt this way before and she wanted to explore its width and breath. They were silent as they walked, hand in hand, down the path. Every one of her senses seemed more acute. Birds were chirping louder. Some small animal made its way through the underbrush. The wildflowers were more vivid than she remembered. And the sun was now a golden ball in the sky while a seemingly transparent moon still hung around. All was right with the world. Her fingers tightened around his.

They reached his porch and went inside. The door was barely closed when his lips caressed hers. Swirling eddies of desire enveloped her, eclipsing everything else. A whisper at the back of her mind tried to caution her, but it was chaff in the wind compared to the power of the intense need inside.

Yesterday, watching him with Luke and Gordon had crystalized so much. There had been the respect the rancher showed Jubal. Even more important was Jubal's patience and an innate understanding of her brother that touched her as nothing else could. It only added to the mind-blowing physical attraction she felt.

Leave, she told herself. *Run before you get in too deep.* He would leave, or she would leave, and there was little chance for permanence. But then, she couldn't resist the magic of the moment.

He reached up and touched her cheek, running his fingers along her cheekbones. Lightly. Gently, as if touching something precious and breakable. His fingers hesitated as they reached her chin, then they dropped away, and his arms went around her and pulled her against him.

She looked up at him. Her body pressed against his hard form and she relished its warmth, even through the clothing. She felt his heart beat and knew hers was pounding, as well. Her hands twisted through his thick hair and then their lips met again and there were new explorations that spun her into a world without boundaries or rules or fears.

Any remaining reservations slipped away as the kiss deepened further, and she felt intoxicated by sensations she'd never known before. She felt him grow hard against her, and she wanted to draw him even closer. Every part of her body ached to connect with his.

A storm was building inside her, feeding on his hungry kisses, on every touch. Her body hummed with all the new sensations—wonderful, delicious feelings as she heard him moan.

"Lisa?" She knew the question and she knew the answer.

"Yes," she said simply. "Do you have...?"

"Yes."

She leaned her head against his hard chest and then she was in his arms again. He carried her to the bedroom, setting her down on the neatly made bed. He was undressing her, and she was unbuttoning his shirt. She saw the scars again, and she hurt for all the pain he'd been through.

She momentarily forgot about them as he finished undressing her and then kissed her again, his hands running along her body, stroking. Her skin was alive with feeling, with wanting.

He hesitated. She saw it in his eyes. "Are you sure?" he asked.

"Don't stop." She ran her fingers along the strong lines of his face, then the scars on his chest, as if caressing them would make them go away.

Their lips touched, this time with a searching tenderness, a savoring of wild emotions. His mouth ignited a warmth that seeped through her, settling into her core.

She wanted more. More of his strength. More of him. She wanted to give and take, and she wanted both things in the most urgent way.

It wasn't her first time, but she'd never felt this kind of connection. It struck her with the power of lightning.

Their lips touched again, and he trailed kisses down her throat, making her shudder with spasms of desire. Every nerve was alive, every part of her responding with hunger.

He turned away for a moment, then returned, arched above her and entered. Slowly, carefully, then his body assumed a rhythm of its own as his mouth caressed hers. Her body responded like a chorus, moving in such complete harmony that it seemed to her they were born to be together.

He plunged in once more and waves of pleasure flowed through her.

She didn't know how much time passed before he rolled over, took her hand in his and kissed her with such tenderness she never wanted to leave his side.

She couldn't speak. Her emotions were running too strong to be properly expressed. She laid her head on his chest and her fingers tightened around his.

They were both silent, then she looked at the clock. It was eight a.m. Only two hours since she'd arrived, but it seemed much longer. Her life changed in those two hours. She didn't know what would happen now, but she did know she had changed.

She needed to go, although part of her wanted to ask some questions first. She didn't know nearly enough about his past, any relationships he might have been in or why he'd landed here in Covenant Falls in the first place. But she didn't have time to ask those things now. She had to get home. She hadn't expected to stay this long. She'd expected to see a sunrise.

Liar.

"How did you get these scars?" she asked, tracing her fingers over them. Something told her they had something to do with him coming here, something that changed his life.

"I was held prisoner by a rebel group in Africa," he said, his tone steady. "Four of us were on a mission to extract a civilian medical group in a dangerous area. I won't go into detail, but the civilians were already dead and we were ambushed. Someone had told them we were coming.

"Two of the team died instantly, another died of wounds several hours later. I was wounded and taken prisoner. I was traveling as a civilian doctor and other members of the team as paid guards. They never knew who we really were.

"The only thing that saved me was one of the rebels was badly wounded and I did a 'hail Mary' and indicated I could save him. I did, and they kept me around to tend their wounded. I was beaten when I didn't succeed."

She listened as he told the rest of the story in an emotionless voice.

"No one knew what had happened to the team until I escaped," he finished. "The team had just disappeared as had the medical unit."

"How long?"

"Two years, give or take a few weeks. I was passed around from one group to another. I finally escaped, but I'd lost a lot of weight and there was permanent damage to my joints. I couldn't qualify as an active SEAL any longer."

"You didn't want to leave, did you?"

His arms tightened around her. "The navy was my family." The words said more than the tone of his voice. She had never met anyone with so much self-control.

She'd settled in his arms now and took his right hand in one of hers, holding it tight. "What about your mother?"

"My mother's family didn't think much of my father—or me, for that matter. We ruined my mother's perfect future. She remarried and her new husband shared those feelings. I guess I didn't help things. But they bad-mouthed my dad all the time, even after he died."

"You don't see her."

"She died in an auto accident while I was in Africa."

"I'm so sorry," she said, tightening the hold on his hand. "How did you happen to join the SEALs?"

"It was all I wanted to do since I was a young kid. I read everything I could about them.

"I was seventeen and had just graduated from high school when I joined the navy. I needed parental consent and my stepfather was more than happy to give it.

"I had to wait until my eighteenth birthday to apply for SEALs training but I had been preparing for years. I ran track and was on the swimming team in high school."

"I would call that determined."

"Probably no less so in your path to become a doctor."

"But why?" she asked.

He shrugged. "Maybe it was in my DNA, or maybe they represented the best to me, and I wanted to be part of that. A hard-ass unit that didn't take crap from anyone. Once you're in, you don't want to get out. The brotherhood is too strong."

"You miss it?"

"Part of me will always miss it. The adrenaline rushes. The friendships. The knowledge you're doing something important for your country, something that a lot of people can't do. But it's no profession for a married man. It's too hard on wives."

"That's why you never married?"

"That's what I believed," he said slowly. "But maybe not. Maybe it was the wreckage of my parents' marriage. I think when my mother left and took me with her, my dad just didn't care anymore. I looked up some guys who'd known him around the same time I joined the navy. They said he became more and more reckless after we left."

"So now what? Where to after you leave here?"

"Honestly, I don't know. I just got in the car and started driving, thinking I would figure it out somewhere along the way," he said with a frankness that no longer surprised her. "I feel like a tumbleweed now."

He hesitated, then added, "I planned to see the families of the other SEALs who died on that mission. I wrote them letters, but I owe it to them to visit in person, tell them about their son or husband or father. I'll still do that."

She snuggled into him. There was nothing to say, nothing to relieve the obvious pain and guilt that he survived and they didn't. She wondered if that was the real reason he swam in frigid water every morning and ran in the middle of the night.

She touched the tattoo of the trident and bit her lip to keep a tear from falling. She could feel the weight of his losses. "Is that why you're so good with Gordon? You knew what it was like to lose people you love."

He rubbed her arm. "Maybe."

"You've been good for him."

He didn't say anything for a minute, then asked, "Are you going to tell him about this morning?"

"I'm going to tell him I came over here and watched the sunrise from your mountain."

"If he asks anything more?"

"I won't give him a detailed report or anything, but I won't lie to him. It just makes things worse in the long run." She stirred herself. "I really do have to go. They usually don't get up early but..."

He nodded and stood. "Want a quick shower?"

She definitely needed one. She probably smelled like sex. He gave her a hand and pulled her up, then kissed her lightly. "I'll have some coffee ready."

Fifteen minutes later, she was on her way home, knowing that her world had been forever changed by Jubal and the connection she felt to him.

Would her siblings notice? Would she look as different as she felt?

She thought about swinging by Maude's to pick up some rolls as an excuse, but they already had so many baked goods at the house. She had done her best to put her hair back in order, and touch up her makeup. Her clothes didn't look too wrinkled after ending up on the floor of Jubal's bedroom. She smiled at remembering how quickly they'd discarded them. Then she smiled at being able to smile. No regrets this time. Not ever.

When she reached home, her sister was up, drinking a glass of orange juice.

"Good morning," she said. "Is your brother up yet?"

"Nope."

Relief flooded her.

"Where were you?" Kerry asked.

She wasn't going to lie. "Watching a sunrise. Mr. Pierce invited me over. He said it was spectacular, and it was."

"Maybe next week I can see it, too," her sister said, obviously accepting her explanation.

"If you can get up that early."

"Where did you watch it from?"

"That mountain at the end of Lake Road. You can see the entire valley from there, as well as the entire town. There's probably a great sunset, too. We can take a picnic up there this evening if you like." She avoided saying it was next to Jubal's cabin. *Was that lying by omission?* She got busy making a pot of coffee.

"Want some eggs? Pancakes? Biscuits?" She had several cans of biscuits that you just popped in the oven. And she wanted to change the subject.

"Pancakes would be great," Kerry said. "Do you like Mr. Pierce?"

"Sure, don't you?" *Was deflection also a form of lying?*

"Yeah, he's hot. And nice, even if he doesn't say much."

"Well, he won't be here long. Neither will we."

Her sister was looking at her with speculation in her eyes. Of course she would.

Gordon walked in, his long hair still tousled. "What's for breakfast?"

"Kerry picked pancakes, so pancakes, it is. Or you can have some of the coffee cake that's left."

"Pancakes sound good."

Lisa saw her sister look startled. Usually it was

a fight. If she wanted pancakes, he wanted eggs and sausage. "Any plans for today?" she asked.

"I thought I would bike over to Mr. Daniels's ranch. Maybe I could do a few things for him, too. Like Mr. Pierce. Earn enough for lessons."

"I'll pay for them," Lisa said.

"I would rather work for them."

Kerry's mouth fell open. Lisa's own stomach dropped. It should have been a good sign but deep down she feared it wasn't. "It's a long way," she said.

"I know, but I need to build up my muscles. I'm thinking about trying out for the track team, too."

Lisa's stomach flopped again. "What about schoolwork?"

"I did it last night. It's easy."

"That's not what you said in Chicago."

He shrugged, went to the fridge and poured himself a glass of orange juice.

She waited for Kerry to say something about this morning, but she didn't. Instead, her gaze was on her brother. They hadn't seemed close in the last few months, when Gordon started ignoring her and running around with boys Kerry clearly didn't like. They teamed up, though, in their opposition to moving to Colorado. Now both of them were settling in, and appeared happier than they'd been since their mother's death.

I'm only going to be here a year. And Jubal? How long would he be here?

She recalled his exact words. *"I just got in the car and started driving, thinking I would figure it out somewhere along the way. I feel like a tumbleweed..."*

An honest answer. A warning. She just didn't think she could heed it, and if not, what damage would she cause her already broken family?

CHAPTER TWENTY

LISA KEPT HERSELF busy most of Sunday morning.
She did some overdue cleaning, then took a lei-
surely bath. Kerry worked on homework so she'd
be finished in time for her riding lesson at Eve's;
she couldn't wait to tell Eve about the new foal.

Gordon asked if he could drive the car to
Luke's ranch. Lisa agreed as long as he, too, finished his homework first.

At two, Eve picked up Kerry, and Lisa walked
to the clinic to do some paperwork which seemed
endless. She wished she could stop thinking about
Jubal but she couldn't. She kept reliving his kiss,
the feel of his body on hers, the ease of being with
him. And yet there was another voice telling her
she was headed for heartbreak.

She'd been working an hour when she received
a call from a frantic husband. His wife had started
labor more than six weeks early. Her contractions
were coming fast, and she'd had a quick labor
with her previous pregnancy.

Lisa asked the husband if he could bring her to
the clinic. Since the baby was so early, she would

have preferred sending the patient to the Pueblo hospital, which had the facilities for preemies, but she didn't think there was time. She checked with an air ambulance but none were available at the time. Better here than on the road somewhere.

The patient, Selma Weeks, arrived ten minutes later. Selma was in transition, the final stage of labor. The moment Lisa got her on the bed, she started pushing and screaming. Ten minutes later, the baby's head crowned. It was small, just five pounds, and its first protesting cry was weak.

"A girl, a beautiful little girl," Lisa told the mother as she laid the baby on the mother's stomach.

Because the baby was more than a month early and appeared to be having difficulty breathing, she told Janie to declare an emergency to get an air ambulance faster. She gave the baby oxygen while Janie made the necessary calls, including calling the police to block off Main Street.

The air ambulance finally arrived and Lisa accompanied the mother and baby.

She waited at the Pueblo hospital until all the tests results were back. The baby would have to stay in the NICU while her lungs grew stronger, but the doctors there were optimistic she'd be fine.

It was ten in the evening before Lisa was ready to go. Except she didn't have her car. It was too late to call anyone, and she didn't want Gordon driving alone this late at night.

After checking in with the kids to make sure they both got home okay, she decided to call Jubal.

He answered after the first ring.

"Do you always answer so promptly at ten p.m.?"

"Your name showed up on the phone. Not many people call me—the ones that do are usually important."

"I'm afraid I'm a bit of a damsel in distress at the moment," she said, relieved that he'd answered the phone.

"How can I help?"

"I'm at the hospital in Pueblo. Not as a patient," she added hurriedly. "I came with a patient in the air ambulance. I need a ride home and you said you don't sleep much…"

"I'm on my way."

"Thank you so much," she said, then gave him rough directions. He hung up right after, which was par for the course with him. He'd said more this morning than he'd said in all their other conversations combined.

She looked in on the baby in prenatal care. She was so small. A surge of satisfaction ran through her. She might well have saved a life today. A new one. She'd thought she would miss that in a small town, miss the rhythm of a large hospital's emergency room, but this was every bit as rewarding.

She went to the urgent care waiting room, knowing there would be coffee. She poured a cup and sat in one of the chairs. Not for long. She was antsy, both from the adrenaline hangover and the fact she'd called Jubal over anyone else.

Why did she do that? Why did she feel so certain he would come? She ended up being right about that, but why did it seem the most natural thing in the world?

Maybe it was the ease of this morning. They had understood each other without many words. Everything about it had just felt right.

There had been a tenderness that couldn't be feigned, in the way he touched her, looked at her. She felt quite sure he hadn't trusted the reason he'd left the SEALs with many people, but he'd shared it with her.

Or maybe a small part of her simply wanted to share the awe that she felt in bringing a new life into the world, just as he'd witnessed a few nights ago in Luke Daniels's barn.

Different but both miraculous.

She had another cup of coffee, then went downstairs to an almost empty front hall. She checked her text messages. There was one from Janie: Are you all right?

She shot back: Fine. I'll be back in the office tomorrow.

She called home for the second time and told Kerry she would be home late and not to wait up.

It was about an hour and fifteen minutes before Jubal arrived. She went outside when he drove up and was inside his car before he could get out.

"Thank you," she said as he turned the car toward Covenant Falls. "I didn't know who to call."

"Glad you called me. What happened?"

She told him. "No matter how many times you deliver a baby, it's always awe-inspiring." She angled her position so she could see him. "I imagine you felt a little like that with the foal."

"Except the mother did all the work," he said. "We were just there for moral support." He glanced at her. "It must be really gratifying to save lives."

She felt she was beginning to know him now, understand the nuances of his thoughts even if he didn't say the words.

"The protectors are as essential as the healers," she said, thinking about how much she'd changed in the past few days. Like so many who didn't actually know warriors, it was so easy to stick to the stereotype. She didn't think anyone could pigeonhole Jubal. He was so much more complex than that.

She studied him. He was dressed in his usual jeans and T-shirt. He glanced over and grinned. It was so unexpected she almost didn't grin back. But she couldn't help it. They were silly, stupid grins, the kind you get when something extraordinarily good happens that you didn't expect.

They were silent for several moments, the easy companionship preventing any awkwardness. The traffic slacked off when they left the city limits and headed on a state road toward the mountains.

"Gordon came to the ranch this afternoon," he said. "He wanted to know if he could pay for lessons by working at the ranch."

"And did Luke agree?"

"You betcha. He loves free labor. But it's up to you."

"What do you think?" She was beginning to trust his instincts with Gordon more than her own.

"I think it would be good for him. His biggest problem is impatience. He wants to do stuff he's not prepared to do, but he definitely has a feel for riding. I think Luke can keep him in line. Track would also be good for him."

Lisa stiffened. She suddenly remembered something he said earlier this morning. He wanted to do track and swimming to prepare for the military. Anxiety bubbled inside her. "He hasn't spoken to you about the military, has he?" The minute the words popped out, she knew they sounded shrill. Not only that, they sounded like a condemnation of all he was.

He stiffened slightly, but didn't say anything. The comfortable silence was gone.

Lisa wished she could take it back or, at least,

change the way it'd come out. But she was scared. She'd already lost so much—a father, a mother, a best friend… The latter to the military. She would fight until her dying breath to keep Gordon from doing the same.

So why was she so attracted to someone who was clearly military stock from head to toe? He was so disciplined. Never a minute late or early. Kept a home so clean you could eat off the floor. That darn competence in everything he did. He never mentioned the military, though; he didn't have to. You looked at him and just knew.

Of course, he was so much more than that, too. The instinctive bond he had with Gordon, the respect he drew from Luke and pretty much everyone who met him. The softening of his eyes when he showed off the foal. His gentleness that morning. He was a good man. An exceptional man.

But none of that changed the fact that he was also military, and her brother was obviously influenced.

It scared her. It really scared her.

They were nearly to Covenant Falls when he spoke again in that neutral voice. "I'm not encouraging him to join the military, Lisa. Track is good for a lot of reasons, mainly self-discipline."

"Why Gordon?" she asked. It was the question she'd been wanting to ask from the beginning. "Why have you taken him under your wing like this?"

"Because he came by my cabin." He took a deep breath. "He was with some other kid I could tell was trouble. I saw myself in him."

"Were you 'up to no good' a lot when you were younger?"

"Hell, yes. I had a lot of rage in me. I channeled it into sports, then the navy. It's not right for everyone. But it was for me."

"Even after…what happened to you?"

"Yes."

That darn simple unapologetic declaration again. He didn't give explanations or reasons or excuses. It was maddening. And unquestioningly appealing.

"Who was the kid with Gordon?"

"I don't know him."

"Then how do you know he was up to no good?"

"Sometimes you just know."

She looked at him, and she knew he wasn't going to give a more complete answer, that he was keeping something from her. So much for the trust they'd shared that morning.

He pulled into her driveway and put the car in Park.

"Thank you for driving me home," she said formally.

He gave her a quizzical look. "Anytime." He started to get out of the car.

"It's okay," she said. "I can make it alone and

it's late." She didn't want to face him at the door. She was sure now he was keeping something from her and it punctured the magical bubble she'd created.

She escaped out of the car and up the steps before he could protest. If he accompanied her to the door, she would only look at him and think of how something so wonderful this morning had turned bad so quickly.

Her fault? Definitely. She let fear spoil that which had made her heart spin.

It was just as well. Jubal would be leaving soon, anyway. *A tumbleweed*, she reminded herself. And she was due back in Chicago in eleven months. How fast the first few weeks had gone.

He had stopped at the car door as she scooted out of the car.

"Thank you," she said as he stood there.

He gave her a speculative look. "You're welcome."

"You don't have to walk me to the door."

He nodded.

She went into the house and locked the door without looking back. But then she looked out the window. He was gone.

Gordon came down the stairs. "Did Mr. Pierce just drop you off?"

"Yes."

"I thought you were in Pueblo."

"I was, but we went by air ambulance. He picked me up at the hospital."

"Why didn't you call me?" There was a definite edge in his voice.

"You've just started driving. That's a long, dark road at a late hour."

"Kerry said you were with him this morning, too."

She could see where this was going, and it wasn't good.

She nodded.

"There were a lot of people you could have called for a ride."

True. "I knew he stays up late."

"Are you two banging?" He said the crude words with anger. "Is that why he lets me hang around?"

"I seem to remember you were hanging around with him before I even met him," she shot back. She was appalled at the way he'd asked her. So disrespectful that her resolve not to lie disappeared.

"You didn't answer the question," he accused her.

"No, and I'm not going to when you act like this. I've had a long day and I'm going to bed."

All the satisfaction in saving a baby's life dissolved when she went into the bedroom. Her private life was falling apart. The joy of this morning was made shameful by her brother, and the progress he'd made threatened to crumble. She'd done and said exactly the wrong things.

When she'd expressed her concerns about Gordon to Jubal, had it even been about Gordon or was it about her? When she talked about Gordon's losses, was it as much about her own? Was she the one who was afraid? Was that why she'd avoided relationships, blaming it on her career?

Although she knew her parents had loved her as much as Gordon and Kerry, she'd always had an ache deep inside that she'd been rejected by her birth mother. Had she subconsciously used Gordon as a reason to nullify the growing feelings she had for Jubal because she was afraid of being left again? She'd taken enough psychology classes to make a case for that scenario.

She turned out the lights but knew she wouldn't sleep.

JUBAL REACHED THE CABIN, went inside and finished off the Jameson whiskey Clint had brought. Unfortunately, there wasn't much left.

He'd almost packed what little he had, thrown it in the car and left for the open road.

But the open road didn't have the appeal it had a few weeks ago—if it ever really had. He'd manufactured enthusiasm for it while in San Diego. Now he had none.

He'd looked at Clint, saw how happy he was these days. Same with Josh and Andy. Where years ago he would've mocked the idea, he now wanted some of that contentment for himself. The time he'd spent with Lisa made him think it might be possible...

But he'd been right in the beginning. She was obviously uncomfortable with the military and that had been his entire life, everything he'd valued. How could they ever reconcile that?

Still, he had commitments now, and he didn't run away from commitments. He would stay long enough for Luke to find someone to replace him, long enough to learn what he needed to buy a ranch somewhere else. That interest hadn't gone away. Riding Jacko had helped soothe some of his demons.

He'd heard how much Clint's dog, Bart, had helped him, and Amos had helped Josh when he'd first came to Covenant Falls. In searching websites about horses, he'd stumbled on several about the role horses played in helping veterans. Maybe there was something to it. The more he read, the more interested he became.

He slept a few hours outside. It was cooler, so he took a blanket. He woke when the sun rose as usual. He decided to skip the swim this morning, and run, rather than drive, to Luke's ranch. It would clear his head as much as the swim would have.

Luke was already busy feeding the horses. He nodded as Luke came in. "I didn't hear your car."

"I ran."

Luke shook his head. "Well, help me feed these critters. They each have their own menu. It's listed in front of the stall."

As they worked, Jubal told him what he had found online about veterans and horses.

"Heard about that," Luke said. "It's a good idea. If you're serious, you might think about getting some rescue horses instead of paying prime prices for blooded stock. You can get both, of course, but it might cut into other income like paid riding lessons and training."

"I thought about that."

"Well, think some more. Talk to Al Monroe about it."

Jubal nodded.

"You may be interested to know the ranch next to ours is going up for sale," Luke said after a pause. "Ben Carroll's wife is sick with cancer and he wants to move to Denver where they'll be close to a good hospital. He's been getting rid of his horses and only has five he's kept for sentimental reasons. He's never ranched for business. It's been a retirement place for him."

Luke paused, then looked straight into his eyes. "He doesn't have the acreage I do, but I've been thinking. And what you just said lines up nicely. If you're interested in buying the property, we can join the land, form a kind of partnership. I like your idea about veterans, and I've always

wanted to do horse rescue. You can handle pleasure riding, adventure riding and maybe some of
that therapeutic work with vets. And I can help
train any horses you acquire."

"What would you get out of it?" Jubal asked.

"Someone close to help if we need it. And I
can use the extra pasture for riding."

It sounded good to Jubal. Perfect, in fact, if it
were not for the fact that Lisa and Gordon lived
here and they'd surely see each other often. He
couldn't say he loved her. It was way too soon for
that. But no woman had affected him as she had.
And poor Gordon would be caught in the middle.

"I'll talk to Monroe," Jubal said. "Thanks."

"What for?"

"For taking a chance on me."

"It's not taking a chance, Jubal. I've seen your
work. I've seen you interact with people. You
don't say much, but when you do, they listen. I've
watched you with the horses. You can tell everything you want to know about a man by watching
him with horses. My wife agrees."

"Appreciate that," Jubal said. "And I'll think
about it."

"You do that. I wouldn't want you if you didn't.
Speaking of propositions, that kid Gordon wants
to work on weekends to pay for lessons with you.
We have a lot of riders and it would take some of
the load off. What do you think?"

Jubal wondered what Lisa would think about

that. He was honest. "He's capable and he does what he says he'll do."

"Good. Another free hand. I'm not sure what's happening around here but all of a sudden I'm getting a lot of free help."

"Looks like I started a trend."

"Yeah, well, I hope it continues. Let me know what you think about the ranch…"

He nodded, his mind in turmoil as he wondered what in hades he was going to do.

CHAPTER TWENTY-ONE

JUBAL DREW A long breath and walked into Al Monroe's office Thursday at four p.m.

For the past three days, his life had been consumed by considering Luke's proposal. Similar to how he used to attack an upcoming mission, he tried to look at all the pros and cons, the risks and benefits. Instead of going to Luke's ranch, he'd spent the last three days on the computer and phone, talking to people involved in equine and vet programs throughout the country. He even talked to the psychologist he'd seen in San Diego and asked his advice.

He wasn't yet satisfied when Luke called to check in.

"The seller has received several calls from interested parties," Luke said. "If you want this, you'll have to act fast."

"Can you ask him to wait just a few more days?"

"Sure thing. Just wanted you to know."

He'd made an appointment with Al Monroe then.

Now he was ready. He'd pulled his financials

together, including tax records and investments, even as questions whirled around in his mind. Was he really ready to risk everything?

He'd taken chances all his life, and survived because he trusted his instincts. They were telling him now that this was his chance for contentment. A happy retirement from the life he'd known.

The stars seemed to be in alignment. The right property, a town filled with vets who could help, the right neighbor who could help him on the equine side...

The last month had convinced him he wanted a life with horses. Maybe even needed it.

And then there was the woman with dark hair and beautiful brown eyes who seemed to linger in his thoughts no matter how hard he tried to shove them out...

Al Monroe greeted him courteously enough, but there were obvious questions furrowing his brow when Jubal explained why he was there.

"Ranches are a risky investment these days," the banker said. "What you want to do is certainly a worthy purpose, but it doesn't generate much income. And ranches aren't cheap to run."

"I don't assume they are. Luke gave me a ballpark figure. I'll lease some of the land to Luke, which will bring in something of an income, and I'll operate it as a working ranch as well as a nonprofit."

"What would you want from me?"

"Advice. A line of credit if possible."

"What's your plan for an initial down payment?"

Jubal handed over the financial statement he'd prepared.

Al Monroe looked it over and raised an eyebrow. "Impressive," he said. "How did you manage this in today's economy?"

"Savings and investments. I can buy the property outright, but it would take most of what I have. I'd rather get a mortgage and a line of credit. I want to build a bunkhouse on the property."

"And you think this will work?"

"I've already talked to several similar programs across the country. There are grants available along with donation streams. I've talked to military psychologists about the program, too, and they're enthusiastic. There's more demand for something like this than there are places."

"And Luke is backing this?"

"All the way. It was his idea for us to share the load." He paused, then added, "I understand others have interest in the property and I have to act fast."

"I think we can arrange something," Al said. "A few years ago I would've tried to discourage you, but I've seen what other veterans have done for this town. I've been pulled, kicking and screaming, along with their plans to grow the town, but now I've become a believer." He paused, then added, "I want you to understand, if this doesn't work out you could lose everything."

"I know. But I want to try. Can't get anywhere without trying, right?"

"Need a new mission, huh?"

"Something like that," he said. He'd doubted the wisdom of staying in Covenant Falls where he would come into daily or weekly contact with the only woman who'd made him want a long-term relationship. But he couldn't turn down Luke's proposal.

Luke would provide the safety net he needed: experience with ranching and horses. His reputation would help in raising funds and enlisting other ranchers in the program. The more Jubal had studied the other horse therapy organizations, the more he felt compelled to do this. At his core, he knew it was the purpose he'd been seeking.

"I can give you a good mortgage rate on the property and a line of credit," Al said. They discussed the details, then Al asked, "You want me to go ahead and arrange the sale?"

"Let me talk to Luke and get back to you, but I'm sure we'll proceed as discussed."

"In that case," Monroe said, rising from his chair to shake Jubal's hand, "I feel it's safe to say, welcome to Covenant Falls!"

Jubal thanked him and walked out. He had made the second biggest decision of his life. The first was joining the navy. Once he was outside, he called Luke.

"It's a go," he said. "Tell your neighbor before he changes his mind on the price."

"Will do. Covenant Falls is finally getting some notice around the state, thanks to Josh. I'll call him now."

Luke called back almost immediately. "Ben's committed to the price and won't entertain any other offers, but he'll need the paperwork ASAP."

Jubal was used to quick decisions, but nothing this fast and certainly nothing involving hundreds of thousands of dollars. There was much to be said about a small community where everyone—well, almost everyone—trusted each other.

He wanted to celebrate. But with whom?

He looked at his watch. It was five p.m. He knew Clint was on duty.

Really, the person he wanted to celebrate with was Lisa, but she'd shut him down Sunday night.

Well, hell, maybe he would visit the Rusty Nail and get happily drunk with new neighbors to be. It had a hollow sound, but so be it.

LISA BURIED HERSELF in work over the next three days after her good-then-disastrous Sunday. It should have been easy to do. There were a number of new pregnancies in Covenant Falls, another football injury, sprained ankles, the list went on. There was even a fight at one of the saloons just outside of town. Clint had brought in a man to set a broken arm before taking him to jail.

When she wasn't treating someone, she was doing paperwork. Janie handled it for the most part, but Lisa had to sign off on almost everything.

The practice was nearly as time-consuming as the hospital had been. But she liked the personal contact with patients. She made follow-up calls to see how they were doing, and some patients who seemed reluctant at first were now quite accepting of her.

She loved walking to work, to lunch, having picnics at the falls. She liked the deep blue sky that was so clear and clean and the nights filled with stars you could never see in Chicago. She loved the fresh, pine-fragrant breezes.

What she didn't like was being on pins and needles, wanting to see Jubal, but also afraid she would.

The phone rang in the afternoon. It was Eve.

"Hey, Lisa, I wanted to invite you to a party at the community center Saturday."

"I'm not sure if I can…" Lisa replied. Saturdays were always busy at the clinic and she was not in a party mood. It had, quite simply, been a dreadful three days.

"It's Andy and Nate's engagement party," Eve continued in her usual cheerful hard-to-say-no-to voice. Okay, make that impossible. "It'll be informal. No presents. Clint has arranged for a small band to play—all vets. Gordon and Kerry are invited, as well. There will be other young people there, too, so they won't be bored."

Lisa couldn't say no. There was no plausible excuse unless she or one of her siblings came down with an illness. Andy and Eve had been too good to her and Kerry.

She finally agreed, unable to find an immediate way to say no. She just hoped Jubal found one, because most certainly he'd be invited, as well. But did she really want that? She hadn't seen him since Sunday night. There had been no reason, and no accidental meetings.

Gordon hadn't broached the subject again, either, but he was back in his guarded mode.

It made sense. Jubal had been Gordon's friend first. Their connection had grown strong in such a short time.

In Gordon's eyes, she'd intruded on that bond, a friendship that was obviously very important to her brother. She'd invaded territory that he'd thought was his. Jubal was *his* friend. Therefore Jubal couldn't be *her* friend. She suspected it went deeper than that—that he knew they hadn't been just friends. And that it had something to do with the mystery of how he and Jubal had got together in the first place. Why had she allowed it to bother her so much? The friendship between the two obviously resulted in good things happening.

Had she just destroyed something valuable because of her own fear of being rejected? It had been buried so deep she hadn't considered it at the time. It was why she immersed herself in books, avoided relationships and kept a distance from her own siblings. They had recognized it even if she hadn't.

She'd hoped Jubal would call. She ached with the need to see that rare smile light his face, even if whatever had happened between them couldn't last.

The phone rang. She recognized the number and her heart beat a little faster.

"Hi," he said.

"Hi yourself."

"Want to celebrate with me?"

"Want to give me a hint as to why?" *That cautious voice in her head was raising its ugly head again.*

"Nope. It's a surprise."

"Okay," she heard herself saying.

"I'll pick you up in twenty minutes."

"When will we be back?"

"Whenever you want."

"Okay," she said again. *Brilliant replies.*

"Should I pick you up at the clinic?"

"That would be fine. I'll call Kerry and Gordon so they know I'll be late. They can find something in the fridge."

"I'll see you shortly." He hung up.

JUBAL HUNG UP before she could reconsider.

Then he swung by the Rusty Nail and talked the owner, another vet who played poker, into giving him a bottle of wine along with two large ham sandwiches.

She was obviously waiting for him. She came out and locked the door to the clinic before he had a chance to step out of the car. She slid inside and looked at him. "Where are we going?"

"I seem to remember something about the falls," he said.

"I like that idea," she said. She hesitated, then added, "You said you were celebrating?"

He glanced at her. She was looking at him intently. "Yes," he said.

"You're going to make me wait?" she said.

"I just wanted to see the falls with you"

"A mystery?" she said.

"More like a decision."

"You like secrets, don't you?" It was a barb and she regretted it the minute she said it.

"No," he said. "I hate them. Particularly when they involve someone I care about." He was silent for a moment, then carefully added, "But sometimes it's the lesser of two evils." He glanced at her quickly before turning back to the road. "Your brother needed someone he could trust. Before I met you, I made a bargain with him. He kept his end of it. If I broke it, he probably wouldn't trust anyone again."

"I'm sorry," she said hesitantly. "But he...he guessed what happened on Sunday. He was up when I returned that night. He asked if I was sleeping with you. No," she corrected herself, "he didn't ask. He suggested it, using some unpleasant language."

"Now *I'm* sorry," he said as he reached out for her hand. "Not for what happened, just that you got grief from it."

They turned up onto a narrow road marked with a big sign.

"We're almost there," Lisa said.

He followed the road to a parking area. There were no other cars. He grabbed the bag from the backseat and they walked to the falls. The sun was dipping behind them. Jubal took her hand, thankful she didn't pull away.

"Remember Sunday when you asked me what comes next and I told you I'd figure it out somewhere along the way?"

She nodded.

"Well, I figured it out. Sooner than I thought."

Her large brown eyes searched his face. "What did you figure out?"

"I'm well on my way to becoming a land owner."

She stared at him. "You don't mean...the Carroll ranch next to Luke's place? I overheard it was for sale..."

"*Was* being the key word. My offer was accepted this afternoon."

"But why?"

"Everything seemed to fall into place, I suppose. It felt right." He watched her carefully. "I wanted to tell you before you heard from someone else."

"So then what about the tumbleweed?"

He grinned. "The wind stopped blowing, I guess."

"What are you going to do with it?"

"Thought you would never ask." He grinned. "I'm going to lease part of the pasture to Luke to run more cattle, and then on the rest, I'm going to build a bunkhouse and start an equine program for veterans."

He saw the shock on her face, then interest as it sunk in. Her fingers tightened around his.

"Luke will be involved, too. I've done a lot of research over the past three days. Looked up a lot of programs. Talked to the people who run them. There's one in New Mexico where a group of ranchers got together and started a program called Horses for Heroes. Most of the volunteers are ex-vets themselves."

"I like it," she said, "but it's a little fast, isn't it?"

"Had to be. As soon as the word went out that property was for sale, there was a lot of interest. Luke got first refusal because they'd been friends and neighbors for years, but he couldn't buy it on his own. He didn't want or need another house or barn, but he did want more land to increase his cattle herd.

"In the beginning we can use his horses, but gradually we'll train and use rescue horses. That was Luke's idea."

Her mouth hung wide open in a mixture of surprise and what looked like it could be joy. Or maybe she thought he was insane.

"I know it'll take months to put together," he said. "I still have a lot of research to do. I would have to provide living quarters or maybe participants might prefer to stay in Josh's inn at a reduced rate. It helps that we have a lot of veterans here."

She looked incredulous. "That's a lot to take in. Had you been thinking about it before the property came up for sale?"

"I'd been thinking about ranching. Working with horses again has helped me. It keeps some of the nightmares at bay."

"I think it sounds like a terrific idea. I think Stephanie will agree."

"Good. I'll need you. I'm going to try to find a psychologist in Pueblo to help design the program. Also…it means I'll be sticking around for a while."

She leaned against him and his arm went around her. "I'm sorry about Sunday night," she said. "I said I was worried about Gordon, but it's more than that." She hesitated. "I was adopted. My parents were told they couldn't have children. Thirteen years later, Mom became pregnant with Gordon and then Kerry. Mom and Dad never tried to hide the fact I was adopted, nor did they treat me any differently.

"Dad used to say I was chosen, a wonderful gift, but it always made me feel apart, a stranger in someone else's house. My birth mother didn't want me, and I always felt so different. My hair is dark while my brother and sister are blond.

"When Gordon started acting up after Mom died, he said he didn't have to obey me because I wasn't his real sister. When you talked to Gordon about his future and he was so secretive about it, I felt it as another rejection. I know it's silly…"

"No, it isn't," he said. "You moved here for his sake. That took a lot of love. You had reason to be concerned."

She stood on her tiptoes, put her arms around his neck and rested her head against his heart. He leaned down and kissed her and, for the first time in his life, felt truly whole.

CHAPTER TWENTY-TWO

LISA COULDN'T CONTROL her nervousness as she dressed for the engagement party.

Jubal had called and offered to drive her and the kids to the party but she said no, fearing her brother would balk at being part of "a date."

In the past week, Gordon hadn't brought up the subject again. He'd attended school, received a B on his first chemistry test, reported to Clint and taken a riding lesson with Luke. All seemed fine—even good—on the surface, but she knew he was avoiding her.

Eve had told her attire for the party was informal, but Lisa still wanted to look nice. She finally decided on a pair of black pants, a pearl-gray tailored top. She added the topaz necklace her father had given her when she graduated with honors from high school. It was simple enough not to be ostentatious, but it complemented her brown eyes and dark hair.

Kerry was excited about the party. Gordon not so much. He'd reverted back to sullenness since

Sunday night. She'd tried to talk to him, but he hadn't wanted to listen.

She knew he was reluctant to go to the party and probably wouldn't have agreed if Luke hadn't encouraged it. Her brother hadn't mentioned Jubal, and Jubal, when he'd called about the party, didn't mention him, either.

In the past two days she knew he'd been busy working out the details of the purchase. She was still stunned by his decision to stay and give it a try.

He was no longer the itinerant ex-soldier. He wasn't going to love and leave. No reason to avoid him now. None but her own fear of relationships. Her birth mother hadn't wanted her. Her adopted father and mother had died. *Admit it*, she told herself, *you're a coward. If you didn't love, you couldn't be hurt.*

"Lisa." Her sister appeared in the doorway with Susie right behind her. She wore a pair of capri pants and a lacy top, her blond hair in a long ponytail.

"Call your brother," Lisa said, looking at the clock. It was a little after seven. "It's time to go."

"He says he's not going."

She went to his room, knocked, then went inside.

"I want you to go," she said. "Luke will be there. So will Clint and Josh."

He shook his head. She saw a kind of despair in

his eyes. Maybe he felt the same way she had—that he was destined to lose whoever he cared about.

She sat down next to him. "I love you, Gordon. If you don't want me to see Jubal, I won't."

"I don't care."

"Yes, you do. He's your friend, too, and you're afraid that will change." She took a deep breath. "You want to know something?"

He just looked at her.

"When you were born, I was jealous of you. I knew I was adopted, and you were truly Mom and Dad's in a way I didn't think I could ever be. You and Kerry looked like them, and the two of you were so close. I felt like an outsider."

He looked at her with questions in his eyes. "But they were so proud of you…"

"I'm not proud of me," Lisa said. "I wasn't there when you needed me most." She was silent for a moment, then said, "Dad was so proud of that fort you built. He knew you were going to be an engineer. He loved you so much. Both you and Kerry."

"You didn't cry when Mom died," he accused her.

"Yes, I did. At night. I was trying to be strong for you guys, but then I failed you because I poured my grief into my job. I told myself I was doing it for you, that as a doctor I could repay Mom and Dad by putting you through college.

But really, I was trying to escape from that grief, just as you were by joining that gang."

She saw tears in his eyes.

"There's nothing I want more than for you and Kerry to be happy," she added softly. "Not only for Mom and Dad, but because I love you." From the expression in his eyes, she knew he understood what she was saying.

"I need to tell you something," he said.

"What?"

"Mr. Pierce didn't hire me to build that bench. Not exactly."

"What do you mean?"

"The night we moved here, I snuck out to meet a kid I'd met earlier in the day. He said no one lived at the last cabin on Lake Road. He said I should set fire to the dock. That it was an initiation."

Lisa couldn't think of anything to say.

"I was so angry," he said. "I tried to do it. I gathered some firewood and had just lit it when Mr. Pierce caught me. He gave me a choice. I could work off the damage or he would report me to Chief Morgan."

Lisa felt her heart beat faster as she tried to absorb what he was saying. Jubal had hinted at something, but not arson. Both Gordon and Jubal had been lying to her for weeks. She tried to justify it. No matter how and why, Gordon had changed for the better because of his influence, but Jubal should have told her. The fact that he hadn't told her he hadn't trusted her any more than Gordon did.

"Anything else you're keeping from me?" she asked in a tight voice.

"No. I resented him in the beginning. I even hated him, but then I realized what he was doing. I wanted to tell you but…"

"You were afraid."

"I didn't want to disappoint you again."

"Why are you telling me now?"

"Because I want you to know Mr. Pierce is a good guy."

But neither of them trusted her and that hurt like nothing else had.

Gordon looked at her for a long time, then said, "I'm sorry. Mr. Pierce told me I should tell you."

The admission didn't help a lot. The secret had been held too long. Both had had a chance to tell her even as she thought the relationships were growing stronger. "Kerry and I are going to the party," she said, trying to keep her voice steady. "I promised."

He just looked at her, regret in his eyes.

"Are you coming with us?" she asked.

"Later, maybe. I can ride my bike."

"Okay." She wanted to hug him but understood he was trying to sort things out himself. "You have your phone?"

He nodded.

"Good." She didn't want to leave. She didn't want to see Jubal. She felt her heart bleeding. The one thing she thought she had with him now was honesty. And now she'd learned that was a lie.

"I'm sorry for what I said about you and Mr. Pierce," Gordon said.

"I know," she said. She felt like a zombie as she joined Kerry at the door.

The parking lot at the community center was almost full, and people were spilling out into the park. She and Kerry went inside, where Kerry immediately left to join a group of kids around her age.

Lisa spotted Nate and Andy and went up to hug them both. "Congratulations! When's the big day?"

"December 20. We're going to see her family next week," Nate said while clutching Andy's hand. They looked at each other with so much love it hurt.

"We're going to try to convince them to move up here," Andy said.

"I hope you succeed. Always nice when family can be together."

She looked around and found she recognized many of the people there—some from Maude's, some from her practice, some who were friends of Eve's.

If it wasn't for the discussion she'd had with Gordon, she would be comfortable. She liked

Covenant Falls. She liked the way everyone cared for each other. There was a warmth in the room that was palpable.

Clint appeared. "Glad you came. Can I get you something to drink?"

"A glass of wine, thank you," she said. She continued to look around as he headed toward the bar, then turned and almost ran into Jubal. He was the tallest man in the room, although Josh came close. She just watched him.

"You look great," he said. His eyes narrowed. "Something wrong?"

"Yes."

Clint reappeared then and handed her a glass of wine. "Where's your brother?"

"He might come later."

"Good, I know a young lady who wants to meet him. My secretary's daughter was asking..." He suddenly seemed to catch a vibe. "I'll catch you two later," he said, and disappeared.

Jubal looked at her for a long moment. "Do you want to go somewhere more private?"

She nodded.

He led the way out of the room, across the hall to the library. It was dark and no one was inside. He turned on the light and closed the door.

"Something's wrong," he said.

"Gordon told me what happened on the dock."

"Good," he said, then paused. "You don't think so?"

"I would have liked to have known about it sooner. I asked. Several times." Tears backed up behind her eyes. She hated that. "Maybe you didn't outright lie but you didn't tell me the whole truth, either. Neither of you trusted me. How can I trust you?"

"And what would you have done if I told you?" he asked, his eyes suddenly cool.

"I don't know, but it was my problem." It was a poor answer but it was all she had.

"That load on your back is going to get very heavy if you never let anyone help," he said. "I didn't know who he was when I first saw him on my dock. All I saw was a kid heading for trouble. I saw myself at that age. I felt his anger. The only way I knew to help was to show him another way. Lectures and punishment weren't going to get through to him. I wanted to tell you," he added, "but this was something he needed to do on his own."

Her cell phone dinged. She checked. A text message from Gordon.

Mr. Pierce's cabin. Someone's setting fire to it.

She handed it to Jubal.

He read it and sprinted for the door and she followed him. He stopped long enough to say something to Clint, then sprinted out the door.

Clint went to Nate and Josh and said something, and the latter two disappeared out the door while Clint made a call, then an announcement to the group about the fire.

In minutes the center was emptied. Most of the guests were heading down down to the cabin, grabbing trash cans or any container they could find. Andy came over to her. "We don't know how bad it is, but it will take time to carry water from the lake to the fire and the surrounding area. There's a fire extinguisher in the hallway. I'll get the one in the kitchen. Meet me at my car by the door. They're fairly heavy to run with."

Lisa ran up the stairs, grabbed the extinguisher and met Andy outside. She jumped in Andy's car, and Andy honked to scatter the men racing down to the cabin.

In seconds, Andy stopped the car on the road and both of them ran toward the cabin with the fire extinguishers. The moon was nearly full and she saw figures struggling on the ground. Clint was hooking up a hose to an outdoor faucet. Jubal had a fire extinguisher in his hands and was aiming it at the flames.

He was too close to them.

The sound of a fire engine grew louder. Several of the oncoming men grabbed the fire extinguishers she and Andy had brought and two others ran over to Gordon. He had a firm grip on another boy, maybe a few years older, who was cursing as he struggled to free himself.

"He did it," the boy said. "He set the fire."

"I was trying to stop him," Gordon said, and glanced around with a panicked look on his face. "I swear."

A fire truck roared into the yard with tanks of water and within minutes the fire was out, but not before half the porch was damaged.

Two men had separated Gordon and the boy he'd held captive. Gordon looked at Lisa with a plea in his eyes.

A police car arrived and a young officer walked over to where Clint and Jubal were surveying the damage. He talked to Clint, who then approached the two boys. "Earl White, you can't seem to stay out of trouble, can you? I don't think the judge will be lenient this time. The whole forest could have gone up in flames."

"I didn't do it." He glared at Gordon. "He started a fire here a couple of weeks ago. I was just driving around, heard all the activity at the center. I was curious, that's all. Then I saw him near the cabin. I seen him there before, trying to set fire to the dock. So did someone else."

Gordon was watching Lisa carefully. He stiffened.

She walked over to him, put her arm around him. "Jubal has my phone," she said as Jubal walked up to them. "It'll prove that Gordon had nothing to do with the fire and actually tried to stop it."

Jubal took the phone from his pocket and handed it to the officer. "Gordon texted us about someone setting a fire. If he hadn't, the cabin would be in flames as well as the woods behind it. Why would he do that if he was the one who'd set the fire?"

"What happened, Gordon?" Clint asked gently.

"I was going to the party," he said. "But I... wasn't ready to go in. I thought I would sit on the bench here for a few minutes to clear my head. I heard voices. I recognized one, and I went closer. Then I saw two guys laughing as they poured gas on the porch. While I was texting my sister, one of them threw a match on the gas and the other came after me."

Earl White tried to protest, but the young officer officially arrested and handcuffed him. He talked privately to Clint for a moment, then hustled the prisoner into the police car and drove off.

"We'll need statements from Gordon and Jubal tomorrow," Clint said. "I think the other kid involved might be Earl's brother. The family moved here a year ago and have been nothing but trouble. I'll have my officers look for him."

Lisa waited more than an hour as the volunteer firefighters soaked what was left of the porch, inspected the interior for any hot spots, then used the rest of the water in the tanks to wet the area around the cabin.

Clint and Jubal walked around the cabin and found an unopened can of gasoline. Clint returned to Gordon and Lisa. "Apparently you stopped them just in time, Gordon. This could have started a blaze that would climb that mountain behind you."

Gordon glanced at Lisa with apprehension. She knew there could be trouble ahead. No doubt, Earl White would tell the police about the dock, and Gordon was on probation. One violation and his record would not disappear, nor would any of the consequences.

"Kerry is still at the community center," she said to Clint. "I should take her home. Is Gordon free to go?"

Clint nodded. "Sure. There won't be any charges. In fact, he should probably get a medal."

Lisa thanked him, then turned her attention to Jubal. "Should you stay here tonight? Is it safe?"

"I usually sleep outside," he said. "Believe me, I'll know if anyone approaches."

She looked at him. "I'm sorry. You were right earlier tonight. I..."

He looked around, then figured *to hell with it* and kissed her. Long and hard. In front of everyone.

There was clapping, and even Lisa felt herself cheering internally.

"The damned cabin did it again," someone said from the remaining onlookers.

Everyone started to leave except for a few men who volunteered to stay and make sure there weren't any sparks left.

She walked with Gordon as he located his bike among the pines. "I'm sorry I didn't tell you about the dock," he said.

"I'm sorry you didn't *feel* you could tell me sooner," Lisa said. "But you saved the cabin tonight and maybe prevented a forest fire."

"But I'm probably why Earl set the fire in the first place. He was really angry when I wouldn't have anything to do with him after the dock..."

She suddenly remembered the black sedan and the way Kerry had shuddered when she saw it. "Did you know he's possibly been bothering your sister?"

"No! I'll kill the little—"

"You will do nothing of the sort..." She suddenly recalled why they were at the community center. *The engagement party...*

When they reached the center, most of the cars were gone. Kerry stood on the steps with a nice-looking boy. "Is everything okay?" she asked anxiously.

Lisa nodded. "The fire's out. There's some damage to the cabin, but it's mostly intact. It seems your brother is the hero of the hour. He not only saved the cabin but caught the guy who set the fire. Clint seems to think he set other recent fires, too."

Lisa put her arm around Kerry and found Nate and Andy. "I'm so sorry about the party and…"

"Don't be. It'll just be a reason for another party," Nate said, holding his arms around Andy. "I'm just grateful Gordon wasn't hurt."

They said good-night, and Lisa drove Kerry and Gordon back to the house. It was already after midnight.

Lisa waited until they both were probably in bed, then changed into jeans and a sweatshirt.

She then wrote a note and left, driving down Main Street to the community center. The lights were off. Everyone had gone home. She continued down the road and onto the drive leading to the cabin.

She stepped out of the car and went around to the back. There was a blanket on a lounge chair but it was empty. Then she felt arms around her. She whirled around.

"Don't you know better than to sneak up on someone in the middle of the night?" Jubal asked roughly.

"Apparently not," she said, lifting up to kiss him. His lips pressed against hers and the need, the yearning, between them exploded. She felt the tension in his body, the barely restrained passion in his hands, which now moved seductively at the small of her back.

Desire enveloped her. She wanted to touch and be touched. "I think we should go inside," he said, a slight shakiness in his voice.

"Is it safe?"

"We examined every corner of the cabin," he said. "It's safe, but the electricity is turned off. We want to make sure none of the wiring was damaged and we can't do that until daylight. There are lanterns, though."

She looked at the lounge chair. "Do you really sleep out here?"

"Yeah. A lot. I don't like feeling cooped up. Sometimes I wake up thrashing at phantoms." He paused and added with a lecherous gleam in his eyes, "I might have to do something to change that."

She couldn't begin to imagine all the pain he'd been through. And yet he'd had the heart to help an at-risk kid he didn't know.

He held her tight. "Speaking of the fire, I received a call from Clint after you left. They found Earl White's brother. He'd parked their truck behind an empty home. A neighbor reported it. When Clint called the dad, the man was furious. Turns out there were traces of manure in the vehicle, and the tires match the tracks found everywhere cattle have been stolen. The police chief is a happy man. Mainly because of Gordon. He's gonna be a hero around here now."

He leaned toward her, his lips brushing her

cheeks. Their lips met and clung with tenderness at first, then passion. It rose between them swiftly and they were clutching each other with a hunger Lisa had never experienced before.

He broke away and led her inside the cabin where they stayed in each other's arms. Lisa felt her body turn molten. She clung to him, her fingers digging into his back, a river of sensation coursing through her.

Once in the bedroom, he hesitated, then they were on the bed, tearing each other's clothes off. His hands were everywhere, stroking and kneading, and she felt her body surging under his touch. Her breasts ached as his tongue replaced his fingers and created a string of fire that ran through her like lightning.

His lips caught her mouth in a kiss that swept away every reservation, and suddenly there was warmth and power reaching into her and she felt sensations she'd never known existed. They clung to each other, savoring the intimacy...

Afterward, they lay together, holding hands. Lisa had not known there could be anything this mind-blowing.

"Is it always like this?" she said.

"No," he said. "I can honestly say this is something special."

"Good." She snuggled in his arms. "Thank you for what you did for Gordon."

"I should have told you."

She shook her head. "No. I wouldn't have understood then. I would probably have just been angry." She tightened her fingers around his. "I'm finding I don't know my brother and sister as well as I thought I did. For nearly half their lives I was in college, medical school or residency. I was seldom at home. Being a doctor was my dad's dream. His daughter, the doctor.

"He'd even established a trust fund for the sole purpose of sending me to medical school. I was just getting started when he was killed. And then when Mom got sick, she begged me not to drop out. I shouldn't have paid attention to her, but I heard what I wanted to hear and I thought my aunt could do what I should have done. I was their sister, and I deserted them when they needed me most. I'm just now discovering who they are, and they're good kids. Just lonely and grieving ones."

"So what now?" he asked quietly.

"I planned to be a pediatric surgeon," she said. "But it would mean another two years, and worse, it would mean a practice that would take me away from them for sixty, seventy hours a week.

"I'm finding my values are changing. I like knowing my patients. I like being available to Gordon and Kerry and I can probably help as many people here as I could as a specialist." She paused to look up at him. "I have another reason now, too. I'm falling in love with you."

Maybe it was too soon, but she had to say it. She'd withheld saying too many things over the years.

A smile curved his lips. "We're on the same wavelength, darlin'. I've been wondering what bolt of thunder hit me since I met you. It's like nothing I've felt before. I can't wait to see what happens next."

That was all she needed to know. He was buying the ranch. He planned to stay and now she could, as well. She doubted Dr. Bradley would ever return to the practice. The stars seemed in alignment. Who was she to deny fate?

They had the time to build on that instantaneous connection that still mystified her, but in a wondrous way.

"I have a lot of learning to do," Jubal said. "I'm discovering that the world includes a lot more than being a soldier." He leaned over and kissed her. "When the foal was born, I saw life as I never have before—full of promises."

She snuggled in his arms. "I heard you were thinking about a name for the foal. What about Promises?"

"Hmm, I like that," he said. He stilled, and his voice turned somber.

"There's something else I have to do," he said. It sounded ominous. She tensed.

"It's going to take a month before I can close on Ben Carroll's ranch and move in," he said. "And I want to give the cabin back to Josh for someone else to use."

Lisa's fingers wrapped around his as she waited. There was something in his tone that kept her from commenting.

"My original plan was to stay here a few days, then visit the families of the guys who died on that last mission. I sent letters when I returned, but it's not enough."

Lisa ached for the pain she saw in his eyes. Guilt was there, too… Guilt that he was still alive and they weren't. She wanted to ease it, but she knew there was nothing she could say or do to help. She could only try to understand.

He hesitated as if uncertain of her reaction, then continued. "I have to do it before I start a new life," he said slowly. "I can do that now. I wasn't sure before coming here, before you and Gordon and Luke and the others."

With her free hand, she traced the lines along his strong face. He was admitting a vulnerability, and she instinctively knew how difficult that was.

"I'll be here," she said. "I wish I could go with you, but I know it's something you have to do alone."

"I'll miss you—a lot—but it's just a few weeks. And you, pretty doctor, have your patients and your clinic and two kids that are growing up fast. And well."

"Yes they are," she said. "Thanks in good measure to you and the town."

She settled back in his arms, relishing the strength in him. Loving him may not always be an easy journey, but she knew it was well worth every step.

Their faces were inches apart. He brushed a lock of hair from her cheek. There was so much tenderness in the gesture that she felt as if she were melting inside.

"When are you leaving?"

"I hope in about five days. I have to contact the families first. It depends on them."

"Then we have to take advantage of those five days," Lisa suggested.

"That's just what I was thinking," he said, and they started doing exactly that.

LISA HEADED HOME before dawn. The house was still, and she looked in on Gordon first. He was sleeping.

Then she checked on Kerry. Susie was curled up next to her, and Kerry's arm was around her. She closed the door softly.

The first golden glints of daylight were filtering through the windows. She would tell Gordon how proud she was of him, of his efforts to make amends, of how much he'd grown in the past few weeks.

She would tell Kerry how much she loved her, and how happy she was that she was in choir and making friends and how she could tell her big sister anything.

She would be there as Jubal learned how to live again.

Just as she was learning what was really important. And they'd get to share that now.

She knew she would make mistakes but she wanted to be better at recognizing them now.

She went outside and looked up. She could still see the transparent moon even as the sun rose, coloring the sky with a spray of color that promised a fine day.

It was her sky now. Hers and Jubal's.

* * * * *

LARGER-PRINT BOOKS!
GET 2 FREE LARGER-PRINT NOVELS PLUS
2 FREE GIFTS!

From the Heart, For the Heart

YES! Please send me 2 FREE LARGER-PRINT Harlequin® Romance novels and my 2 FREE gifts (gifts are worth about $10). After receiving them, if I don't wish to receive any more books, I can return the shipping statement marked "cancel." If I don't cancel, I will receive 4 brand-new novels every month and be billed just $5.09 per book in the U.S. or $5.49 per book in Canada. That's a savings of at least 15% off the cover price! It's quite a bargain! Shipping and handling is just 50¢ per book in the U.S. and 75¢ per book in Canada.* I understand that accepting the 2 free books and gifts places me under no obligation to buy anything. I can always return a shipment and cancel at any time. Even if I never buy another book, the two free books and gifts are mine to keep forever.

119/319 HDN GHWC

Name	(PLEASE PRINT)	
Address		Apt. #
City	State/Prov.	Zip/Postal Code

Signature (if under 18, a parent or guardian must sign)

Mail to the **Reader Service:**
IN U.S.A.: P.O. Box 1867, Buffalo, NY 14240-1867
IN CANADA: P.O. Box 609, Fort Erie, Ontario L2A 5X3

Want to try two free books from another line?
Call 1-800-873-8635 or visit www.ReaderService.com.

* Terms and prices subject to change without notice. Prices do not include applicable taxes. Sales tax applicable in N.Y. Canadian residents will be charged applicable taxes. Offer not valid in Quebec. This offer is limited to one order per household. Not valid for current subscribers to Harlequin Romance Larger-Print books. All orders subject to credit approval. Credit or debit balances in a customer's account(s) may be offset by any other outstanding balance owed by or to the customer. Please allow 4 to 6 weeks for delivery. Offer available while quantities last.

Your Privacy—The Reader Service is committed to protecting your privacy. Our Privacy Policy is available online at www.ReaderService.com or upon request from the Reader Service.

We make a portion of our mailing list available to reputable third parties that offer products we believe may interest you. If you prefer that we not exchange your name with third parties, or if you wish to clarify or modify your communication preferences, please visit us at www.ReaderService.com/consumerschoice or write to us at Reader Service Preference Service, P.O. Box 9062, Buffalo, NY 14240-9062. Include your complete name and address.

HRLP15

LARGER-PRINT BOOKS!

REQUEST YOUR FREE BOOKS!
2 FREE WHOLESOME ROMANCE NOVELS IN LARGER PRINT
PLUS 2
FREE
MYSTERY GIFTS

✽✽✽✽✽✽✽✽✽✽✽✽✽✽✽✽✽✽✽✽✽✽✽✽✽✽

HEARTWARMING™

✽✽✽✽✽✽✽✽✽✽✽✽✽✽✽✽✽✽✽✽✽✽✽✽✽✽

Wholesome, tender romances

YES! Please send me 2 FREE Harlequin® Heartwarming Larger-Print novels and my 2 FREE mystery gifts (gifts worth about $10). After receiving them, if I don't wish to receive any more books, I can return the shipping statement marked "cancel." If I don't cancel, I will receive 4 brand-new larger-print novels every month and be billed just $5.24 per book in the U.S. or $5.99 per book in Canada. That's a savings of at least 19% off the cover price. It's quite a bargain! Shipping and handling is just 50¢ per book in the U.S. and 75¢ per book in Canada.* I understand that accepting the 2 free books and gifts places me under no obligation to buy anything. I can always return a shipment and cancel at any time. Even if I never buy another book, the two free books and gifts are mine to keep forever.

161/361 IDN GHX2

Name	(PLEASE PRINT)	
Address		Apt. #
City	State/Prov.	Zip/Postal Code

Signature (if under 18, a parent or guardian must sign)

Mail to the **Reader Service:**
IN U.S.A.: P.O. Box 1867, Buffalo, NY 14240-1867
IN CANADA: P.O. Box 609, Fort Erie, Ontario L2A 5X3

* Terms and prices subject to change without notice. Prices do not include applicable taxes. Sales tax applicable in N.Y. Canadian residents will be charged applicable taxes. Offer not valid in Quebec. This offer is limited to one order per household. Not valid for current subscribers to Harlequin Heartwarming larger-print books. All orders subject to credit approval. Credit or debit balances in a customer's account(s) may be offset by any other outstanding balance owed by or to the customer. Please allow 4 to 6 weeks for delivery. Offer available while quantities last.

Your Privacy—The Reader Service is committed to protecting your privacy. Our Privacy Policy is available online at www.ReaderService.com or upon request from the Reader Service.

We make a portion of our mailing list available to reputable third parties that offer products we believe may interest you. If you prefer that we not exchange your name with third parties, or if you wish to clarify or modify your communication preferences, please visit us at www.ReaderService.com/consumerschoice or write to us at Reader Service Preference Service, P.O. Box 9062, Buffalo, NY 14240-9062. Include your complete name and address.

HW15

LARGER-PRINT BOOKS!
GET 2 FREE LARGER-PRINT NOVELS PLUS
2 FREE GIFTS!

✦ HARLEQUIN®

I N T R I G U E
BREATHTAKING ROMANTIC SUSPENSE

HILP15